THE RHYTHM OF THE RAIN

Dannie was mesmerized by the water that ran over Jake's powerful shoulders, down his chest and stomach. He reached for her and pulled her close to him.

She let her hands slip over his wet skin and hard muscles. She tasted the rain as it mingled with their kiss.

Her damp clothes clung to her body, and she could feel the pattering of droplets on her shoulders as he worked the buttons on the front of her dress. Her back arched of its own volition, and the rain beat on her forehead and slid between her parted lips.

When he lifted her off the ground, she swallowed a cry of longing. The storm raged on, within and without.

Also by Suzanne Elizabeth

When Destiny Calls
Fan the Flame
Destined to Love°

Available from HarperPaperbacks

°coming soon

Kiley's Storm

≥ SUZANNE ELIZABETH ≤

HarperPaperbacks
A Division of HarperCollinsPublishers

This is a work of fiction. The characters, incidents, and dialogues are products of the author's imagination and are not to be construed as real. Any resemblance to actual events or persons, living or dead, is entirely coincidental.

HarperPaperbacks *A Division of* HarperCollins*Publishers*
10 East 53rd Street, New York, N.Y. 10022

Cover illustration by R.A. Maguire

First printing: February 1994

Printed in the United States of America

HarperPaperbacks, HarperMonogram, and colophon are trademarks of HarperCollins*Publishers*

❖ 10 9 8 7 6 5 4 3 2 1

To Vickie Good (*my evil twin*), a playmate and fellow writer who always understands.

To Linda Miller-Reed, a loyal friend, and devoted "Uncle" to my three children.

To Yvette ("Betty") Palting-Spieldenner, for giving me my first romance novel in high school.

And to my wonderful editor, Abigail Kamen, who really can squeeze a diamond out of a chunk of coal.

1

Colorado, 1859

The entire town had gone stark raving mad.

Dannie Storm strode down the main street of Shady Gulch, kicking up clods of dirt as she went. The afternoon air was heavy and thick with moisture, tempting her hair out of its tie to spring annoyingly against the sides of her face.

It had been a hot, dry summer, and the Colorado hillsides, which were normally rich with vegetation this time of year, had become parched, not to mention that Spangle Creek was down to no more than a slow, thin trickle. But today the sun was blotted out by a haze of gray clouds, and the town was hoping for a few blessed drops of rain for the first time in over two months.

Dannie wasn't overly concerned about the weather, however, and she'd had about all the trouble she could take from Spangle Creek. That one, darn, stretch of water had given her more headaches in the last two weeks than a lifetime of heatstroke, frostbite, and sunburns put together.

She passed by the weathered walls of her father's gun shop, noting that the sign above the door needed a fresh coat of white paint. Her father's clerk, Joseph Hardy, stepped into the threshold and raised his hand to her in greeting.

"Afternoon, Dannie."

Dannie waved as she walked past, not willing to waste a single moment to stop and chat.

Rawlins Beekman appeared in the doorway of his barber shop and dentistry. Casting a disapproving glance at the two old-timers smoking pipes on his boardwalk bench, he called, "How's it goin', Dannie? Looks like rain, don't it?"

"Appearances can be deceiving," she replied sharply.

"Your pa back from Denver yet?" Smithy Anderson hollered from the blacksmith shed on the other side of the street.

"No." *I should be so lucky*, she added to herself.

"I suppose you heard about Douglas?" Smithy continued, wiping his greasy hands on a rag as he stepped toward her.

Dannie paused just long enough to give the thick-armed man a glare. "Where the heck do you think I'm going, Anderson?"

"Yeah, Anderson," Joseph Hardy said. "Where the heck do you think she's goin'?"

"Well, has Donovan heard about Douglas yet?" Rawlins Beekman asked.

Dannie pressed her lips together and resumed her trek toward the jail at the end of the street. She hated it when people assumed her older brother Donovan could handle things better than she could. And she hated it that these men suddenly found it in their best interests to follow her every move. If it weren't for the gold, the three of them wouldn't even have greeted her.

That blasted creek was going to be the end of her sanity—if she didn't dynamite it right out of her life first. In the past two weeks it had done nothing but stir up trouble for her family, and for the rest of Shady Gulch as well. Spangle Creek ran directly down the border of Storm and Potter lands, and two weeks ago her father had found a gold nugget the size of a hen's egg nestled in its rocky bed.

But instead of a town celebration, questions had been raised. Whose nugget was it, the Storms' or the Potters'? Was it finders keepers? Or share and share alike?

The Storms claimed it was their gold. After all, they'd found it. The Potters claimed it was theirs, since they'd owned *both* properties before selling half to the Storms a while back. The truth was, nobody knew which family owned the place where the gold was found. And nobody would know until the state surveyor decided to ride out to the gulch and settle the whole mess.

But the people of Shady Gulch were willing to take a good guess whom the gold belonged to, not to mention place a few healthy bets. The town appeared to be divided right down the center. Half were rooting for the Storms, and half were rooting for the Potters. Sherman Potter had gone so far as to disallow anyone "in cahoots with that thievin' Storm family" from entering his mercantile. And Dreyfuss Storm refused to sell even a single bullet from his gun shop to a soul who sided with the Potters.

In Dannie's astute opinion everyone had fallen off their rockers. But for the residents of Shady Gulch, life had finally taken a sharp turn toward interesting.

There were fights every night on Aspen Street among men eager for a chance to stick up for their chosen victors. Women were whispering rumors about their counterparts, and the seamstress shop had gone so far as to hang a sign in the window that said NO STORM SYMPATHIZERS. Schoolchildren were beginning to join in on the feud, slapping tags on the backs of one another that said STORM LOVER or POTTER PICKER. Sundays were such a total disaster that Minister Stevens was now giving a double service, preaching to the Potter camp at eight in the morning and the Storm camp at ten. Sheriff Wingate had gotten so fed up with the people of Shady Gulch, he fled for the hills last week and hadn't been heard from since.

Which was why Dannie was now striding down Aspen Street, heading straight for the town jail. There was a new lawman in town, a marshal that the governor of the state of Colorado had sent to keep order until the state surveyor could clear up this mess. And to think Dannie had been so relieved at

this news. To think she'd believed that at last law
and order would be returned to the normally quiet,
friendly little town.

But at the moment Dannie had not law, order, or
friendliness in mind. The new marshal had arrested
her little brother, Douglas, that morning, and either he
was going to set Douglas free or she was going to see
the good marshal shackled to the cow catcher of a
hell-bound train.

She reached the jailhouse and paused to knock
the dust off her boots before stepping up onto the
boardwalk. People milling about the street had begun to
stare, no doubt waiting to see if she could take care of
this problem on her own or if she'd have to run to her
big brother, Donovan, again. She gave a particularly
interested group of women an icy glare. Then she
thumbed the latch on the jailhouse door and pushed her
way inside.

The interior of the office was dim and sparsely
furnished. There was a big black potbellied stove
warming against the wall to her left and a cluttered cot
not three feet from that. She eyed the gun rack next to
her, where her younger brother's holster and six-shooter
were hanging.

A movement behind the desk on the far side of the
room drew her attention to a small, grisly looking man
with a scar running down the center of his forehead. He
watched her closely as she walked toward him.

"Marshal Kiley," she said. "I've come to negotiate the
release of my brother."

The man's tiny eyes narrowed, turning his scar

into a deep crease. He slid lower into his chair and rubbed the gray bristle on his chin. "You must be Daniella."

His voice surprised her. It was soft and smooth, nothing like his appearance. "That's right. And once I've explained the situation to you I'm sure you'll agree that Douglas does not belong in jail."

The man grunted. "You know how many times I've heard that in my career?"

Dannie placed her hands on the desk and leaned forward. "I don't care what you've heard before, Marshal. This time it's the truth. My brother is innocent of these charges."

The man's hand paused in the process of rubbing his stubbly beard. He took in her stubborn stance and the determination glittering in her eyes. "It don't matter," he finally said.

"What do you mean it doesn't matter? Of course it matters! Douglas hasn't done a thing wrong!"

"What I mean, lady, is that it don't matter whether ya go on spoutin' his innocence to me nigh onta the next forty years. I cain't do a damn thing about it."

Dannie stood quietly for a moment, letting his words sink in. "Explain *cain't*," she finally said.

"Cain't. Cain't listen to a plea. Cain't make a decision. Cain't open the dag blurned cell. Need it any plainer?"

"But you're the marshal!"

The man in front of her opened his mouth to respond but at that moment the front door swung open, drawing their attention to the threshold. Dannie squinted into the bright daylight as a tall broad-shouldered stranger stomped into the jailhouse and closed the door behind him.

"Did ya catch him?" the older man asked.

"Naw. The kid scurried under an overturned wagon and hightailed it down an alleyway."

"Miz McIntire's gonna be set to spit."

"Mrs. McIntire can take her spit and—"

The stranger's eyes settled on Dannie and stayed there longer than the simple second it should've taken for him to see her. Dannie couldn't hold his stare. His almost black eyes were so unnerving that she looked down at the floor. She wondered what the devil he was finding so interesting and hated herself for not having the courage to ask.

Finally, the man at the desk cleared his throat. "This here is—"

"Don't tell me." The tall man took two steps toward her and peered down into her face. "Miss Daniella Storm."

Dannie looked up and swallowed. His eyes were like twin pieces of hard coal, and by the way his nostrils were flaring he looked about half-ready to ignite. He tilted his head, probably waiting for her response. She wondered if his jaw was always so tight, or if that had something to do with the anger she could practically see steaming out of his ears.

"What the hell do you have to say for yourself?" he demanded when she said nothing.

She froze. Obviously she'd been caught doing something, but she had no idea what that something was.

Again the man was waiting for her response, and again one wasn't coming. She wasn't ignoring him on purpose, she just couldn't seem to get a sound past her dry throat.

"Cat got your tongue, lady?"

"Seemed to have a purty good handle on it not five seconds ago," the other man said.

The stranger took off his hat, revealing thick hair as black as night. He tossed the hat on a coatrack in the far corner. "What is it we can do for Miss Storm this afternoon? As if I couldn't guess."

"Claims her brother's innocent."

The tall man laughed as he moved to sit on the edge of the desk. Dannie found herself looking down at the floor again, anywhere but into his condemning eyes.

"Says he don't belong in jail."

"In jail, Miss Storm, is exactly where you, your family, and half this town belongs."

Dannie stopped examining the cracks in the floor and looked up at him. "If you have such a problem with this town, mister, then maybe you should ride on."

He laughed again, and even the man behind the desk was starting to grin. "If only I could. How I would love to climb back onto my horse and leave all this craziness behind. But, unfortunately, I have a job to do in this godforsaken town. And from what I'm gathering, you and your family seem to be at the heart of its problems."

Dannie felt the color slip from her cheeks. A thought was beginning to dawn on her, and she had only to glance at the old man behind the desk to find her answer. Her eyes flicked back to the dark man in front of her. "Am I to assume that *you* are Marshal Kiley?"

He looked over his shoulder at the older man. "Have you been stealing my job out from under me again, Bean?"

"Folks jist keep wanderin' in here promotin' me all over the place. 'Spose that's what ya git for playin' outside all the darn day long."

"My brother is innocent, Marshal—"

"Don't!" The marshal's sharp voice made Dannie flinch. "Don't you even start with me."

"I told her we heard that kinda talk a thousand times before," the man named Bean said softly.

"I caught your brother myself down by the creek. He had his face stuck so far in the water I could've drowned him if I'd had a mind to—which I probably should have."

Dannie clenched her teeth. "Did it ever occur to you that he might be getting himself a drink?"

"That creek is off limits to anything and everything on two legs, lady. I don't care if he was washing out his soiled britches, he's in jail and that's where he's staying."

It was becoming increasingly apparent to Dannie that this new marshal wasn't going to give in to a reasonable plea.

"Can I at least see him?"

The marshal studied her for another long moment before giving her a curt "No."

"You won't even let me speak to him, see if there's anything he needs?"

"I only do favors for friends, Miss Storm, and people I like, neither of which lives in this town." With that he slipped off the desk and walked to the other side of the room.

As he passed her Dannie wished she had the nerve to stick out her foot and trip him onto his face. Instead she turned to the man called Bean, but he only shrugged and went back to rubbing his chin.

She wanted to shout down the rafters out of frustration, but she managed to keep her voice calm. "Marshal Kiley, my baby brother is only sixteen years old. Chances are he's in that back room scared out of his wits. Are you telling me that because I am not a personal friend of yours, nor am I *liked* by you in any way, that I will not be allowed to see to his welfare?"

The marshal set a metal teapot of water down onto the potbellied stove. "I think that about sums it up."

"Why you pompous—"

"I'd bite down on that tongue if I were you, lady, or your *baby brother* might not get anything but bread and water for the next week—"

"Week!"

"He'll be in jail until the surveyor gets here."

"But that could be a month for all we know!"

"He should have thought of that before he bent his back to get a . . . *drink,* did you say?"

"He wasn't stealing gold! How can a person steal gold from his own creek!"

"Whether or not it's your creek has yet to be determined."

"Oh, this is the most ridic—you can't just keep him here indefinitely!"

He gave her a calm look that infuriated her. "Would you rather I charged him formally and saved him for the circuit judge? Stealing gold oughta get him a few good years."

Dannie clenched her fists at her sides, wanting nothing more than to kill the marshal. Instead, she plucked his black hat from the coatrack, dropped it on the floor, and gave it a good grind with her boot heel. "Stick that on your head and wear it!"

Jake Kiley ignored the sound of the door slamming shut. Instead he focused on bringing the water in the kettle to a boil so he could fix himself a cup of strong coffee. He turned from the stove only when he heard Bean's cackling laugh.

"That filly done stomped on your hat!"

"I've always said you've got the worse sense of humor this side of cow shit."

"You're not gonna mope now, are ya? I know how you can git when a lady gits the better side a you—"

"That redheaded hurricane that just blew out of here was no lady. Ladies don't coddle men who break the law. Ladies don't cause street fights between their neighbors. And ladies certainly don't wear pants!"

"Jist the same, I commend ya for holdin' on to your

temper till after she left. You purty near scared the Holy
B. Jesus out of her the way it was."

Jake jiggled the teakettle impatiently. "Maybe she'll
think twice next time before she saunters in here crying
foul play. Damn. What the living hell are we doing here,
Bean?"

Bean sat forward and the chair beneath him creaked
in response. "Seems to me I recall we brought in the
wrong man, stone-cold dead, in fact."

"Damn McBride, that son-of-a-bitch." Jake glanced
around at the bare room. "I'd rather be banished to
China."

"I warned you about Marshal Duff McBride. He'd
shoot his own mother for the gold in her teeth. But you
were set on havin' things your own way, jist like ya
always are. And I suppose we best get to keepin' things
real quiet here or we jist might find ourselves headed to
China." Bean jabbed a finger at the ground. "The hard
way, if ya know what I mean."

"I'll keep it quiet here, all right, if I have to lock the
whole town in that back room to do it."

"The way things been lookin' the past few days,
wouldn't be surprised if ya have ta."

"Have you ever seen such a crazy bunch of people in
your life, Bean? It was one lousy nugget of gold, for
Christ sake. You'd think Spanish treasure was found in
that damn creek."

"The Gulch ain't Denver. Folks out here, so far from
big town excitement, tend to git bored. Tend to make
their own fun."

"Yeah, and families like the Storms and Potters

make it real easy for them. I just picked a ten-year-old boy up off the street out there. He had a black eye, a bloody nose, and all because his daddy placed a bet at the Rolling Spur on the gold belonging to the Storms."

"I hear the McIntires are in this thing deep. They're not only rootin' for the Storms, they're campaignin' fer 'em."

"So I'm supposed to say that kid deserved it? 'Hey kid, better luck next time on your pa's bets?' No wonder the previous sheriff ran for the hills. Hell, I'm probably going to end up shooting them all just out of sheer frustration!"

Bean pursed his thin lips. "The girl's right. Could be a good month till the surveyor gits here, what with all the gold bein' found in these mountains lately."

"Denver's a veritable zoo," Jake grumbled.

The kettle went off and he spooned a generous amount of ground coffee beans into the boiling water and left them to simmer. Then he sat down on the cot, with all its blankets strewn about, and rubbed his forehead.

"How you fairin' over at the Merriweathers'?"

He looked up at his deputy. "You're sweet on those two old ladies, aren't ya?"

"Those two lovely flowers a spring are not old ladies, and I was asking to yer welfare, not theirs."

Jake shrugged. "The food's good, the bed's soft."

"They, uh, ask about me a'tall?"

"The food's pretty closed-mouthed, but I swear I heard the bed whispering your name last night—"

A wad of paper flew through the air and bounced off

Jake's head. "Yer jist jealous 'cause I got me some female companionship during our lengthy stay."

"What you've got, Bean, are two women who think you need a bath, a shave, and about a hundred pounds added to your skinny body."

Bean sat up straight. "They say that?"

"Yup."

"Dag blurnit." He scraped the bristle on his cheek. "I ain't had a bath nigh onto three weeks."

"I know." Jake paused. "How's the boy doin'?"

"Storm? He's fine considerin'. Was sweatin' it out fer a while, thinkin' you was gonna hang him. Now, where in the world would he a'gotten an idea like that?"

"I might have mentioned a noose once or twice during our trip into town from the creek." Jake reached his arms over his head and stretched his back. "That kid's greener than a spring grasshopper."

"And 'bout twice as jumpy. Did he tell ya what he was doin' at the creek?"

"He said he was getting a drink."

"Now there's a tale with a familiar ring."

"Don't even think it, Bean. Chances are they worked that line up together just to corroborate stories and give us second thoughts."

Bean went back to slumping in the chair. "Things around this town bein' the way they are, probably better off where he is anyway."

"And I plan on keeping him there." Jake stood and took a dipper of cool water from the barrel in the corner. He added the water to the coffee to settle the grounds, then poured himself a steaming mug and sat back down on the cot.

Bean was watching him with expectant eyes. "You're thinkin' that boy's family's gonna try and break him out, aren't ya?"

"You saw the look on Miss Storm's face. She's not about to settle for waiting for the surveyor."

"She's got spunk, that one does."

Jake sipped his coffee, feeling the heat run all the way down his throat. "Yeah, well, spunk can't pick locks, Bean. And spunk sure the hell can't get her past me."

2

Dannie marched down the road toward home cursing loud and fluently. Her eyes fixed on the cracked ground in front of her, she was so angry she thought she might explode. What would folks say if they found her tattered body spread from here to Kansas?

The ominous sound of thunder rolled in the distance and she glanced up at the cloudy sky. Maybe it would finally rain. Maybe it would pour, and the creek would swell and wash the gold straight down the mountain and out of her life. And maybe the gold would take that smug lawman with it.

She was going to have to tell Donovan about Douglas, and that meant making things ten times worse than they already were. Donovan Storm didn't believe in fixing things the quiet way. To him a good knuckle sandwich topped a mouthful of words any day. The previous sheriff would have found a way to cool Donovan down before things got out of hand, but Marshal Kiley was not Sheriff Wingate. Marshal Kiley was nothing short of Satan himself, and, as far as Dannie could recall, Satan wasn't known for his patience or his understanding.

Dannie found herself wishing that her mother were still alive, as she kicked a rock out of her path and watched it skip into the dried grass and bounce against a willow tree. Her mother would've known exactly how to handle this situation: with a cool head and a calm heart. Unfortunately none of Colleen Storm's children had inherited her passive nature or her sweet temper. Sighing, Dannie sent up a silent prayer that her father would be back from Denver when she got home. At least he had the ability to box Donovan's ears if her brother refused to see reason.

The road narrowed, and she turned up the drive to her house just as another rumble of thunder rolled across the sky, taunting the dry earth. Dannie hoped Donovan wasn't back from hunting yet. She was going to need some time to prepare a convincing argument that would keep him from running off to town half-cocked.

She pushed opened the white picket gate, crossed the yard, and went into the one-story house. As she stepped into the front room, she knew at once that her father wasn't home, but Donovan sure was. He was standing by the front window with his Winchester carbine rifle in his hands, and she could tell by the murderous look on his face that he had definitely heard about Douglas.

"It's good you're home," he said. "I got somethin' to do and I want you safe here while I'm doin' it."

Dannie shut the front door, threw the sturdy lock into place, and spun around to face her brother. "You're not going anywhere, Donovan Storm. Not until I've had my say."

"Whatever you got to say is gonna have to wait—"

"Will you sit yourself down and *listen* to me for once!"

Her older brother could display the pure mean stubbornness of a spiteful mule at times, and he had very little tolerance for anybody who didn't take his side in matters, but things were more serious than Donovan realized. Somehow Dannie had to make him understand that.

"Dannie, our brother has been locked up in jail and I aim to get him out."

"You will aim yourself straight down into that chair, Donovan Storm. You will listen to what I have to say if you know what's good for you *and* what's good for our brother!"

There was a brief moment of silence as Donovan took a deep breath. "I'm gonna pretend you're not raisin' your voice to me. I'm gonna pretend that you aren't standin' there blockin' my way out of this house. But I won't be pretendin' my hand is connectin' with your backside if you don't heft yourself out of my way."

His voice was soft, almost calm, and Dannie knew from experience that he was simmering, brewing like a pent-up tornado. "You have to listen to me, Donovan. I've already been to the jail."

He took a step toward her. *"What?"*

"I knew Douglas hadn't done anything wrong so I figured I'd handle it myself!"

A muscle in Donovan's jaw worked rhythmically. "You figured you'd handle it yourself? How many times do I have to tell you to leave the man work to the men?"

"Since when is making a plea to free an innocent brother *man* work?"

"You're never gonna learn, Dannie. And one of these days you're gonna get yourself hurt . . . Well?"

"Well what?"

"Well, where is he? Where's Douglas?"

Dannie swallowed and looked away. "He's . . . he's still in jail."

A long breath of air hissed out from between Donovan's teeth. "I shoulda known."

"And what's that supposed to mean?"

"It means it don't surprise me none that you walked out of that jailhouse without our brother! A woman don't have half the guts of a rabbit!"

"Well, you don't have half the brains of a turkey if you think you're just going to barge in there and take Douglas back! That new marshal isn't a pushover like Sheriff Wingate was, Donovan. He'd sooner shoot you than mess with you."

"Tell me what he said."

"He said Douglas was going to stay in jail until the surveyor gets here. And that because we aren't friends of the marshal's, we can't even see Douglas."

"Yeah? Well we'll just see about that."

Donovan reached for the knob, but Dannie pressed back against the door. "He's got a deputy. A scurvy-looking man with a scar running straight down the middle of his forehead. And he's mean, Donovan, this marshal is really mean. I get the feeling he hates everything that has anything to do with this town."

"Get outta my way, Dannie."

"He's smart as a whip. You'll never get the keys!"

Donovan laughed. "Who said I need the keys?"

Well, that was that. She'd given him her best speech and it hadn't changed a thing. In a last-ditch effort, she clamped her arms over the door frame. "You're not going. Barreling in there is only going to make matters worse—"

In one smooth motion he picked her up and dropped her into the brown horsehair chair by the front window. On his way out the door he paused to point a finger at her. "You had better be sittin' in that same spot when I get home, or you ain't gonna sit for a week."

A few moments later, Dannie shut her eyes against the sound of Donovan's horse clamoring out of the barn. Through the front window she watched her brother ride from the yard just as a dagger of heat-lightning streaked across the sky. There was nothing she could do but wait, as Donovan had instructed. Wait and hope that his fierce temper didn't wake the beast that she knew lived and breathed inside the new marshal of Shady Gulch.

Bean pulled the shutters together on the one window in the jailhouse and latched them tight. "Sun's goin' down."

Jake set his elbows on the scarred desktop and rubbed his eyes. Just once he'd like to have a calm night in this town, one good night's sleep that wasn't interrupted by shooting and brawling. "I don't suppose it would be too much to ask these people to spend the evening in their homes?"

"It's either this or have 'em knockin' each other silly in broad daylight in front of the womenfolk."

"Oh, I think the womenfolk would gladly jump into the fray."

The deputy scratched his chin and cackled. "Probably right. You makin' the rounds tonight, or should I give her a go?"

"Naw." Jake shoved aside his plate of half-eaten chicken and stood to reach for his greatcoat. "You must be all worn out from playing marshal all day. Get yourself some rest. I'll look after the barnyard."

"Just so long as ya don't start shootin' the chickens."

Jake smiled wryly. "Killing half-witted, defenseless animals ain't my idea of fun."

He stepped out onto the boardwalk, noting the orange-and-pink cast to the cloudy sky. A cool wind touched his face and he reached to tug his hat low over his eyes—and remembered that the hat was now lying in the garbage pile, thanks to Daniella Storm. Muttering a curse, he set off into the growing darkness, anticipating the first scuffle he was bound to have with either a Potter or a Storm sympathizer.

He walked down the east side of Aspen Street, passing the relatively quiet Rolling Spur Saloon, passing the blacksmith shed, and crossed the street toward the closed doors of Potter's Mercantile. The store was quiet and dark. Mr. Potter and his son had already called it quits for the night. A smart move, as far as Jake was concerned.

He walked on toward the seamstress shop, pausing only a moment to shake his head at the sign hanging in the window: NO STORM SYMPATHIZERS.

He wondered what it was going to take to make this town move on to a better pastime. Would the state surveyor's naming of the winner make any difference?

Suddenly, shouts and gun shots echoed down the street toward him. Jake took off in a dead run in the direction of the Bull Horn Saloon. What greeted him there were two men, both drunk, slugging it out in the middle of the street, while groups of men on either side whooped and fired their guns in the air.

Jake moved into the fray and pulled the two men apart by the backs of their shirts. They both took swings at him, and he quieted them down by knocking their heads together. The shouts and shooting had stopped, and he found himself standing in the center of a crowd of half-drunk, incited men who'd been enjoying themselves just fine until he'd shown up.

One big man stepped forward, teetering on his feet. "I reckon I don't like you very much."

Jake figured if he blew hard enough he could knock the man over. "I reckon about now nothing looks particularly good to you."

A yell came up from the crowd. "Who you rootin' for, Marshal?"

"Yeah, Marshal! You puttin' your money on the Potters, or throwin' it away on them Storms?"

"Them Storms got justice on their side!" another

voice shouted. "And I'll clobber the first man to deny it!"

"I'll take that bet!" another yelled.

Before Jake could stop it, another fight, this one thirty-men deep, started in the middle of the street. He looked up at the glowing sky and cursed. Sweaty, swinging men began shoving him in every direction, and no matter how hard he yelled or how many punches he threw, it became clear that nothing was going to stop this clash of fools.

He made his way out of the tangle, getting hit a few times in the process, and stood beside a group of saloon girls who were watching the show. The crowd was transformed into a sea of bodies, heads bobbing and arms swinging.

Wondering if they'd all fit in the jail, Jake glanced up at the jailhouse that sat in the faint glow of twilight down the street. A flicker of movement caught his attention and he narrowed his eyes. Someone was slipping through the door to his office. The image of Daniella Storm's determined green eyes flashed through his mind.

He strode toward the jailhouse, wondering if Bean was still awake. He doubted Daniella Storm would hurt an old man, but after what Jake had experienced so far in this town he wasn't about to leave anything to chance. He slid his gun out of its holster and thumbed the hammer. Douglas Storm was in jail for a reason, and damn if he was going to let some fiery-haired troublemaker break him out.

The interior of the jailhouse was as black as pitch. Jake slipped in the door, much the same way Daniella

Storm had, and crouched against the wall, waiting for his eyes to adjust. Soon he was able to make out the drape of blankets on the cot against the far left wall. A narrow beam of light sifted through the shutters on the window and outlined the edge of the desk to his right.

He heard a faint shuffling beside him and turned to find Bean crouched down next to him. His deputy pointed to the open door of the cell-room and Jake nodded in understanding. Daniella Storm had snuck into the office, tiptoed past the deputy, who hadn't been as asleep as she'd thought, and headed right for the cells in the back of the building.

Jake edged past the desk and toward the far door. The interior of the cell-room was as dark as the office, and stealing a peek around the door didn't earn him a thing. He could hear soft voices, could hear the subtle clinking of metal against metal. Damn, if she wasn't picking the lock!

He pushed through the door, grabbed the shadowed figure by the arm, and shoved it against the wall. Then he pressed his gun against a surprisingly firm chest. "You're gonna regret messing with me, lady."

Bean barreled through the door with a lit lantern in his hand, and its bright yellow light spilled over the occupants of the room. Jake's eyes rounded in surprise and Bean let out a startled laugh. "That is *the* ugliest woman I have ever seen."

Jake pressed his arm against the man's throat. "I don't take kindly to people breaking my prisoners out of jail, mister. Now, who the hell are you?"

The man's jaw clamped tight, and Jake pressed a little harder with his arm. "You gonna start talking or am I gonna take away your right to breathe?"

But Jake knew by the reddish color of the man's hair and the familiar glint in his green eyes exactly who he was. It was another Storm, another troublemaker come to make his life more difficult.

"Donovan," the man finally rasped. "Donovan Storm."

"Well, it's so kind of you to check into my jail, Mister Donovan Storm. Hell," Jake added, "the more the merrier."

3

Dannie woke with her face pressed against an arm of the horsehair chair. She lifted her head and squinted into the morning sunlight coming in through the front window. Sitting up, she began to work the stiffness out of her neck. The house was quiet except for the ticking of the mantel clock.

"Donovan?" she called, rising up from the chair. "Douglas?"

Frowning, she went from the front room down the long hallway toward her brothers' rooms, where she happened to catch her reflection in a hanging mirror. She adjusted her hair and then paused at Douglas's door. "Douglas? You awake?"

She rubbed the sleep from her eyes and waited for Douglas's response. After getting no answer by rapping on his door, she eased it open only to find the bed empty and the sparsely furnished room looking the same as he'd left it the morning before.

"Blast-it, Donovan," she muttered. "Men's work is it?"

She strode to Donovan's door and didn't bother to knock before pushing it open. "You left him there yourself, didn't you . . ." Her voice faded as she took in the sight of yet another empty room.

Donovan's bed hadn't been touched, nor was there a plate lying on his night table as evidence that he'd eaten breakfast in his room as usual. Something was wrong. Dannie could feel it all the way from her tightening throat to her twisting stomach.

A loud barking in the yard startled her. She spun around and headed for the front room, tripping over a throw rug and almost knocking a lamp to the floor before she reached the door and threw it open. Joseph Hardy was just climbing down from his horse, and one of the town dogs was bounding excitedly at his feet.

"Joseph?" She watched his face carefully as he approached her, looking for some telling expression that might prepare her for the reason he'd left his post at the gun shop.

"I've got some bad news." He took off his hat and twisted it between his hands. "Some mighty bad news."

Dannie took a deep breath and gripped the porch post. "Is it about Donovan?"

Joseph nodded. "Yes, ma'am."

There was a long moment of silence as Joseph tried to come up with the right words, and Dannie felt tears burn her eyes. She was getting a vivid picture of what must have happened the night before. Donovan had probably charged like a raging bull, at the marshal, and Marshal Kiley had shot him down in the street.

"Is he . . . is he dead, Joseph?"

Joseph's head came up. "Oh no, ma'am. Not at all. He's just been . . . well . . ."

"Injured?"

Joseph shook his head.

"Run out of town?"

"No, ma'am."

"Then what! *What is wrong?*"

"Donovan's been jailed."

"He's been—he's been *what!*"

"Jailed, ma'am. Right alongside Douglas."

Dannie darted back into the house and came out a few moments later carrying her father's Remington shotgun. "I need a ride into town, Joseph."

"I don't know. I think you better wait for Dreyfuss to get back from Den—"

Dannie lifted the shotgun and tweaked Joseph Hardy's nose with the tip of both barrels. "You are not my daddy, you are not my big brother, and you are not my conscience, Mr. Hardy. Keep your damned advice to yourself and give me a ride into town!"

Joseph eased the shotgun away with his finger. "Sure thing, Dannie. But might I make one little recommendation? You waltz into that jail wavin' this thing around, and your pa's gonna come home from Denver only ta find each and every one of his children behind bars."

"Your advice is noted. Now are you going to share that horse, or am I going to take it from you?"

Dannie kept the shotgun tucked up under her arm and held onto the back of Joseph's shirt with both hands as they galloped toward town. She knew Joseph had a good point, but she also knew that reasoning with the marshal hadn't worked, and whatever Donovan had tried the night before had obviously failed miserably. It was time somebody shoved a long-barreled piece of persuasion in Marshal Kiley's face and insisted he take a different view on things.

They raced into town and stopped in front of the jail-house in a choking swirl of dust. People had heard the news and were already gathering on both sides of the street to watch the show. Dannie purposely landed on the toes of one spectator as she slid off the back of Joseph's horse.

Joseph cleared his throat. "You want I should come in there with ya, Dannie?"

Dannie eyed the people crowding closer. "No, you stay out here with these buzzards and try to keep them from swarming. Me and my daddy's Remington will do just fine by ourselves."

She marched up onto the boardwalk, amid murmurs and whispered speculations, and barged straight into the jailhouse, the shotgun raised and ready. "I've come for my brothers, Marshal!"

She slammed the heavy door shut behind her and, ignoring the deputy who rolled into a sitting position on the far cot, turned her attention to the formidable man sitting behind the long oak desk. "Are you going to give them to me, or am I going to take them?"

The marshal rose to his full height, a good six feet in Dannie's estimation, and pinned her with a dark, fathomless gaze. "You got a bug up your butt, Miss Storm?"

"Yeah, and he's got sin-colored hair and demon black eyes." She gripped the shotgun tighter and aimed it at his chest.

The marshal leveled his eyes on the bores of the twin barrels. "If you've come to wave that thing around under my nose, darlin', you better be prepared to use it."

"I learned how to shoot bothersome rodents by the time I was five years old. Of course you're a much bigger rat than I'm used to, but I figure it's the same principle." She glanced toward the cell room door. "Do you open it or do I?"

The deputy on the other side of the room cleared his throat. "Yer brother was caught jail breakin', Miz Storm. That's a grievous offense. Cain't neither one of us let him go."

"If that's the case, then Donovan was trying to break out an innocent man."

The marshal grunted.

"Douglas is innocent, Marshal! And that means Donovan isn't guilty of anything either!"

"Well, damn, Bean, why didn't we see all this before? Those men are innocent—*innocent*, she says! So, hell, let's let 'em out!"

Deputy Bean edged away from the cot and crossed the room toward them. "Holy B. Jesus, boy-o. Don't you know you're tauntin' the wrong end of the rattler here? Don't pay any attention to him, Miz Storm. Sometimes his brain just sorta stops all of a sudden."

"If he's *got* a brain, he'll let my brothers go."

Slowly, the marshal came around the edge of the

desk. He leaned over the length of the shotgun at her. "Go to hell, lady."

Dannie's anger and frustration mounted. Her breath started coming hard and fast, making her heart thunder against her ribs. She moved her hand over the stock of the shotgun and thumbed back one of the hammers. The marshal didn't budge, didn't even bat an eyelash at the faint *click* of the weapon being primed.

"Jake? You git shot and blood splatters all over my new two-dollar shirt, I'm gonna be mighty unhappy with you!"

A muscle worked at the back of the marshal's jaw and he arched his black brows. "Well, Miss Storm? Do I die? Or do you join your brothers in my jail?"

Dannie felt the color drain from her cheeks and a nervous cackle came from Bean. "He's jist joshin' ya on that one, Miz Storm. Ain't no women gonna be locked up around here, no sir-ee. Why, you put that pellet-blower down right now and I'll see to it that he don't even glance yer way the rest of the time we're in yer fair town."

Dannie felt a sweat break out on her forehead and she risked a hesitant glance at Bean, who stood just to the right of the marshal. She hadn't figured on things going this far. She hadn't figured on the marshal being so darn stubborn that he'd sooner die than give up his prisoners.

She looked back at him and stared deep into his eyes, and that's when she knew that there was no way she could win. "I'm not going to jail," she blurted out.

"You're not walking out of here, either."

She licked her dry lips. "I could kill you right now."

His hand slid down his hip, to the six-shooter she hadn't noticed until now. "And I could kill you."

Dannie would have liked to think the odds were even the way they stood. However, good sense told her they weren't. The one thing that stood between her and victory was the cool stamp of experience she saw in the marshal's expression.

"Looks to me like it's a standoff," Bean announced. "A dead even heat. What's say we all throw in the towel and call it a draw before somebody ends up shootin' me?"

Dannie stared at the hand the marshal was resting on the handle of his gun. One flick of his wrist could mean the end of her life—but she wouldn't be dying alone. She slid her finger to the trigger of the shotgun.

"Whoa, now," Bean jumped in. "Things appear to be escalatin'. Miz Storm I know you don't have a hankerin' to die. Am I right?"

Dannie nodded carefully.

"And dammit, Jake, I know ya don't wanna shoot a woman. . . . Say I'm right, Jake, just to make an old man happy."

A cold smile curved one side of the marshal's mouth. "You're right, Bean."

"All right, then let's all move our fingers from the triggers of our various weapons. . . . Miz Storm?"

Her heart racing in her ears, Dannie eased her finger away from the trigger of the shotgun. In response, the marshal placed his hand on the desk beside him.

"Now how 'bout if you lower the peashooter, Miz Storm?"

"First he's got to swear he won't put me in jail."

"Swear, Jake—"

"I'm not doing anything of the sort."

Dannie jerked her finger back to the trigger and the marshal's hand slipped back down to his gun.

"Jake Jedediah Kiley, *swear!*" Bean shouted.

The marshal's upper lip twitched. He pulled back his hand and clenched it into a fist against the scratched surface of the desk. "I swear," he said through his teeth.

Dannie gave him a cautious look. "No jail. Not now. Not ever."

The marshal only glared at her, but Bean nodded earnestly. "You gotcha self a deal."

The deputy's compliance alone wasn't good enough for Dannie, though, and she poked the marshal in the chest with the shotgun. "Not now. Not ever. Swear!"

"I swear," he finally said, soft and slow.

With a sigh, Dannie leaned back against the door, letting the shotgun nose toward the floor. She'd never played chicken before, but she'd just been initiated to the game by a man who had to be a true master.

"I want to see my brothers."

"I gave you my answer yesterday."

"Well, I'm not settling for what you told me yesterday!"

Bean stepped forward and took the shotgun out of her hands. "I'll just set this over here by the stove 'til yer set ta leave."

"Lady, you're lucky I'm a man of my word, otherwise I'd be tossing you into one of my cells headfirst! The way things stand, you'd do best just to gather up your stupid tendencies to irritate me and get the hell out of my office!"

Dannie crossed her arms and looked him square in the eye. "I am not leaving here until I've spoken to my brothers. Now, you can either let me in to see them or drag me out of here kicking and screaming. Of course I don't know how much respect this town is going to give their new marshal after they witness a spectacle like that. It might make it rather difficult to keep the peace."

"She's gotcha there, boy-o."

The marshal gave his deputy a silencing glare and then returned his attention to Dannie. "All right, I'll give you five minutes, lady. Five, *fast* minutes."

Dannie fought the urge to smile. It was a small victory but a victory nonetheless. She pushed away from the front door and crossed the floor toward the cell room.

"*But . . .*"

The one word stopped her and she glanced back at the marshal only to see a vindictive glint flicker in his dark eyes.

". . . you'll have to submit to a weapons search."

"That shotgun is the only weapon I have."

He laughed. "Now, what in the world makes you think I'd believe a single word you say?"

Dannie contemplated her options. A weapons search was understandable, she supposed, and a small price to pay to see her brothers. "All right, Marshal. Search away."

He took a step toward her and then paused. "Bean?" he called over his shoulder. "Maybe you should step outside and see to the gathering I hear shuffling around out there."

Bean hesitated, and then shoved his short-crowned

hat down onto his head. "You two behave yerselves, ya hear?" He opened the door and went outside.

The marshal turned back to her. "Turn around and put your hands against the wall."

Dannie did as she was told, knowing the sooner she got this whole thing over with the sooner she could see her brothers. The marshal's hand came down hard on her shoulder, and she let out a small yelp when he kicked her feet apart. Then suddenly it hit her what circumstances she'd unwittingly placed herself in: She was alone and unarmed with a man whose life she'd just threatened. And he was holding her in place very effectively with only one hand.

"I figure with pants this tight," he said softly against her neck, "the only place you could hide anything would be beneath this shirt."

"I told you, Marshal. I don't have any other weapons besides the shotgun. So this search is pointless."

"You could always leave, Miss Storm."

"Not until I've seen my brothers."

His free hand skimmed over her back and she went rigid as a thin line of heat raced up her spine. His other hand moved from her shoulder and came to rest on her lower back where he splayed his fingers and skimmed both hands from the arch of her back all the way up to the base of her neck. "Nothing here."

Dannie tried to remain still, but a shiver was attempting to wrap itself around her. "I told you—"

"Turn around."

She did so immediately, relieved to have the search over with. But she drew in a sharp breath when he clamped his fingers around her rib cage. She stepped back and slapped away his hands. His arms dropped to his sides and she glanced up to see an unrelenting look in his eyes. His point was clear. She could either submit, or leave.

Swallowing her pride, she lowered her arms and lifted her chin. He met her stare for stare as he put his hands on her hips. Her chest was beginning to heave from the effort it was taking not to run, and when his palms slid up her ribs, underlining the rise of her breasts, she bit her lip to hold back a biting curse.

His fingers eased to the side to search beneath her arms and then his hands came together, slowly. She couldn't move, she couldn't speak, and for the life of her she couldn't look away from the challenge in his eyes.

"I guess I can't call this nothin'."

She drew back her hand and slapped him, the sharp crack echoing against the walls of the dim room. He barely flinched, although even in the meager light she could see the reddening of his cheek. "You've had your search, Marshal. Now open this door."

Without another word, he lifted a ring of keys off the desk and unlocked the door that divided the cell room from the front office. "Five minutes," he said. "And then I lock this door whether you're out or not."

Her heart hammering, Dannie stepped into the room whose only source of light was three barred holes cut in intervals in the cement ceiling. She heard the scrape and the thud of the door closing behind her, and had to shake off a feeling of being trapped.

"Goddammit to high heaven, Daniella Storm!" Donovan shouted. He rose from his cot and strode toward the bars of his cell. "I told you to stay put in that chair until I got home. When I get outta here I'm gonna blister you somethin' fierce!"

"If I had stayed put, I would have rotted in that chair by the time you got home!" She looked into the next cell. "How are you doing, Douglas? Are you being fed well enough?"

Her younger brother pushed a hand through his thick mess of reddish-blond hair. "I'd be a whole lot better if Donovan would quit shoutin' at me all the time."

"Shut the hell up!" was Donovan's response.

Dannie finally smiled. "Not in a real good mood this mornin' is he, Douglas?"

"Never heard of a real good mood where Donovan was concerned."

Donovan grumbled something neither one of them heard and Dannie stepped back against the wall so she could see into both cells. "I don't suppose one of you would like to tell me how all this happened?"

"Donovan screwed up—"

"*Donovan's* gonna tear off your head when he gets outta here!" the older brother snapped back.

"He snuck in last night to break me out, but he didn't wait long enough for the deputy to fall asleep or for the marshal to go off duty. The marshal caught him tryin' to pick the lock here." Douglas snickered. "He thought Donovan was a woman. You're lucky he didn't give ya a big wet kiss and a tweak for your trouble, big brother."

"You ever seen the inside of your butt, boy?" Donovan threatened.

"You want the chance to describe it to me!"

"Boys!" Dannie shouted before they could erupt into a heated argument. "The marshal is only allowing me a five-minute visit. I won't have you wasting it on bickering. Do either of you have any ideas on how to get you out of here?"

There was a moment of silence as each man pondered the notion. Douglas brightened. "You could get the keys and let us out."

Donovan groaned and dropped his head into his hands. "Why, oh, why did God give me such a stupid brother? She can't just waltz up and ask for the keys, you *re*-tard! And if she tries to take 'em, she'll end up in here with the both of us!"

"Oh, Lordy, Lordy—I told you that marshal was the devil himself! He's gonna see us both hanged! He wasn't kiddin' when he told me that."

"Don't get yourself all worked up, Douglas," Dannie said. "He isn't going to hang you. He just plans to keep you here until the surveyor gets into town, and God only knows how long that could be." She shook her head. "If you're not out of here by the time Daddy gets back, the fur is really going to fly."

Douglas looked as though he were about to cry. "Do something, Dannie—"

"Don't you do a goddamned thing, Dannie Storm! You just go back to the house and wait until Daddy gets home. He'll take care of everything just fine!"

"We could be hung by then," Douglas protested. "I don't wanna die, Donovan."

"Ah, for Christ sake. We ain't gonna die! Stop your fool-headed whinin'! You want that marshal comin' in here and seein' what he's done to your pride?"

"I'll head out for Denver in the morning," Dannie announced. "Maybe Daddy's already on his way back and—"

"You will go straight home!" Donovan repeated. "You will sit yourself into that chair I told you not to vacate and you will wait!"

"Just what do you plan to do if she disobeys ya, Donovan? Make her drop her drawers and stick her butt through the bars so you can paddle her?"

"Who the hell's side you on, anyway? You want her traipsin' across the wilderness by herself?"

Douglas hesitated. "She's as good a rider as the both of us. She'll be just fine on her own."

"You're forgettin' the time Willie Potter nearly had his way with her. If I hadn't happened by the gazebo that night, our little sister would no longer be as pure as the driven snow. She's a woman, you idiot. She don't have half the strength of a ten-year-old."

"I learned my lesson from that!" Dannie snapped.

"The only lesson to be learned there, dear sister, is that you don't stand a chance against a determined man. The trail between here and Denver is full of woman-hungry men who'd give their big toe for a crack at a female like you." He reached through the bars and pointed a finger at her. "You mind me and get on home."

Dannie stood back and evaluated the situation. For once her brother couldn't force her to obey him.

She turned and walked to the office door. "Riding all day and night I should be in Denver by tomorrow noon. Try not to do anything stupid before Daddy and I get back."

She left the room, ignoring Donovan's ensuing bellow, and retrieved her father's shotgun. She knew what she had to do and nobody was going to stop her.

"Goddammit, Daniella Storm, I said get back here!"

"Sounds like the three of you had a real nice visit."

She glanced toward the desk to see the marshal tipped back in his chair, staring intently at her. "They hate to see me go," she replied.

"Come back anytime, Miss Storm. Just keep in mind the conditions."

Dannie reached a shaky hand for the front door, hoping she'd never have to endure another of the marshal's weapon searches. She stepped out onto the boardwalk and was instantly bombarded with shouted questions.

"Is it true that Donovan has been locked up?"

"Was Douglas really caught trying to steal gold from the creek?"

"Does this mean all the gold will be forfeited to the Potters?"

Dannie ignored the noisy crowd and edged toward the deputy. "Where's my brother's horse!" she shouted above all the voices.

"Boarded him up at the livery!" Bean hollered back.

She touched his arm. "Thank you! For everything!"

Bean scratched his stubbly cheek and nodded toward the office. "You leave him alive?"

"This time!" she replied, smiling.

She pushed through the crowd, leaving Bean to answer all the questions, and headed down the street toward the livery. She'd bring her father home. And then Marshal Jake Kiley would regret ever having heard the name Storm.

4

Dannie took some corn dodgers from the pantry, filled a canteen with water, and started out on her trip to Denver. The afternoon sky was a bright clear blue, and it appeared that Shady Gulch would have to wait yet another day for that needed drencher of rain.

She rode east, keeping the sun at her back and Pikes Peak to her right. Traveling through daylight and the long dark night, she hoped to reach Denver by noon the next day, if she didn't meet her father already on his way home. He'd headed for Denver to check up on the surveyor and had been gone for almost a week, but she knew he wouldn't stay away from Spangle Creek any longer than he had to.

The day wore on endlessly as she rode over crackling hillsides, thick with dry weeds and grass, and wound through endless stands of aspen. It had been years since she'd ridden this far and this long, and by nightfall her thighs had begun to ache, and her knees felt like they'd never bend any way but sideways again.

Though summer days in the mountains tended to be warm, the nights could turn dangerously cold. Fortunately, Dannie had thought far enough ahead to bring along a coat, but she'd neglected to wear her gloves. As a result, her fingers were red and sore from controlling Donovan's horse, and now they were cramping from the cool night air.

When the moon had reached its zenith, she had gotten to the point where the trail wound downward toward the eastern Colorado plains. She reined in Donovan's horse at the top of a rise and looked out on the vast ocean of darkness.

Denver lay out there somewhere, nestled against the base of the Rockies. The boomtown city served as a haven for those about to forge the treacherous mountain passes and a refuge for those who had somehow survived the perilous eastward crossing. By tomorrow she'd be moving among Denver's busy street traffic and probably having a tasty lunch in one of its fancy eating establishments.

She settled herself tightly into the stirrups and nudged the horse toward the steep, winding trail that would lead her to her father. The horse shied at first, unsure as to where to place its feet in the darkness, but Dannie persisted, gently but firmly, and succeeded in getting the animal to move forward.

The going was slow. She leaned as far back in the saddle as she dared to help keep the horse balanced, but he paused before each step.

"Come on, boy," Dannie whispered. "The trail flattens just a little ways ahead."

The horse snorted in response to her voice and kept up its vigilant pace, skidding on loose rocks while avoiding objects in its path. When the trail finally began to level out Dannie sighed with relief. The remaining ride to Denver would be a gradual decline as opposed to a sharp drop.

She gave the horse an affectionate pat on the neck and a vigorous rub of the ears. "The worst is over—"

Suddenly the horse squealed and reared, and Dannie caught the fleeting sight of red gleaming eyes before they darted into the enveloping darkness. She felt herself sliding backward and screamed while grabbing frantically for the pommel of the saddle. The horse bounced and gave a frightened kick with its hind legs and her fingers clutched nothing but air.

She flew out of the saddle. The ground came at her with a deadly force. The breath whooshed out of her lungs. Then everything went black.

The acrid smell of smoke filled Dannie's nostrils. The sound of sharp, cracking pops registered on her dulled mind. She opened her eyes, groaned at the pounding in her head, and stared in bafflement at a camp fire.

She glanced down at the heavy wool blanket covering her, and her frown deepened. She knew she hadn't brought a blanket from home.

A twig snapped from somewhere behind her and she lunged to her knees. She would have jumped to her feet

but her knees were as far as she got before her head
exploded in a blinding burst of pain. She brought her
hands to her head and peered into the darkness.

"I guess the dead *can* rise."

She went still at the sound of the unfamiliar voice.
Then Marshal Kiley walked into the circle of firelight.

"What the—!" She stopped short. The sound of her
own voice had made her head pound even worse.

"What the hell am I doing here? I've asked myself
that same question numerous times over the past two
hours, Miss Storm."

"Two hours?"

"That's how long you've been lying there like a chunk
of wasted buffalo meat."

She probed at the goose-egg-sized lump on the back
of her head. Grimacing, she sank back down to the
ground. "How did you find me?"

"I followed you."

His frank answer startled her. "Why?"

"Because your brother asked my deputy to do the honors
and for some reason Bean has taken quite a shine to you."

"Darn that Don—"

"Your brother seemed to think you'd be stupid
enough to try the steep trail in the dark. . . . Looks like
he was right."

"I wasn't thrown navigating the trail, Marshal. My horse
got spooked by a coyote. Where is that horse, anyway?"

"Halfway home by now, I'd guess."

She sighed and rested her forehead on her bent
knees. "So, where is Deputy Bean?"

"In his cot at the jailhouse, probably."

Her head came up again. The marshal had crouched down by the fire. He was wearing a black greatcoat and looked like the angel of death hovering over the ground.

"You came after me alone?" she asked with no small amount of surprise.

"The last thing that old man needs is to get into a tangle with—"

"Thank you."

His startled dark eyes met hers, and the flickering shadows thrown by the campfire danced across his face.

"If you hadn't come along," she continued, "I don't know what I would have done."

He shuffled and straightened. "Died, probably."

As he walked away from camp a quick feeling of fright trickled down Dannie's spine. "Where . . . where are you going?"

"You said your horse was spooked by a coyote. Somebody has to keep watch."

As if to protest his intention, a low mournful howl rose up in the night, gliding across the cool air to raise goose flesh on Dannie's arms. Reaching down to pull the blanket to her chin, she peered into the darkness, trying to make out a pair of ferocious glowing eyes, imagining herself sound asleep with a dozen snarling jowls snapping at her helpless form. A loud *who who who-who* came from the trees overhead, and she started.

"It's an owl."

She turned to her left to see the marshal sitting in the shadows a few yards away. "Wouldn't it be better if you were a little closer to the fire?" she inquired sweetly.

"Better for who?"

"How do you expect to protect me from all the way over there?"

"Who said I was protecting you?"

She clenched her teeth. "Didn't you just say you were going to keep watch?"

"Yeah. Over my horse."

Pain nudged the back of Dannie's head and she brought her hand up to cover her eyes. "I should have known . . ."

"What was that?"

"I said, I should have known I couldn't rely on you!" She grimaced and continued more softly, "It shouldn't surprise me at all that you'd put more value on the life of a dumb animal than that of a fellow human being."

"That dumb animal has carried me through a thousand miles of hostile Indian territory for a nice bucket of oats and a solid pat on the rump. Not only would I not get two good feet on you, Miss Storm, you'd probably buck me off before I even got settled in the saddle."

Despite the pain, her head shot up. "You even touch my *saddle*, mister, and you'll be shaking hands with God."

"Oh, don't worry, lady. I like my mounts well trained, with a sizable amount of experience."

"You're disgusting—and you're obviously still angry that I slapped you this morning. Well, you deserved it. And I won't apologize!"

There was a moment of silence, and then he said, "If I'd wanted retribution for your little swat I'd have taken it at the time. Now shut your mouth and go to sleep."

"*Sleep?* How am I supposed to sleep knowing that your first priority is your horse?"

"You clamp down on that flapping tongue of yours for one solid minute and I'll consider making an exception for tonight."

"Now what in the world makes you think I'd believe a single word you say?" she mocked, using his exact words from that morning.

"Don't push your luck, sweetheart. I suggest you cuddle up there and snatch a few winks before I change my mind."

At those disquieting words, Dannie burrowed down beneath the blanket and closed her eyes. He could promise he'd watch over her until the moon turned to cheese, but she wasn't going to trust him long enough to get one single ounce of rest. She yawned loudly, tucked her hands beneath her chin to keep them warm, and in the next moment fell fast asleep.

The whicker of a horse woke her the next morning, and she opened her eyes to the soft violet color of the dawn-touched sky. The sun was just cresting the mountains, and she imagined she'd slept maybe three hours. A cool breeze brushed against her cheeks. She shivered and burrowed deeper beneath the blanket.

"Come on, lady. It's a half-day's ride back to town and I'm not wasting a drop of sunlight on your beauty rest."

The previous night came back to Dannie like a bad dream, and she slid the blanket past her eyes and down her nose to stare up at the marshal. Not surprisingly, he was already on his horse and ready to ride. "And I suppose I have to walk?"

"You hold your tongue and I'll let you ride behind me." He gave her a direct look. "But if you start jumping all over me this early in the morning I'll leave you right where you lie."

Dannie gave him a hateful glare and rose with the blanket wrapped around her shoulders. For a minute her head spun and she had to steady herself against a tree, but then everything settled down long enough for her to offer her hand to the marshal.

The rough leather of his glove felt cool against her palm as he lifted her. She swung her leg over the back of his horse and settled in behind him, holding on to the cantle of his saddle as they rode off with the rising sun at their backs.

They traveled home on the same path she'd ridden the day before. As they traversed the hills she was forced to lean close to him to afford herself a better grip on the cantle, and as they wound through endless stands of aspens she found she had to tuck her legs behind his calves to protect them from slapping branches.

The sun gradually grew hot and beat down on her bare head. She watched as a damp film of sweat broke out on the back of the marshal's neck, and wondered if the sun was bothering him at all. Of course if he'd been wearing a hat—she suddenly realized that it was solely because of her that he wasn't wearing a hat, but instead of feeling guilty, she broke into a grin.

Without warning, his horse stumbled and she was

thrown forward, smashing her face against the hard planes of the marshal's back. He steadied the animal, but not before his warm, musky scent had filled Dannie's nose. She jerked back, her heart pounding.

"Sorry about that," he mumbled.

His head was tilted to the side as he waited for some response from her, and she tried her very best to answer, but her throat had gone dry.

After what seemed like a very long moment of silence, he returned his attention to the trail and clicked to his horse, sending them on their way again, and leaving Dannie feeling completely ridiculous. It was only the dust that was making her throat so tight, she told herself. Only the heat that was making her feel so light-headed. But from that moment on, she made a point of keeping her back straight and not leaning on the marshal the slightest bit.

They rode in silence throughout the morning and into the afternoon, and Dannie kept her complaints to herself, despite the fact that she felt every step the marshal's horse took in the bruises she'd sustained from her fall the night before.

"Aren't you getting hungry?" she finally asked around midafternoon.

"I ate before we left."

Anger rose up in her from the empty pit that was her stomach, and she glared at the back of his head. "Why wasn't *I* able to eat before we left?"

"You shouldn't have slept so late."

"Well, forgive me, Marshal, if I was a little tired. It isn't every day a girl rides for ten hours straight, is thrown from her horse, knocked silly, and then is rescued by a man who puts about as much stock in her life as he would an insect's."

"Maybe that girl should've stayed home where she belonged instead of traipsing off to Denver."

Dannie grunted. "You sound just like Donovan. He'd have every woman in the world shackled to a stove and with a child hanging from every finger and toe if he had his way."

"A man after my own heart."

She arched a brow. "You know, my late mother once said that any man who keeps a woman under his thumb is just plain scared of the competition."

"The day you can pee your name in the snow I'll start worrying."

Dannie's stomach growled loudly. She looked down at the hard ground below her. "I suppose if I faint from hunger and fall off you won't even pause?"

"Not even to wave good-bye."

She clamped her fingers tighter around the cantle, determined not to give him the satisfaction of leaving her in the middle of nowhere. "Are you at least planning to stop soon for water?"

"There's a creek up ahead. My horse will need watering. Take advantage of the time to eat if you want."

Dannie fought her irritation that once again his horse was coming first, and contented herself with the knowledge that she'd soon be eating something. A few minutes later, the creek emerged out of the dense, dry underbrush, racing over smooth rocks like a thousand diamonds in the sun. Because of the drought, it was only a few inches deep, but Dannie wished she could take a long, cold bath.

She slipped off the back of the marshal's horse and headed for a patch of wild blackberries growing by the water's edge. She filled her mouth and then her hands, relishing the feel of food as it settled in her painfully empty stomach.

From behind her she could hear the fading sound of clacking hooves as the marshal's horse wandered down the shallow creek bed while drinking. Then the thought occurred to her that the unconscionable lawman could simply mount up and ride on without her. But with a fist full of blackberries and a creek full of clean mountain water, Dannie decided she'd take her chances.

After a few minutes of contentment, she moved toward the water to wash the berry juice from her lips and chin. And that's when the loud *bang* of a shotgun sent her diving, belly first, into the creek. She felt the icy cold water seep through the front of her clothes, and the shock of it knocked the air from her lungs. Another shot exploded behind her, and she scrambled to her feet, dashing for shelter on the opposite bank.

She caught her breath behind the safety of a thick pine. A cool breeze drifted over her wet clothes and a chill raced across her soaked skin. She peeked around the edge of the tree and saw Marshal Kiley standing on the other bank, leaning on the stock of his shotgun.

He'd tried to kill her! She wrapped her arms around her chest to ward off another chill and prayed he wouldn't ford the creek to finish the job.

"You can come out now, Miss Storm."

Her first impulse was to scream when she heard the merciless sound of his voice. But she was out in the middle of nowhere. Who would hear her?

"I'm not going to wait forever," he called to her again.

Good. If she stayed right where she was maybe he'd go away. She heard him grunt, then heard the sound of his boots crunching on the bank as he made his way to his horse downstream. She let out a relieved breath and leaned her forehead against the rough bark of the tree. It would be a long walk home, but at least she'd get to town in one piece.

When she heard the crunching of rocks again she stiffened. He was coming back, and, by the sound of the heavy steps, he was getting angrier.

"The goddamned thing's dead, lady! Now, I'm giving you one more chance to come out from behind there!"

Dannie paused. What "goddamned thing"? Cautiously, she peered around the edge of the tree again. The marshal was standing where she'd been eating berries on the opposite bank and nudging a huge mound of yellow fur with the bore of his shotgun. The pieces began falling into place and Dannie edged out a little farther.

"It's dead," the marshal repeated.

"What . . . what is it?"

"Mountain lion. You eat the berries, it eats you."

Stunned, she stumbled into the creek and stood in the cold water, letting it rush against the sides of her boots. "You . . . shot him?"

"My horse would have done the honors but he was out of range," he said wryly.

Dannie raised a hand to her spinning head. She'd almost been attacked by a mountain lion, devoured by a sharp-toothed, iron-jawed, beast.

Swirling sparks of light began dancing in front of her eyes and she felt her legs begin to weaken. She heard a soft curse and the sound of the marshal bolting toward her as she was suddenly pulled into a narrow tunnel of darkness. Her knees buckled and she started to fall . . .

She came around to the feel of cold water being patted to her cheeks. A sturdy arm was keeping her on her feet, and she lifted her heavy lids only to stare straight into a pair of deep brown eyes accented by heavy black brows. He was a study of contrasts, this man. One minute he was threatening to leave her in the wilderness, and the next he was saving her from a deadly animal.

"You all right?"

Her gaze moved from his eyes, to his slightly flared nose, to the fullness of his lips. His mouth had always seemed hard and drawn, but standing this close to him, it looked soft . . . almost inviting, and she couldn't take her eyes from it.

His eyes narrowed, and he said something that didn't register in Dannie's mind. Then, surprisingly, he lowered his head and kissed her. Even more surprisingly, she didn't push him away.

The feel of his hard body against hers was like a heady drink of wine to Dannie's senses. The kiss was gentle, almost careful, but then a surge of warmth spread up from her stomach and she arched into him, curling her fingers over the rounded muscles of his shoulders.

In response, he pressed closer, and the kiss grew more insistent. He was urging her mouth open, refusing to accept less. And she gave in, allowing him to deepen the kiss.

Suddenly there was a loud crunching on the bank behind them, and they instantly pulled back from one another. Dannie glanced over the marshal's shoulder and saw a familiar man on horseback. It took a moment for her head to clear, but once it had, she cringed at the shocked expression on her father's face. Horrified, she turned to the marshal and did the first thing that came to mind. She slapped him. So hard, in fact, that it scorched her palm.

Her father cocked his rifle. "Do you suppose I oughta shoot ya now, fella, or wait until you've explained to me just what the hell yer doin' to my daughter?"

5

Jake rode into Shady Gulch with his back straight and his eyes forward. Despite his hope that he wouldn't be recognized, the people on the boardwalks began to notice him right away. They pointed their fingers and whispered behind their hands, and before long the entire main street had come to a grinding halt.

He figured he could lie to himself and say they were all awed by how well he sat a horse with his hands tied to the pommel. But more than likely they were shocked to see their new marshal riding into town with a Storm rifle nudging his back.

After practically cracking the side of Jake's face open, Daniella Storm had informed her father of every event since his departure. She'd told of a vengeful marshal who had ridden into town and tossed her exalted brothers in jail "for no good reason," and then how that same marshal had come riding after her to compromise her now that she had no family to protect her.

Jake hadn't missed the desperation in Daniella's green eyes as she'd made up her story. Her cheeks had gone redder with each elaborate lie, and her father's eyes had gone colder with each passing second.

Yeah, she'd dug herself in deep with this one. Jake knew from experience that if you gave a woman half a chance she'd attempt to lie her way out of anything, and being caught kissing the man who'd locked up her brothers had to be more than enough excuse for Daniella Storm to start with the stories.

Jake was directed toward the jailhouse in the soft glow of twilight. He'd been riding tied up for four hours and during that time Miss Storm hadn't said a word. He wondered if she was feeling guilty for putting him in this situation, but then he caught a glimpse of her face as she walked forward to untie his hands. She looked nervous, but not remorseful as she bent to the task.

Bean dropped his feet from the desk as the three of them walked into the office. His old eyes skipped over Daniella, then her father, and then narrowed on Jake. "What the hell did ya git yerself inta now?"

Jake pulled off his coat and slung it over the coatrack. "Deputy, meet Dreyfuss Storm."

"And Mister Storm's rifle," Bean added dryly.

Jake poured himself a cup of coffee. He turned his back to the potbellied stove, feeling the heat as it began to work its way through his shirt. "Shall we get down to business, Mr. Storm?"

"You get them keys and you set my boys free." Storm jostled the rifle in his hands. "You ain't gonna just waltz into town and jail my boys for no good reason. And you ain't gonna start takin' liberties with my only daughter! Just who the livin' hell do you think you are?"

"Unfortunately, I'm the marshal."

"Yeah? Well, this here's my scales of justice." He nudged the rifle toward Jake's chest. "Open the door!"

Bean slapped his hands down onto the desk and stood. "Now, hold on there jist one second. Who says them boys were jailed for no good reason? The younger one was caught stealin' gold from the creek and the eldest was captured while tryin' to break the little 'un out of jail!"

Jake took a sip of coffee. "Things like that are against the law, Mr. Storm. Much like holding a loaded rifle on a marshal."

Dreyfuss Storm turned his head to give his daughter a questioning look. "That right, Daniella? Was Douglas stealin' gold from the creek?"

"Of course not, Daddy! Douglas would never do a thing like that. And as for Donovan, he knew Douglas hadn't done anything wrong—and the marshal wouldn't even let us see him!"

Dreyfuss Storm seemed to hesitate, but then with a cold glare in Jake's direction he leveled the rifle once again. "That don't explain you attackin' my daughter in the creek."

Jake glanced at Daniella. "I don't suppose it does."

Bean spoke up again. "Hold on, now. What's this attackin' business?"

"I saw him with my own two eyes! He had hold of my daughter, his mouth all pressed to hers. Looked to me like he was tryin' to wrestle her down into the water!"

Jake saw the look that came into Bean's eyes and knew he wasn't going to live this one down anytime soon.

"Are you tellin' me that this fine upstandin' marshal was swapin' spit with your daughter in some cold mountain creek?"

"That's right! Who knows what mighta happened if I hadn't wandered upon them when I did!"

Bean shook his head and scratched his bristly chin. "Well, I'll be damned."

"Mr. Storm, I'm going to tell you the same thing I told your daughter when she came in here waving a shotgun under my nose yesterday morning. They're in jail, and that's where they're staying until the surveyor gets here—"

"I'm about fed up to my nostrils with folks tellin' me what to do! My whole life's been tossed up in the air until some short-pants government man decides to ride in and give me what is rightfully mine!" The man moved forward until the bore of the rifle was pressing hard against Jake's stomach. "You may have dealt with a Storm woman yesterday mornin', Marshal. But now you're dealin' with a Storm man. You open up them cells or we're all gonna see firsthand what you had for breakfast."

Jake finished his coffee and tossed the empty cup onto the cot. "Fine. The keys are in the drawer." He crossed to the desk, but only made it as far as the edge before the man stopped him.

"Hold it right there, Marshal! Dannie girl, you get the keys from the drawer."

Jake put his hand on the desk and casually closed his fingers around the handle of a razor sharp letter opener. Daniella pulled away from the front door and edged toward him. She was wary but had to look away from him in order to find the handle on the drawer. And that's when Jake made his move. He reached out and took her by the arm, hauling her up against his chest and pressing the letter opener to the slim column of her throat.

Dreyfuss Storm gasped but kept a tight grip on the rifle that was now pointed directly at his daughter's chest. "You . . . you wouldn't."

Jake nudged the tip of the letter opener against the pale flesh beneath it until a tiny droplet of blood appeared on the sharp blade. "Try me."

With a defeated sigh and a prideful lift of his chin, Dreyfuss Storm let his rifle drop to the floor. Bean rushed forward to secure the weapon and said, "You're under arrest, Mr. Storm, for assaultin' a peace officer."

Daniella went slack in Jake's arms and he had to tighten his grip to hold her up. "Go along quietly with the deputy, Storm, and you can have a nice long visit with your boys."

"You're gonna regret this, Marshal!" Dreyfuss Storm warned him.

Remembering the way Daniella had reacted the last time he'd jailed a member of her family, Jake didn't doubt it.

Bean and Dreyfuss Storm went into the cell room and closed the door. Jake was now alone in the office with Daniella, and her entire weight was pressed back against him. She didn't appear inclined to move, and he wondered if she'd fainted again. "Lies tend to make things worse, lady. Next time remember that."

She sniffled. It was the only sign that she'd heard him. When she shifted, he tightened his hold, not ready to let her go just yet, not while he had the chance to examine the disturbing burst of desire he'd felt at the creek when he'd held her in his arms.

Hell, he'd kissed a hundred women a hundred different ways, but none of them had ever been able to make his heart race like the sweet, unassuming kisses of Daniella Storm. Even now, the memory of their unexpected embrace was sending a shock of heat racing through him, and making his pants feel unbearably tight.

He glanced down at the small red mark he'd made on her otherwise perfect neck and fought the irrational desire to kiss it away. She was trouble, pure and simple. He needed to remember that. The smartest thing he could do was to take the kiss for what it was, a quick moment of pleasure, and forget Daniella Storm.

"You're a bastard," she whispered, hoarsely. "And I've never despised anyone as much as I despise you."

That statement brought a bitter taste to the back of Jake's throat and, setting aside his decision to forget her, he pulled her tight against his chest. "For a woman who hates me you sure the hell are snuggled in."

"The last thing I need is to be another victim of your jail," she responded in a soft voice. "Frankly, I'm afraid to move."

"You wrestled a promise out of me not to put you in my jail, remember? Now or ever?"

"Any man who can throw three innocent people in jail without a backward glance can hardly be expected to stick to his word."

Jake clenched his jaw. He considered his honor to be his one decent quality, and no redheaded brat was going to say otherwise. He dropped his arms to his sides, but Daniella still didn't move, and with her calm submissiveness she was making him feel like the bastard she claimed he was.

He put his hand to the small of her back and nudged her away from him. "Get outta here."

She took a few halting steps and then continued on to the front door, where she rested her hand on the knob and looked back at him. There was a faint glimmer of despair in her eyes, but she wasn't crying. No, stubborn-willed, fiery-tempered Daniella Storm probably never cried.

"You haven't heard the last of this," she said evenly.

Jake gave a faint nod. He could still feel the warmth of her in his arms, and he knew he'd probably never hear a more truthful statement than that one.

"You haven't heard the last of this by a long shot."

As the door closed behind her, he swallowed hard and then turned his head toward the cell room only to find Bean standing there watching him. "All right. Go ahead. I know you're dying to get it out, old man."

Bean relocked the cell room door and turned to put the keys back in the desk. "Woulda never thought that girl to be your type."

"And just what is my type?"

"The poofy-skirt and poofy-headed type. The ones

what *ooh* and *ahh* over your big strong muscles and giggle incessantly at every stupid thing ya say."

"For your information I don't have a type. I slake the urge when the need arises and then I move on. Plain and simple."

"I gotta tell ya, I ain't never seen a woman go toe to toe with ya the way that one does. She's got character. Mettle. Boy-o, if I was ten years younger . . ."

"Try twenty."

". . . I'd snap her up quick as a wink." Bean settled himself back down in the chair behind the desk.

"Then the next time she gets herself into trouble, which is bound to be within the hour, *you* can go save her."

"I woulda done that yesterday but you was all fired up to go after her yerself. At the time I thought you was savin' this tired old body the effort, but now I suppose I need to rethink that—"

"Don't waste the energy, Bean. Rethinking ain't gonna do either one of us a bit of good. I kissed the girl, all right? What's a man supposed to do when a woman is staring at his mouth like it's the only water within a hundred miles?"

"So you didn't attack her?"

"Oh, hell, do you really think I'd do something like that?"

"Known ya fer a long time. . . . Never seen ya take somethin' somebody else wouldn't gladly give ya. 'Course I never come across a female what wouldn't gladly give it to ya."

Jake pushed himself away from the desk. "This conversation is over."

"I'm jist tryin' to understand yer reasons—"

"Maybe I don't have any reasons! Maybe reasoning just sort of jumped out of my brain for one, brief second in my life!"

There was a pause, and then Bean said softly, "I hope you don't holler at her like that. A tone with that much bite could hurt a woman's tender feelin's."

Jake let out an impatient sigh and went to get his coat. What he needed was a night on the town caught up in the middle of a few Storm versus Potter fights.

"I ain't never heard of wooin' a woman by throwin' her family behind bars. Suppose it has its possibilities like everything else, but how do you propose to get on Miz Storm's good side?"

Jake paused in the doorway, noting the laughter brimming in Bean's eyes. This one incident was bound to be a great source of entertainment to the deputy for a while to come. "I have yet to meet her good side, Deputy. Let me know if it drops in unexpectedly."

Dannie felt empty inside, as if somebody had reached in and yanked her heart right out. And it was all her fault. If she hadn't lied, if she'd only told her father the truth from the start, that she had let the marshal kiss her, then maybe her entire family wouldn't be in jail. She rubbed the nose of her father's horse and leaned her head against its soft, warm neck. Night had fallen on the town and with it had come a uneasy sort of quiet, softened only by the sounds of chirping crickets and tree frogs.

She would be going home alone, to a dark, empty house that wouldn't be giving shelter to the rest of her family for a week, maybe more. Because of drinking from a creek, trying to rescue a brother, and protecting an only daughter, her family would be sleeping on hard cots with nothing but tattered woolen blankets to keep them warm at night. They'd be forced to pace a tiny cell for entertainment, and they'd get little more than mealy bread and thin, meatless soup for their meals.

An idea came to her. She glanced down the street toward the Merriweather house. She might not be able to free her father and brothers, but maybe there was something she could do about those tasteless meals from the Rolling Spur. She climbed onto her father's horse and rode toward the end of the street.

The Merriweather sisters had the fanciest house in town. It had been built by their father, the founder of Shady Gulch, as a present for his wife some thirty years ago. Ever since she was a child, Dannie had admired its neat little rose beds and blue shuttered windows. She loved its arched doorway and two red-brick chimneys, and had wondered countless times what the house might look like on the inside. She'd heard there were treasures from all across the world tucked in the house's cozy walls, presents from Captain Cyrus Merriweather to his wife and two daughters.

She slipped down from the horse and pushed open the wrought-iron gate. She went up the walk, climbed the three wooden steps up to the blue painted porch, and knocked firmly on the carved oak door. A shuffling came from inside, and then the front door opened.

Suddenly she was surrounded by the fragrance of mint.

Maybelle Merriweather's blue eyes crinkled. "My stars! It's Daniella Storm, Louisa! My dear, my dear, come in. You must be freezing out there in the dark."

Dannie edged past the billowing silk and taffeta of Maybelle's voluminous blue skirt and slipped through the door. "I'm sorry to barge in on you like this—"

"Nonsense. Louiiisaaa!" Maybelle called.

Louisa Merriweather swished into the foyer with a sparkling silver tea service gripped in her hands. "I'm here, already. I swear, you are going blind!"

"I simply wanted you to bring the child some tea, sister. Who knows how long she's been standing out there in the cold."

"Well, if she had to wait for you to respond to her knock it could have been hours."

"Come, come, my dear. Sit with us in the parlor."

"Oh, yes. It's been so long since we've had a lady over to share tea."

"Louisa, it was only yesterday. Abigail Drummond called to tell us about her son in the army. Your memory is about as solid as cream."

Dannie followed along behind them, trying to be polite and not stare at all the colorful objects piled, willy-nilly, in every corner. They led her to a room at the end of a long hallway and Dannie gave into an impulse to reach out and touch the red curtains and golden tassels on the threshold.

"Don't touch!"

Every muscle in Dannie's body froze at the sharp reprimand, and she turned to the two women, who had seated themselves on a plush red settee in a room whose walls were covered with gold silk. A fireplace edged in smooth white stone stood at the far side of the room, and a painting—of the late Siras Merriweather, Dannie supposed—hung majestically above the mantle.

"Harvey!" Louisa Merriweather chided. "Don't be so impolite. Daniella can certainly touch whatever she likes."

"Don't touch!"

Dannie looked toward the far corner of the room where a gold cage housed a white bird with a fluffy crown of feathers. She peered at the bird, trying to figure out if she'd really heard him talk or if it was just some sort of trick.

"Beady little eyes! Beady little eyes!"

"One more remark from you, young man, and I shall toss a quilt over your room!" Maybelle warned the bird, which promptly hopped to the highest perch in its cage.

"Do sit down, Daniella. I don't think we've ever had you in our home before. . . . Have we, sister?"

"We certainly haven't," Maybelle said, smiling. "Do you prefer one lump or two?"

After one last look at the astounding bird, Dannie crossed a red-and-gold oriental carpet and sat down in a wing-backed chair across from the matching settee. "One, I suppose." She accepted her cup of tea.

"Tell me, Daniella, how is your father? I understand he grew tired of waiting for the surveyor and rode off to Denver to check into matters himself."

"Actually, that's why—"

"Goodness, Maybelle, the child hardly wishes to speak

about all that infernal gold business. She's obviously here on some important matter, so why don't you let her get a word in edgewise?"

"Yes, I wanted—"

"*Me* let her get a word in edgewise? You haven't stopped talking since the poor thing stepped in our door. And gold, dear sister, is not infernal. Daddy happened to feel it was the basis for a happy, healthy life."

"Speaking of daddys—"

"He also believed it was the root of all evil in man, let us not forget that, Maybelle. It turns saints into sinners and sinners into devils."

"I couldn't agree—"

"Of course you can agree, my dear. This is, after all, a free country."

"Free country!"

"Hush!" Louisa snapped at the bird.

There was a pause in the arguing and Dannie took a deep breath, wondering when it would be her turn to talk. She only knew the Merriweather sisters from church, but their kindness, along with their eccentricities, was well known throughout town. She hoped she'd be given the chance to ask them a favor before morning.

"Well?" Louisa said, her gray brows arching over her clear blue eyes. "You certainly are a quiet child. Isn't she a quiet child, Maybelle?"

"I remember Mary Lambert was quiet. Remember Mary Lambert, sister?"

Louisa nodded and looked at Dannie. "She died stuck up in a tree."

"She was too quiet to yell for help," Maybelle added.

"So don't be afraid to speak your mind, Daniella."

Dannie took the advice and jumped into the conversation. "I was wondering if you might make meals for my family at the jail."

Both women's faces drew into confused frowns and Dannie wondered if she'd violated some social custom. Maybelle was the first to speak. "Did I hear her correctly, sister?"

"I believe she wants us to cook meals for her family at the jailhouse."

"I wasn't even aware they had a kitchen at the jailhouse. Why doesn't she want us to make the meals here?"

"I do want you to make them here at your home, if you would, and then take them to my family at the jailhouse. Remember when Smithy Anderson was locked up for two days, after he got drunk and shot up the saloon? The two of you made him meals during his stay in jail. I'd do it myself, but I'm not much of a cook. Daddy and the boys would probably prefer the slop from the Rolling Spur to whatever I could scrape out of the bottom of a pan."

The two older women exchanged a bewildered glance. "Daniella," Louisa said, "why would your family want to eat at the jail? Is there something wrong with your home?"

Dannie blinked. How could they not have heard about her family's jailing? By now the news had to be spread clear to Denver. "The new marshal has locked up both Douglas and Donovan. And he has just jailed my daddy."

Both women's jaws went slack. "That nice Kiley boy?" Maybelle muttered.

"*That nice Kiley boy* has left me with nothing but a horse and an empty house."

"Oh, my dear," Maybelle said softly. "That's really quite horrible."

"So horrible. . . . It reminds me of the time Willoughby Barns was tripped by that runaway pig as he was crossing the street. Remember that, sister?"

Maybelle nodded. "Willoughby wanted to have the pig slaughtered, but our father demanded to buy the poor animal. Wouldn't let Willoughby lay a hand on it."

"Father was fined five dollars for that."

Perplexed at how any of this figured into their conversation, Dannie glanced from one woman to the other. "Your father was fined five dollars for protecting a pig?"

"Certainly not," Louisa said, laughing. "For bashing ol' Willoughby over the head with a beer keg. Oh, of course we'll make your family meals, dear Daniella. But we really should be talking about you, I think. Don't you agree, Maybelle?"

"Oh, yes. We can't have you staying out there in that dark, empty house all alone."

"She'll stay here," Louisa announced with a note of determination.

"Yes, yes. You'll stay here. Oh, it'll be such fun having a young lady in the house."

Louisa and Maybelle were already on their feet and heading for the foyer when Dannie called, "No, really, I couldn't stay."

Louisa paused in the parlor doorway and turned back to her. "Of course you can. We've just invited you, my dear."

Dannie stared after them as they left the room, not sure what to do. She supposed it would be handy staying so close to the jail, it would certainly make her visits to her family a lot easier, but it seemed to her to be an awful intrusion.

She hurried after the two women and found them climbing the stairs, arguing about what color linens they should use in her room. "Wait," she called. "I—I appreciate the offer, but, really, I can't trouble you like this."

The sisters exchanged odd smiles and then continued up the stairs. "The matter, my dear," Louisa called, "is settled."

6

Bright sunlight flickered through the curtains and drifted over Dannie's face. Her first thought was that it would be another day without rain. She threw her arm over her eyes and allowed herself to wake up slowing as she listened to the jangling of harnesses outside and the steady rise of voices. The daily activity on Aspen Street was moving into full swing.

She'd need to pick up some things from home that morning if she planned to stay with the Merriweathers for any length of time. But first she needed to visit her family at the jail. Maybe since last night they had thought of a way to get themselves free, because, for the life of her, she hadn't been able to think of a thing.

She sat up on the bed and stretched, and then her eyes widened in alarm. There, in the far corner was an enormous metal suit of armor. And it was staring directly at her.

She took a calming breath, wondering if she'd ever

get used to all the oddities in the Merriweather house, including the women themselves. She got out of bed and dressed in the clothes she'd had to wear for the past three days. Her pants were stained with grass and mud, and her shirt was stiff from sweat and dust. She glanced down at her dirty arms and realized that not only did she need clean clothes, she needed a good bath. She was embarrassed to be seen looking like she did.

She peered in the mirror at her reflection and tried to smooth her fingers through her tangled hair. Finally braiding the unruly mess, she tied it with a piece of string and went downstairs to breakfast.

She could hear the Merriweather sisters arguing in the kitchen as she walked through the foyer. They were discussing lightning and whether or not it would hurt to be struck by a bolt.

"Honestly, sister. A little jolt of electricity would probably add some color to your ruddy cheeks."

"Yes, Maybelle, a nice shade of burnt brown."

Dannie pushed the swinging kitchen door with her elbow, while tucking her shirt farther down into her pants, and said "Good morning."

Unless Louisa or Maybelle had suddenly swallowed a pond full of frogs, the deep voice that answered her did not belong to either sister.

Dannie's head came up and she was stunned to see the marshal, sitting at the kitchen table, his fork poised over a plate full of flapjacks. "What are you doing here?" she demanded.

The marshal's eyes narrowed. "I was about to ask you the very same question."

"Come, come. Sit down, my dear," Louisa called. "I'll fetch you a plate."

As Louisa Merriweather moved toward the stove, Dannie glanced suspiciously at him again, trying to figure out just why he was eating breakfast at this particular table. He was staring at her which she assumed was meant to intimidate her, and so, lifting her chin, she slid out the chair beside him and sat down.

"Daniella," Louisa called from the stove, "you've met Marshal Kiley, haven't you? He's been delighting us as our houseguest during his stay here in the gulch."

Dannie's heart all but stopped beating. The marshal was staying *here*? With the Merriweathers? Well that settled it. If she hadn't had a good reason for not staying with the sisters the night before, she certainly did now!

"You'll be happy to hear, Marshal," Maybelle said, smiling, "that we've invited Daniella to stay with us as well."

The marshal's face turned downright pale at this bit of news. "Wonderful." He shot Dannie a glare. "And whose bright idea was that? As if I couldn't guess."

Dannie wrinkled her nose and glared back. Did he honestly think that she was any happier with this predicament than he was?

"*We* invited Daniella to stay with us," Maybelle responded. "Considering the unfortunate situation with her family, we thought it best that she not be alone in that empty old house so far from town."

"You never know what type of scoundrels wander about the countryside, Marshal," Louisa added. "They roam around at night, attacking poor helpless women in their sleep."

"Daniella is very welcome to stay here with us until she feels she's ready to go home."

"Wonderful," the marshal mumbled. "I don't suppose she might feel ready this morning?"

Far from hurting her feelings, the marshal's reluctance to have her underfoot gave Dannie an evil thrill of delight. "My, my," she said, glancing down at the plate full of flapjacks and fried potatoes that Louisa had set in front of her. "I suppose I'll have to get used to these bearish moods you obviously wake up in."

"Come, sister," Louisa suddenly said to Maybelle. "I need to speak with you about something in the parlor."

"Speak to me about it right here."

"Sister," Louisa said in a warning voice.

"Oh." Maybelle blinked. "Louisa needs to speak with me about something in the parlor. Something . . . private?"

"Yes." Louisa smiled. "Something private."

The two sisters left the kitchen and the marshal turned on Dannie. "You're doing all this just to irritate me, aren't you, lady?"

Dannie brought a forkful of fried potatoes to her smiling lips. "Don't flatter yourself, Marshal. I wouldn't waste a single moment of my time doing *anything* to you."

His response was a smug smile, and she knew exactly what he was thinking. It was that kiss—that darn kiss that they'd shared.

"Sometimes," she said, "a girl will do just about anything for the sake of her family. Even tangle with a viper."

His smile turned cool. "They're in jail, Daniella, and that is exactly—"

"Where they're staying. Yes, I know. And, well"— she sighed—"you're the marshal. It's your jail. You put them behind bars, and I guess they'll have to stay there until you've changed your mind." She smiled at him again and forked a piece of flapjack into her mouth.

"That's right. And there isn't a *thing* in the world you can do that will make me change my mind. They get released when the surveyor arrives and not a minute sooner. And let's not forget, Miss Storm, that I'm going to have just as much access to you in this house as you will have to me. In other words, any revenge you might decide to take will be visited upon you, two-fold."

She paused with her fork at her mouth. "Are you threatening me? Because if you are, I'll be forced to defend myself. Maybe even carry a shotgun."

"Christ," he muttered. "I don't know why I didn't toss you in jail a long time ago."

"I believe it was because of your sterling word of honor. Sometimes a promise can be such an inconvenience," she added sarcastically.

"I may have promised that I wouldn't toss you into jail, lady, but I didn't say anything about not tossing you over my knee and blistering your butt with the palm of my hand."

Dannie had been bullied all her life by an older brother, and she wasn't about to put up with such treatment from a total stranger. She set down her fork and slowly turned toward him. "And I may have backed down to you a few times before, Marshal, but you raise a hand to me and I'll see to it that it's the last thing on you that *ever* raises."

A soft gasp came from the vicinity of the door, and the two of them looked over as the sisters came back into the room.

"Don't mind us," Maybelle said as they headed for the sink. "You two go on about your business and pretend we're not even here."

"How are they supposed to pretend we're not here, sister, when you gasp at every little thing they say? You'd think a bag of hot air was listening at the door beside me."

Maybelle picked up a dirty dish and dipped it in the bucket of water on the countertop. "At least I'm not staring at them like an old buzzard."

Louisa turned away from where Dannie and the marshal were sitting and focused on the pile of breakfast dishes. "That's only because you could barely see them if they were standing on your toes."

"At least *I'll* remember what they said to each other in ten minutes time," Maybelle retorted.

"There is nothing wrong with my memory. I simply choose to ignore certain things you do that have no meaning whatsoever."

"And I suppose you chose to ignore the invitation Minister Stevens had for supper last week? And the name of our cleaning woman, who has worked for us for over twenty years?"

"Oh, Henrietta is so tiresome. I only do that to keep her on her toes."

"Her name is Harriet, sister."

"Yes, but I prefer to call her Henrietta."

Maybelle suddenly looked over at Dannie. "Eat, my dear, eat."

"You're a very pretty young lady, Daniella. But, frankly, you have the build of a porch rail."

Dannie heard something that sounded like a strangled laugh come from the marshal, and she glared at him.

"We'll be journeying into town after breakfast to visit the bakery, Daniella, if you'd like to accompany us for some air."

Dannie was still trying to get over the remark about the porch rail. "No, thank you. I'll be heading to the jail to visit my family."

Maybelle perked up. "Oh? Perhaps the marshal would like the privilege of escorting you."

"I'd rather have the privilege of escorting her into a deep ravine."

"I am not a lemming, Marshal. I think I'd have brains enough to pull up if I saw the tail end of your faithful steed careening straight down."

"I'm willing to take that risk, lady."

"Goodness, children. If we're all to live here in peace, then we are going to have to learn to get along. Isn't that right, Louisa?"

"Honestly, sister, life would be a complete bore if we all got along. Let them have their fun, for pity's sake."

The marshal shoved back his chair. "I have a town to see to. Thank you for breakfast, ladies. If I'm not back for lunch or supper"—he gave Dannie a direct look—"don't be too surprised."

He marched out of the kitchen, and Dannie's shoulders

tensed as he slammed the front door. Staying under the same roof with the marshal wasn't exactly her cup of tea, but if it bothered him this much . . . ?

She glanced up at the two ladies at the sink. They were watching her expectantly. "Well, I suppose I'll be here for lunch and supper. I'm not one to pass up a good meal, or a soft bed."

They smiled at her and Dannie hoped she was making the right decision. Besides, her family had probably already come up with an ingenious plan to free themselves.

"That is the craziest idea I have ever heard in my life, Donovan! And you have come up with some loo-loos before!" Dannie stood, exasperated, in the cell room, facing her brothers and her father through the bars of their cell. "I may be willing to do just about anything to get you out of there, but I will not seduce that low-down marshal!"

"Dannie's right," Douglas said. "We got no call to ask her to do somethin' like that."

"Oh? You'd rather sit here and wait for the Potters to steal all our gold?"

Douglas's eyes rounded, and he said, "Well, maybe it ain't such a bad plan, Dannie."

"It's not like I'm askin' ya to do somethin' you haven't already done," Donovan pointed out.

Dannie gave her father an accusing look. "You told them?"

"Well, it ain't every day a man comes upon his daughter lockin' lips with the bane of his existence. 'Course I told 'em. It was family business."

"It was my business, Daddy. And now look at the fool idea you've given Donovan! He wants me to throw myself at that man just to protect a creek of gold that might not even belong to us!"

"You hush your mouth, girl!" her father ordered. "If there is one thing in this world I'm sure of it's that gold is ours!"

"And that the Potters are gonna steal every shiny granule now that we're not there to stop 'em," Donovan added.

Dannie shook her head. "I think that nugget Daddy found is bigger than all three of your brains put together."

"It's not as though we're askin' ya to play slap and tickle with the man," Douglas said. "Just smile a bit. Talk sweet to him. Give him a little kiss—"

"Like hell!"

"Keep your voice down, Daniella," Donovan said. "You want that deputy to hear us?"

"I am not kissing him. I don't even *like* him."

"Well, you surely had to like somethin' about him if you were lettin' him climb into your mouth like that—"

"Donovan Storm, he was not climbing into my mouth! He was taking advantage of my faint."

"Yer what?" Douglas asked.

Dannie bit her lip. "My . . . faint. I fainted."

"You fainted?" Donovan repeated, shocked. "You ain't never fainted in your whole life!"

"I was tired and hungry. Your stupid horse had thrown me and I'd hit my head. I started to faint and the marshal caught me. When I woke up he was . . . he was kissing me."

"See there? What did I tell you? You don't have any defense against a man that takes you unaware. None of this would have happened if you'd just stayed the hell home like I said."

"Don't you start in on me, Donovan Storm, or I'll leave the three of you to rot in that cell. I may not have succeeded in my attempts to get you out, but at least I didn't get myself locked up in jail!"

Donovan's eyes narrowed. "One would wonder why that is, little sister. I hear tell that you, yourself, held a shotgun on the good marshal not two days ago. The same crime that got our Daddy locked up, if I recall."

Dannie gave him a hard stare. "Just exactly what are you suggesting?"

"Could it be that you're sweet on that lawman. Could it be that he's already seduced you—directly over to his side!"

"I am going to pretend that you didn't just suggest that I have turned my back on my family. The same way I'm going to pretend that this conversation has never taken place."

She turned for the door, but her father's voice stopped her. "Dannie girl, I'm ashamed to admit it, but you could be our only chance. If the Potters take all the gold it won't make a whit of difference if every surveyor in the country marks that creek as ours. We're a strong, proud family, but we've never really had much. That gold could buy us a fancy house, a hundred gun shops, it could send Douglas to school back East. With money, Storm will finally be a name to reckon with. Without it, we'll be nothin' for the rest of our lives."

Dannie swallowed hard. "If Mama heard you talking like that she'd whop you with a skillet. We were fine, happy, until gold came into our lives. And now, that's all you three think about: fancy houses, fancy clothes, money. Look at yourselves. You're in jail, for crying out loud. And it's all because of that one darn nugget!"

"Ah, Daddy, ya made her cry."

Dannie sniffed. "I'm not crying, Douglas, I'm just disappointed, that's all. . . . All right. I'm not going to promise you anything, that lawman doesn't even like me, but I'll see what I can do."

"Woo-wee, Dannie," Douglas shouted. "I knew you'd come through for us! And you're not gonna regret this either, right, Donovan? When we get outta here, we're gonna buy you the prettiest dress in Denver with all that gold!"

Donovan snorted. "First she best take herself a bath."

"Don't press your luck, big brother. I wouldn't smell so bad if I hadn't been chasing after other people's problems for the past three days—yours included."

"Another fine argument as to why you should have listened to me and kept yourself put in the house!"

"I'm sorry, Donovan, when was it that you became my father?"

"A sassy handful like you could use all the fathers she can get in my point of view!"

"And we all know how sound your point of view is half the time!"

"That's enough!" her father interrupted. "How's the nugget?"

Dannie was still glaring at Donovan. "It's fine."

"When was the last time you checked it?"

Her eyes wavered. Then she looked at her father. "I haven't."

"Then how the hell do you know that it's fine!" Donovan practically bellowed.

"Because the only person who ever messes with it has been locked up in here for the past two days!"

Donovan gave his father a guilty shrug. "I like to look at it every now and then."

Dannie rolled her eyes. "He practically sleeps with the thing."

"I told all three of you to leave it alone. What if Potter had seen ya takin' it out of its hidin' place? What then?"

"I'm heading over to the house this morning, Daddy, so I'll check on it. I'm sure it's just fine."

"Wait a minute," Donovan said. "Wait just a gal-darn minute. What do you mean, *heading over to the house this morning*? Didn't you just come from the house?"

"The Merriweather sisters have invited me to stay with them while you're in jail. I thought it was very kind—"

"You slept under the same roof last night as that marshal! My God, he did seduce her!"

"He did not seduce me!" Donovan made a move to open his mouth again but Dannie cut him off by saying, "You better stop accusing me, Donovan Storm, or I'm going to come in there and sock you in the nose!"

Her father was smiling. "This only makes things easier, Donovan. Don't ya see? She's livin' right there in the same house with him. She'll have all kinds of opportunities to play with the fella's mind."

"As long as that's all she plays with—"

"This wasn't my idea in the first place!" Dannie retorted.

Donovan pointed a finger at her. "You just watch yourself, girl. You let that marshal get you into his bed and you'll be pegged as loose, easy pickin's. I don't wanna be spendin' my days splittin' lips. No sister of mine is gonna be the town toy."

Dannie clenched her teeth. "I'm leaving. I'll check on the nugget, and I'll do what I can with the marshal. But may I suggest that while the three of you are in here you attempt to unscramble your brains and get straight what is really important in life. Here's a hint: It *isn't* heavy and shiny."

7

The sky was still refusing to open up, and as Dannie rode to her house late that morning she wondered if it would rain again in her lifetime. However what the citizens of Shady Gulch needed even more than a good cloud burst was a strong dose of humility. Not only was their inexcusable behavior corrupting one another, it was corrupting their children.

Dannie pitied Joshua Hill, whose father had been the first man in town to take Sherman Potter's side. Kincaid Hill had trounced a man for claiming the Potters had no right to the gold, and now little Joshua, who really was too young to have much of an opinion on anything, was being bullied daily on his way to and from school.

Dannie had come upon the six-year-old standing in the middle of the road with a Snider boy on either side of him, their fists clenched at their sides. She had taken one look at Joshua's wide blue eyes and swung down from her father's horse.

"If I didn't know better, I'd say you two boys were ganging up on this young man."

Jimmy and Teddy Snider had relaxed their stances and turned bright smiles on Dannie. "Heck no, Miss Storm. We was just asking Joshua, here, if he wanted a piggy ride to school. Ain't that right, Joshua?"

Little Joshua shrank back from Jimmy's glare. "Y-yes 'um."

"Well, isn't that refreshing. All the other children in town treat each other like dogs, but the three of you appear to be the best of friends. I'm proud of you, boys. You're growing into fine, responsible young men."

Teddy, whose bottom Dannie had wiped when he was a baby, looked down at his shoes and shuffled. Of the two Snider boys, Teddy had always been the most transparent, and the easiest one to humble.

"I'm going to recommend to Minister Stevens that he call you up to the podium on Sunday for special recognition," she added, and turned toward her horse.

"Miss Storm?"

"Teddy," she heard Jimmy say in a warning whisper.

"I ain't standing up there on Sunday with everybody staring right through me," Teddy whispered back. "Miss Storm, actually, we *was* sorta pickin' on little Joshua, here."

Dannie put on her best shocked look and turned back toward the three boys. "Picking on him?"

"They was gonna give me a finger sandwich!" Joshua cried.

"I think that's a knuckle sandwich, sweetie."

"And then they was gonna strewn my innards all the way ta Kin-tucky!"

Dannie arched a brow. "Not exactly a friendly way to speak to your neighbor."

"He wants the Potters to get the gold!" Jimmy accused. "He thinks what you folks found don't rightly belong to ya!"

"I don't think nothin'," Joshua said, shaking his blond head. "My pa says thinkin' just gits me inta trouble."

"Your pa cottons to thieves!"

Dannie took a calm breath. "The Potters are not thieves, James Snider. They simply expect justice, just like you and I. And you picking on a boy half your age and size is hardly fair."

"But they want to take your—"

"I can look out for myself and my belongings just fine, thank you. I don't need you or your father, or anyone else in this town for that matter, fighting over what does or does not belong to me. Do you understand me, James Snider? Stop all this stupid bickering and fighting, or so help me I'll get a thick switch and take it to your little bottom!"

The Snider boys paled. "We were only tryin' to help," Jimmy said.

"Do you really think my family wants you picking on Joshua? Gold may be valuable, boys, but friends are priceless. Now, how about if you give him that piggy ride?"

Jimmy balked, but Teddy stepped forward, and after

patting Joshua on the head and apologizing, he swung
the little boy onto his back. Jimmy reluctantly accepted
the task of carrying Joshua's lunch pail.

If only reasoning with her family could be so easy,
Dannie thought as she rode up to her house. She went
directly to her bedroom, packed her yellow cotton
dress, her blue gingham dress with the tiny flower
buttons, and her pale green muslin. She dumped her
whole underwear drawer into the canvas bag, along
with her brush, hair pins, and the tintype of her mother
that she always kept by her bed. Then she went to the
kitchen and pried up the loose floorboard under the
table to check on the gold nugget, as she'd promised
her father.

She had to admit it was spectacular, all glittery and
jagged. It was so big it practically filled her palm. She
found herself staring at it, wondering how many dresses
and how many soft pairs of leather shoes she could buy
with this one chunk of gold . . .

Blinking, she shoved the nugget back into its hiding
place and replaced the floorboard. She refused to get
caught up in it. Gold fever could be a crippling disease—
Shady Gulch was proof of that. She'd remember what
was important in life and never forget the trouble that
creek and its "priceless" treasures were causing.

When she arrived back at the Merriweathers' house,
lunch was on the table and the marshal was nowhere in
sight. There was a place for him set at the table, and
Dannie thought him rude not to show up just because
she was there. Louisa and Maybelle Merriweather
didn't seem a bit bothered, though, and the three of

them enjoyed a delicious meal of roast beef and sweet potatoes.

"Daniella, were you aware that Gladys Colby does not allow Storm sympathizers in her bakery?"

"*Sister,*" Louisa reprimanded.

"It's all right, Louisa. Yes, Maybelle, I am aware of that."

Louisa sighed and shook her head. "Gracious, what has come over this town?"

"Gold, sister. That's what's come over it." Maybelle looked across the table at Dannie. "When Gladys Colby heard that you were visiting with us, Louisa had to practically wrestle the muffins we'd already paid good money for right out of Gladys's hands."

Louisa stabbed a neatly sliced piece of roast beef with her fork. "Nobody cheats *me* out of a muffin."

"A young man threw a dirt clod at us outside the hotel."

Dannie stopped chewing. "Did he hurt you?"

Louisa snorted. "He was a horrendous aim."

"Louisa whopped him with her parasol."

"Right on the noodle."

Dannie set down her fork and wiped her mouth with her linen napkin. "You know, I can always stay at my own house—"

"Nonsense!" Louisa said. "We've invited you here, and no muffin war or spiraling dirt-clod battle will change our minds. Right, Maybelle?"

"Correct, sister." Maybelle's tiny blue eyes began to gleam. "As a matter of fact, we thought we might take you along the next time we visit the bakery."

Louisa smiled. "Yes. And, sister, don't we need some lace to edge that lovely shawl you're knitting?"

"Hester Jones's seamstress shop has the best lace in town," Maybelle reminded her with a grin.

Dannie watched them carefully as delight brightened their eyes, like two children planning the best way to nab Santa Claus. "You two are very naughty, which is probably why I'm growing so fond of you."

Maybelle clapped her hands. "Then it's settled. Tomorrow morning we storm the front lines. Isn't that funny, sister? *Storm* the front lines?"

Dannie cleared her throat. "I think I'll head out to the pond for a quick bath."

Both women looked at her. "I should say not," Louisa exclaimed. "We shall heat the water for you and you may use the tub in the pantry."

Dannie rose and pushed in her chair. "Then I'll start bringing in the water."

Maybelle stood. "I'll stoke the fire in the stove. Sister, I believe we have some bars of honey soap in the linen cabinet upstairs."

"Right you are, sister. And some fine oriental bathing salts that Father brought back from Asia."

The three of them worked like an organized cotillion of ants moving back and forth from the pump to the stove to the copper tub in the pantry. Within an hour, Dannie was easing herself down into a tub of hot water that was murky with the essence of cinnamon bathing salts.

She took her time washing and scrubbing out her hair, soaking until the water had turned cold and her skin was pink and wrinkled. She dried off with a white towel that was as soft as a cloud and then slipped on her yellow cotton dress. She'd spent the last three days in pants, and it felt good to have her legs free again.

The sisters had finished with the dishes, so Dannie followed their voices down the hall to the red parlor. She found them sitting on the settee and working over a patchwork quilt while discussing the merits of hair dye.

". . . has the appearance of a blue-headed woodpecker with that long nose of hers."

"Stella Goodwin dyed her hair yellow, and I happen to think it looks like sunshine."

"Oh, Maybelle, it looks like a giant lemon swallowed up her head. I'll keep my gray hairs, thank you very much. I worked very hard for every one of them."

"Gray hairs are not trophies, Louisa. They're a sign of impending doom."

Louisa stilled her needle and looked up at her sister. "Sister, we're half-blind, half-deaf, our bodies have shrunk down to half their normal size, and we can barely remember our own names. Should we really be worrying about a few gray hairs?"

"Get out!"

Both women turned to look at Dannie and she glared at the annoying parrot. "I didn't mean to interrupt. I was just wondering where I can wash out my clothes."

"Oh no, my dear. Henrietta—"

"Harriet."

"Harriet will do that for you."

"I can do it myself," Dannie replied.

Louisa was insistent. "Harriet will do it. Now sit down here and we'll teach you to daisy stitch."

Dannie spent the rest of the afternoon mastering the daisy stitch. While Louisa and Maybelle prepared supper, she continued to ply a thread into tiny daisylike knots all along the border of their beautifully crafted quilt. And she continued to throw glares at the parrot in the corner whose insults only increased when the two sisters left the room. According to Maybelle, Harvey was able to repeat any word said to him clearly, and with the maliciousness of a vengeful child Dannie began chanting, "Stupid bird, stupid bird . . ."

It wasn't until the door knocker thudded just before six that Dannie was called away from the quilt. She walked to the front door, not sure who would await her, and was stunned to find Sherman Potter standing in the foyer, admiring a medieval tapestry.

He was dressed in a broadcloth suit of navy blue, with his gold, fobbed, pocket watch dangling from his vest pocket. Dannie could remember sitting on his lap as a little girl, staring at the face of the watch as the tiny hands ticked away the minutes. On top of Sherman Potter's head sat his customary black bowler hat, and he had waxed his gray moustache until the ends curled.

"Daniella," he said, tipping his hat.

"What can I do for you, Mr. Potter?"

He laughed coldly, as if her words held a special meaning for him. He wasn't the same kind man she'd known as a child. Of course the tension between their families had hardened her heart to him, but she'd noticed that lately the luster had gone from his eyes and the carefree bounce had slipped from his confident stride.

Dannie hadn't actually spoken to Sherman Potter in almost a year—not since William had attacked her and she and Donovan had gone to his house to accuse the young man. She'd never forget the look of hatred and rage that came up in Mr. Potter's brown eyes.

And now, with her family behind bars, he was paying her a visit? He was up to something. Although she hated to think he meant to take advantage of her family's situation, the arrogance of his crooked smile left little doubt that she should be prepared for the worst.

"Sources tell me both your brothers are in jail, my dear," he said. "And Dreyfuss as well, I'm told."

"Let's not beat the bush for dead birds, Mr. Potter. You're well aware that my family is in jail. There isn't a soul within a hundred miles who hasn't heard all the particulars by now."

"That's what I've always liked about you, Daniella. There's no slipping anything past you. No siree—"

"What do you want?"

His eyes narrowed. "And you always get right to the point. All right, have it your way. You know precisely what I want and I've come perfectly willing to negotiate, although you don't appear to have a lot left to bargain with."

"Don't count on that."

"Oh, but I am counting on that. You see, without

your brothers or your father keeping watch over that creek, I could dredge it and bleed it dry of every drop of gold dust from here to Denver."

Dannie was half-tempted to say, "Be my guest." But she knew how much that gold meant to her family, and it was her duty to do everything she could to stop Sherman Potter. "What do you want?" she repeated.

"I want you to marry my son."

Dannie almost laughed. She should have known it would come to this. "We've been over this before. Marriage to William doesn't appeal to me."

Potter's nostrils flared. "Even now, with your family in such dire straits?"

"And what good would it do any of them if I married William?"

"Ahh, there's the bargain. You marry William and I'll forfeit the gold, the creek, and the nugget included."

"That doesn't get my family out of jail."

"No, but it does protect the gold while they're there."

Dear God, how she hated that gold. "I gave William my answer two years ago. I haven't, and I won't, change my mind."

"Now, you listen to me, missy. I love my son. I give him everything he wants. And for some odd reason *you* are what he wants—"

"Only because I'm something he can't have."

Potter leaned closer, and the sharp tang of his cologne burned her nose. "How do you think Dreyfuss is going to feel when he finds out you let all that gold slip through his fingers?"

"If you recall, my family stood behind my decision

two years ago. They'll stand behind it now." She hoped.

"Oh, yes, I recall. I recall how Dreyfuss was as eager as I for a Storm and Potter union. And I also recall how he let you and your asinine notions run full steam over him and a lifetime friendship. You not only destroyed my son, you destroyed two entire families!"

"Don't you dare blame me for your narrow-mindedness! William proposed to me, not my father, and the choice was mine to make. You're the one who took it personally! You're the one who let my decision come between you and my father! You can threaten me and that worthless creek bed all you like but I'm not going to change my mind!"

There was a moment of silence while Sherman Potter considered her. "You're as stubborn and willful now as you were as a child. . . . I can see why my boy's so fond of you."

Dannie crossed to the door and opened it wide. "Please leave, Mr. Potter."

Sherman Potter turned to leave but paused in the doorway. Dannie looked around him to see Marshal Kiley and Deputy Bean coming up the walk.

"Mighty determined man, our new marshal," Potter said. "I'm sure, Daniella, that once a few more days have gone by, without the comfort of your loving family, you'll want to talk with me again. My regards to your father."

Dannie allowed the man to walk away without giving him the scathing response he deserved. She heard the three men greet one another on the walkway and, leaving the door half-open, moved back into the security of the parlor and the distraction of the quilt.

The conversation she'd had with her family earlier began spinning around in her head. Her father had been right. The threat Potter posed to the gold was very real. If she wanted her family to have their dreams of wealth, she'd have to get them out of jail—quickly.

She heard the *thunk* of Marshal Kiley's boots as he came through the front door, followed by the calming sound of Bean's smooth voice. "I dunno, Jake. I'd swear that was her. Who else you know in town's got hair like that?"

"I think you're getting old, Bean. You and Maybelle Merriweather should share a pair of spectacles."

"Two-bit law man! Two-bit law man!"

Dannie smothered a laugh at the bird's sharp cry. It was nice to know she wasn't the only one suffering from Harvey's poor sense of humor.

"Damn bird," the marshal muttered.

"I say we go find her and see jist exactly who it was. Then we'll be seein' who needs spectacles."

"Be my guest, Bean. Chances are you'll find Miss Storm upstairs cleaning her shotgun, and dressed in those stiff-with-dirt pants she never takes off."

Dannie clenched her teeth, but the sound of their approaching footsteps made her steady her rising temper and concentrate on her daisy stitches.

"She's a clever little thing," Bean said with a laugh.

"Yeah, well her kind of intelligence I can do with . . . out . . ."

Their conversation faded and Dannie knew they were standing in the threshold staring at her. She could practically feel the marshal's eyes boring into her.

"Holy B. Jesus," Bean muttered.

She looked up, feigning a lack of interest in the fact that they were finding her change of appearance so fascinating. The marshal's slack jaw was practically resting on his chest, and she took a great amount of satisfaction in that.

"Good evening, gentlemen."

Bean elbowed the dazed Marshal. "I told ya it was her," he said, his smile widening. "She sure cleans up nice, don'cha think?"

"I was under the impression that you'd be eating your meals somewhere else, Marshal."

The marshal snapped his mouth shut and frowned.

"Had himself a good taste of the Spur's food this afternoon and decided nothin' was worth sittin' through another calamity of burnt steak and undercooked potatas."

Dannie set aside the quilt and stood up. "I see." The marshal's gaze drifted down her dress and settled on her bare feet. She felt a flash of embarrassment. "Then I'm sure you'll be happy to hear we're having cottage pie for supper and the Merriweathers make the best in town."

Bean's eyes rounded in delight. "Oooh. Cottage pie. Did ya hear that, Jake? Cottage pie. . . . Jake?"

"This little charade isn't going to work, lady."

She blinked. "Excuse me?"

"I don't care if you strip that damn dress off and parade around in front of me bare-ass naked!" he bellowed.

She flinched and then scowled. The bird in the far cage squawked something about battening down the hatches. "Excuse me?" she said sharply.

"They are staying in that jail, and that is that!"

"Jake, I think yer paddlin' without an oar here—"

"Why, you arrogant son of a bitch," Dannie said, completely amazed. "You think I took a bath and put this dress on for you?"

Bean slid his hand over his face and shook his head. "Boy-o, if there's a pile a dung ten feet up in a tree you're bound ta get yer foot sunk in it."

"Oh, and I'm supposed to think this amazing metamorphosis is just a coincidence!"

"I call it just good sense!" she shouted back. "What? Do you honestly think I never take baths? That the only clothes I own are the pants I do chores in? Do you honestly think I raced to the seamstress shop this afternoon, the one that won't even let me press my nose against the display window, and bought this dress just for you? Is that what you *honestly* think!"

"Lady, with you half the time I don't know what the hell to think!"

"So you're making it up as you go along?"

There was a lull in the shouting and the three of them heard Maybelle's soft voice calling them to supper. With a final disgusted shake of her head, Dannie brushed past the marshal and his deputy and headed for the dining room. Grumbling to herself, she vowed that Jake Kiley had insulted her for the very last time.

Tonight she was going to show him just exactly what she was capable of!

8

Jake wasn't buying into it. Not one bit. Clever little Miss Storm was up to something, and he wasn't about to be caught off guard when the true motives for her sudden physical transformation surfaced.

He stole a glance at Bean, who was sitting next to him at the mahogany dining room table. It seemed to be a night for changes. In honor of supper with the Merriweather sisters, Bean had taken a bath and shaved off his trademark whiskers. The Merriweather sisters approved of his new appearance, but Jake thought the old man looked awkward, like a bald raccoon.

Bean tore his gaze away from Maybelle Merriweather long enough to smile at something Daniella Storm said. Jake grimaced at that toothy smile, wondering why the old man was allowing himself to be taken in by a pair of wide green eyes and a dimpled cheek. Planning to have a nice long talk with his deputy when the evening was finally over, Jake turned his attention back to his plate.

"We missed you at lunch today, Marshal."

Jake swallowed his bite of cottage pie and looked up at Maybelle Merriweather. He had every intention of responding politely, but before he could even open his mouth Bean was answering for him. "I insisted the marshal eat with me at the Spur this afternoon, ma'am. I hope you don't mind. I figure it ain't right for a man ta eat angel food like this here, before he's right an able to appreciate it."

Jake gave his deputy a dubious look, and Bean answered with a shrug.

"You should avoid that establishment at every opportunity, gentlemen," Louisa Merriweather said. "Rumor has it that the late Wilfred Grimley died not of a tired heart, but of a greasy leg of Rolling Spur chicken."

Maybelle was nodding. "And they sugar their water to make the customers eat more."

"No!" Bean looked as if he might fall out of his chair. "Do ya hear that, Jake? Sugared water!"

Jake couldn't believe Bean Toomey was making such a fuss over a couple of women. "Maybe you should head on over there, Deputy, and arrest the unscrupulous charlatans."

"Oh, Deputy, no," Maybelle pleaded. "The Christys really are nice people. And I would so hate to be the cause of any trouble for them."

"Honestly, sister. If you don't want to cause trouble, then you should think before you open your mouth. You're lucky Mr. Toomey isn't over at the Spur this very minute bringing in his man. There could have been a shoot-out for all you know."

Maybelle let out a horrified gasp. "Oh, my!"

Bean's chest puffed up so much that one more compliment would have made him burst for sure. "Don't worry, ladies. I'll let the bounders go fer now. But don't you think I won't have my eye on 'em."

Jake looked across the table to find Daniella Storm suppressing a giggle with her hand. Their eyes met, and his heart quickened. Her hair was like a cloud, the rich red color of a sunset, and his fingers began to itch to test its softness. Damn, if she wasn't pretty.

He locked his jaw. *Pretty* is exactly what she wanted him to think. And if there was one thing he hated more than lying women, it was women who played games with him.

She gave him a hesitant smile and he looked away. Bean Toomey may be leaning toward the gullible side tonight. But Daniella Storm could smile, bat her long eyelashes, and wiggle her cute ass till doomsday and Jake Kiley still wasn't going to let her family out of jail!

Dannie tucked her fingers into the lambswool of her thick coat and pulled it tighter around her neck to ward off the evening chill. She pushed off with her feet and sent the porch swing into motion, listening to the faint creaking of the chain in the darkness.

Her eyes were on the wrought-iron gate at the end of the walk. Marshal Kiley had left on his rounds over two hours ago, and any minute now he would be coming down the street toward the house. After supper she'd gone up to her room and formulated her plan, and now she was ready for him. Her heart tripped with excitement just at the thought of finally bringing the smug marshal to his knees.

Time marched on slowly and her courage began to waver, along with her ability to stay awake. She sat up straight and looked up at the stars while winding and unwinding a lock of her hair around her finger. She found the Big Dipper. She found the Little Dipper. She found the winking brilliance of the North Star.

Still the marshal didn't come.

Yawning, she finally laid her head back against the rim of the swing and unintentionally rocked herself to sleep.

When she opened her eyes a little while later to find a shadow looming over her she let out a soft cry of alarm.

"Strange place to be spending the night, Miss Storm."

She brought her hand up to where her heart was pounding in her chest and took a deep breath. "You scared me half to death."

The marshal shifted, and the moonlight caught the angles of his face. "Why are you sleeping on the porch?"

"I wasn't." She rubbed the kink out of her neck. "I mean, I didn't mean to fall asleep."

"Go to bed." He moved to the porch rail and leaned against the narrow ledge. Hiking up the collar on his long dark coat, he turned his attention from her to the front walk.

Dannie gritted her teeth. If things were going to work out in her favor, she would have to put up with his arrogance tonight. "Actually, I think I'll stay. I've been enjoying the evening."

"Through your eyelids?"

"It's a little chilly out, but the sky is clear. I even found the Little Dipper earlier."

"Now you're an astronomer? Next thing I know you'll be wallowing in mud and trying to convince me you're a whelping sow."

She gave him a tight smile, fighting down the irritation he always aroused in her. "I am sorry about our misunderstanding earlier, Marshal. If I had known that my taking a bath would annoy you so much I—"

"Would have taken one sooner?"

"You're making it very hard for me to apologize."

"Forgive me if I don't take that apology too seriously."

She allowed a bit of her anger to surface. "Do you have any idea how rude you are?"

"Without a doubt."

"I take that to mean you act this way on purpose?"

"I don't act, period. Games aren't my style," he said with a pointed glare.

A shiver of apprehension raced up Dannie's spine, but she forced herself to relax. He couldn't possibly know what she intended. She pushed her foot against the porch and sent the swing into motion again, gliding back and forth. "How's the town tonight?"

He sighed loudly. "The town, Miss Storm, is quiet except for the few normal skirmishes. The shops are all locked tight, and all the people with sense enough to stay off the dark streets have made it safely to their homes. Next should I tell you about my long, hard day, or can we end this game right now?"

"Why are you so suspicious of a simple conversation?"

"Oh, I don't know. Maybe it's because of the fact that we're sitting here alone, in the middle of the night, you want something very badly, and I'm the only one who can give it to you."

Alarm raced through her as she realized that he might know exactly what she intended. She swallowed at the tightness in her throat. "Which adds up to what, Marshal Kiley? I'm sure you're dying to tell me."

He stepped away from the porch rail and reached out to grab her coat lapels. With a slow, deliberate motion, he pulled her to her feet. "Which adds up to I have something you want, lady, and I am damn anxious to find out how far you're willing to go to get it."

She stared at his chin, feeling the warmth of his breath on her face, the strength of his fisted hand at her throat. "You think you can see right through me, don't you?"

"Like polished glass."

"And if I tell you you're wrong?" She forced herself to look up into his eyes. "That what I want from you is not what you're expecting?"

It was hard to see his expression in the darkness, but she knew he was watching her closely. "Then I'd have to question my good judgment for the first time in my very long life."

She brought her hand up to his wrist but didn't try to push him away. The next words she uttered were the hardest she'd ever had to say. "I—I want you to kiss me again."

There was a long pause, and then the steady, deep sound of his laughter. She'd expected his scorn, yes, and maybe even his wrath, but his amusement was almost too much for her to bear.

It was time to raise the stakes.

She pressed her cheek against his cold hand and nibbled at the rough pad of his thumb. His laughter was cut short by a sharp intake of breath, and the lustful look he gave her made her feel shameless, completely immoral.

"All right, lady," he said softly. "I'll play along. You want a kiss? Fine. But I did the honors last time. It's your turn."

Dannie hesitated. That was the last thing she'd expected him to say. She'd assumed he would either flat out refuse to kiss her or at least lead the way.

She took a deep breath and raised her hand to his chest. The edges of his unbuttoned greatcoat had separated and her hand came down on the thin linen of his shirt. The heat of him felt like fire against the coolness of her palm, and she curled her fingers against the muscles of his chest. She was sure she felt his heartbeat quicken.

"Do you kiss me, or do I fall asleep on my feet?" he said.

She lifted her face. He was standing so close to her she bumped her nose on his chin. "I—I'm not sure I know how to go about kissing."

She'd been kissed before, by William and most recently by the marshal himself, but never in her life had she been on the giving end.

He bent his head toward hers. "It's all in the mouth."

Her eyes centered on his mouth, on the strong yet soft lips she'd found so fascinating while standing in the creek the day before. She'd let him kiss her then, and even though she'd been forced to slap him afterward, she had to admit that she'd experienced an incredible burst of sensations during the few seconds that his mouth had been on hers.

She licked her dry lips and leaned up to him. Then she paused. "What if I do it wrong?"

"Then I'll correct you."

Her eyes flickered closed and she pressed her mouth to his. For just one moment she forgot her ploy, her plans to trick him, and let herself enjoy the surprisingly pleasant feel of his body, strong and solid, against hers. Their lips parted, met again, and then parted a final time. She opened her eyes and couldn't hide her smile. Kissing wasn't so difficult after all.

"I'm ready to start anytime you are, lady."

The smile slipped from her face and she blinked. "I thought that kiss was very nice."

"I've gotten better kisses from Bean."

Her pride stung, she attempted to move away from him but he still had a firm grip on her coat. "Hold on, sweetheart. I've got a turn coming."

He backed up, dragging her with him, until he was leaning on the porch railing. Then he parted his legs and brought her solidly into the V of his thighs. Dannie pressed her palms against his chest, trying to keep at least a breath of distance between them, but he kept her against him by placing his hand at her back. The other hand he moved to her chin. "Open your mouth."

She stared at him in amazement. "What in the world for?"

"You claimed you wanted a kiss, Miss Storm, and now I'm going to give you one. Those tight little smacks you just gave me could shrivel a stone."

Now he wanted to kiss her? Well, he'd certainly squelched any urges in her that might have been there before. She stiffened and leaned away from him, and in the pale moonlight she saw one of his dark eyebrows arch. "I assume this means that you've gotten what you wanted from me?" he said.

With those mocking words Dannie's resistance waned. So far she hadn't gotten a thing except her pride bruised. She looked back at him warily, wondering at his compliance with this whole situation. "What I wanted, Marshal, was a simple kiss. But you insisted that *I* kiss *you*. And when I did, you insulted me."

His fingers fanned over her jaw in an almost caressing motion. The moon had climbed high overheard, shining down on the two of them, and she could just make out the slight smile on his face. He was obviously finding this all very funny.

"All right, you smug, pompous—give me your best shot! Go ahead! Knock my shoes off! Curl my knickers! Braid my—"

He caught her midsentence—with her mouth open—and when his lips closed over hers, she realized why he'd wanted it open. Instead of smacking, their mouths melded together this time. And with her lips parted he was able to slip his tongue inside her mouth. She felt the warm thrust of it and, after a moment of shock and hesitation, touched it tentatively with her own. The hand he had in her hair gripped tighter and she grew bolder.

She heard him groan, and was surprised—no, disappointed—when he took her head in both his hands and pushed her away from him. They were both breathing hard, and Dannie realized then that she'd placed one of her hands beneath his coat on his hard back and twined the other in his thick dark hair. She'd lost control.

He was watching her intently, his eyes burning with something she couldn't name. She barely had the time to wonder what he was thinking before he began peeling the soft lambswool away from her neck and buried his face against her throat.

His hot lips scalded her senseless, and she took hold of the back of his shirt. Her skin seared where he nipped her with his teeth, soothed only by the hot moisture of his tongue as he burned a path to her ear. The sensation was so incredible that she arched her neck and offered him more.

"Damn you, Daniella Storm," he whispered raggedly.

"Damn you, Jake Kiley," she whispered back.

He took her earlobe between his teeth. "Is this what it's come to?" he whispered. His industrious hands were finding their way beneath her heavy coat. "You, offering yourself up in exchange?"

Her fingers were immersed in the silken strands of his hair, holding him to the promise of something so very sweet. She groaned and arched further against him as one of his strong hands found and cupped the curve of her bottom.

His lips grazed along her jawline, his breath hot against her cheek. "I get you?" His other hand found its way up the front of her coat and skimmed over her breasts. "And the Storms go free?"

"Yes." The word slipped out on a gasp. But that wasn't right. He wasn't supposed to *get* her. One kiss. Hadn't that been the original plan?

He leaned back against the porch railing and locked his ankles around hers. Then she watched him, unmoving, as he began to loose the frogs that held her coat together. When it hung open, leaving only her yellow dress to keep her warm, he took hold of her coat's lapels and pulled her back to him.

His mouth claimed hers again, hot and seeking, while his hands began mapping the curve of her hips, her waist, her ribs. Then he pulled back and cupped her breasts with his palms.

The expression on his face, combined with the delicious pressure of his hands, elicited a groan from the back of Dannie's throat. His thumbs flicked at her nipples, and her knees went weak. "A virgin sacrifice," he murmured. "I'm honored."

Something deep inside her flinched at that remark. She wondered why he'd stopped kissing her and wanted to ask him to continue. But, confused as to what was expected of her next, she kept quiet.

"Shall we find a bed, or should I just throw your skirt up over your head here on the porch?"

Reality began to return, and with it a sense of disbelief. What had he said? That she was to be a virgin sacrifice? She pulled her hand out from beneath his coat, away from the tight muscles of his back.

"No? Then how about the porch swing? You sit, I kneel?"

He caught her around the waist before she could

move away from him. "Do I sense hesitation, Miss Storm?"

"Let go of me." Her voice was choked with the remnants of desire and the seeds of disgust.

He pulled her closer, forcing her breasts against his chest. "It was your game, lady. Don't tell me you're a sore loser."

She struggled but he wouldn't let her go. The thought of kneeing him in the groin flitted through her mind, but he was half-seated on the porch rail. So she raised her hand to slap him.

He caught her wrist in midair. "Once . . . maybe twice . . . but never three times."

She was staring at his mouth, the mouth that she knew was warm and soft and could make her feel the most amazing things. The tears that pooled in her eyes surprised her. "This was a mistake."

"Too bad you didn't realize that before we started playing. I don't like to stop before the last move is made."

"This isn't a game of chess, Marshal. And if it were, it would be over. Finished!"

His lips curved into a half smile. "So is it check?" He raked his eyes over the front of her dress, over her breasts which still ached from his touch. "Or is it checkmate?"

She yanked her wrist out of his fingers and was finally able to wrench herself away from him. The cold air of the night crept in through her open coat and chilled her to the bone. She'd lost. Somehow he'd anticipated and countered her attack. She rubbed her wrist where his fingers had bruised her skin. "You're depraved."

"You asked *me* to kiss *you,* remember?"

"No gentleman would have taken me up on my offer."

"No lady would have offered."

His point was well taken. She drew the edges of her coat together to cover the form he'd just so expertly traced with his hands. "I'm tired, and I'm going to bed."

She headed for the door, always aware of him watching her, of his intense gaze burning into her back.

"Daniella?"

She paused on the threshold but couldn't bring herself to turn around to meet his penetrating dark eyes.

"I'll await our rematch with eager anticipation."

She practically flew up the stairs to her room. She tore off her coat, peeled off her dress and underclothes, pulled a nightgown over her head, and scrambled into bed as if the hounds of hell were nipping at her heels. She lay there, breathing hard, the blankets pulled up to her chin, wondering if he was still sitting out there mocking her or if he'd gone to bed as well.

Damn, but she'd messed up this plan! She was supposed to have teased him, tormented him into giving her what she asked for. But he'd seen through her all along, probably from the moment he'd found her asleep on the porch swing.

She heard the steady thump of boots on the staircase and in a burst of fright pulled the blankets up over her head. What would she do if he barged into her room and demanded they finish the game? She could be attacked, even raped. Her only possible saviors were two little old women who wouldn't stop arguing long enough to find out what was going on in front of their myopic eyes.

He came toward her door and paused. She held her breath, in a panic but still not able to deny the thrilled pattering of her heart. After a moment, he moved on and she took a deep, relaxing breath.

She listened to the sounds of the marshal undressing in the room next door, heard the telltale creak of his bed, and then wondered how long it would take him to nod off. She could still feel the damp heat on her neck where he'd kissed her, tasted her. And she knew, despite how much she hated herself for it, that she wouldn't be falling asleep for a very long time.

9

Jake strode out of the cell room and yanked the door closed on the shouts and curses that followed him. With an irritated flick of his wrist, he tossed the ring of keys onto his desk, where they collided with a heavy inkwell and a slightly askew stack of wanted posters. With all the noise emanating from his irate prisoners, he was surprised Bean could even get a wink of sleep.

In the gloom of the early morning light, his deputy looked up from where he stood by the warm stove. "No luck, huh?"

"No luck."

"I suppose we can't blame 'em fer bein' uncooperative, considerin'. I told ya that Dreyfuss Storm ain't nothin' but a mule-head."

Jake dropped down into the chair behind his desk and leaned his head back against the wall. "Now I know where Daniella gets it."

Bean grinned broadly. "She sure is somethin', ain't she?"

Somethin' didn't quite cover it: Daniella Storm was about as restrained as a Dodge City tornado—and twice as unpredictable. He couldn't believe she'd actually tried to seduce him last night! She was a flirt and a conniver, and he sure could come up with better hobbies for those luscious lips of hers besides telling fibs and weaving webs.

Bean was still grinning, and Jake gave him a glare that could have withered a mighty oak.

"Holy B. Jesus, boy-o, you got all the humor of a cow pie in the heat of summer this mornin'."

"I'd say that pretty well sums up my mood."

"That cute lil' thing really did git yer goat last night, didn't she?"

"I am about fed up to my eyeballs with you finding that woman so goddamned *cute* all the time!" He came forward in the chair. "Wasn't it you who told me once that a woman's sole intent on this earth is to catch herself a man? *'And if you've got any sense at all, boy-o, when one comes huntin' you'll run faster than a flushed-out jack rabbit.'*"

"Sure ya run." Bean smiled crookedly over the rim of his cup. "But only from the ones who ya don't want ta ketch ya."

"Well, you, my friend, are acting like a man who wants to be caught."

"Never happen. Haven't been caught for fifty years, won't be for at least another fifty."

Jake arched a brow. "And what about the Merriweather

sisters?" He could tell by the way his deputy grew quiet that he was hitting close to the meat of the matter. "The last time I saw you act like this was five years ago, down in Texas."

"Don't start in with me on that, Jake. I don't wanna hear it, I don't wanna—"

"She was tall, and silver-blond, as I recall. She had a handful of ass, and a chest out to here, and she had you slobbering all over her within ten minutes of us riding into Abilene."

"I was wounded. She dug a damn bullet outta my shoulder—"

"And you fell head over heels. She almost had you convinced into settling down, until you found out she planned to save her ranch with every penny you had stashed in the bank. But back then, I don't recall you ever bothering to shave."

Bean rubbed the bristle that was just starting to sprout again on his chin. "The Merriweathers are different."

"How so?"

"They're sweet and kind—and they don't have no use for any of my money. Anyway, my life ain't none of yer goddamned business! Just 'cause yer havin' problems with little Miss Shotgun, don't mean you git ta start pokin' that long nose of yers into my matters."

"I am not having problems with Miss Storm," Jake replied.

It was Bean's turn to look skeptical. "Oh really? Then what was all that ruckus last night about the poor girl takin' a bath and puttin' on some decent clothes?"

"The only reason she took a bath was so she could seduce me into letting her family out of jail!"

"That is a load a—"

"She tried it last night on the Merriweathers' porch."

"That sweet little thing tried to cuddle you into lettin' her family go?"

"That *sweet little thing* would have rolled around naked at my feet if it would have freed her family."

Bean was silent for a moment. Then he started shaking his head. "That poor helpless little girl."

Jake grunted. "Daniella Storm is anything but a helpless little girl. You should have heard her, Bean. You would have been so proud. 'All I want is for you to kiss me again,'" he mimicked, batting his lashes. "How about some sympathy for poor little Jake for a change?"

"She must really be in despair to resort to seducin' you."

"Oh, well, thank you very much."

"You know what I mean. It jist don't seem to be in her nature to do somethin' like that."

"Deputy, you have known that woman just short of five days. How could you possibly have a clue as to what is in her nature?"

"It's all in the eyes, Jake, ol' pal. Sure she may be stubborn and hotheaded and scrappy on the outside, but ya take a look into her eyes sometime and you'll find a timid little girl scared half to death of failin', of takin' the wrong road in life and fallin' flat on her face."

Jake studied his friend for a moment before saying,

"That is the biggest load of crap I have ever heard."

Bean shrugged. "Sounded good when Maybelle said it. You didn't take advantage of her, did ya?"

"Of Maybelle?"

"Of Daniella, you jackass."

"No, I didn't take advantage of her. Although I did make it perfectly clear that I knew exactly what she was up to, and that I was going to counter any move she made."

"I'm afraid ta ask."

"I kissed her."

"And?"

"And the little scoundral kissed me back."

Bean looked less than approving. "Ya know, messin' with Dreyfuss Storm's daughter ain't exactly gonna beholden the man to ya. And if we don't secure that nugget by the time the surveyor gits here, we best start gettin' used to bein' kicked in the fanny."

Jake rested his chin on his steepled fingers. "Well, Dreyfuss Storm isn't going to help us one way or the other. As far as he's concerned that nugget is his, and he's not giving it back no matter who comes out the winner."

"I hear that's a mighty big chunk a gold."

"Stories tend to expand with every teller."

"Dreyfuss Storm sure has put high value on this particular story. If you were him, where would you hide a gold nugget?"

Jake shook his head. "I don't know. And neither Dreyfuss Storm or either of his boys are talking."

Both men grew silent, and then they suddenly looked up at each other.

"You thinkin' what I'm thinkin'?" Bean asked.

"She's not likely to give it up without a fight."

"She's not likely ta volunteer the information either."

Jake nodded thoughtfully. "Asking her about it will only put her on guard."

"Maybe you should jist follow her. She's bound to check up on it every now and then what with all them Potters wanderin' around free."

"She could lead me right to it."

"And then we wouldn't have to worry about gittin' our butts put in a sling."

"It's sneaky," Jake warned.

"It's low-down dirty," Bean agreed.

Jake broke into a slow smile. "It's exactly what Daniella Storm deserves."

Dannie stood by the front door of the bakery letting the mingling scents of yeast, flour, and lemon tease her nose. She was keeping a careful eye on the woman behind the counter, wary of any sudden moves that might be misconstrued as aggression. Gladys Colby was an intimidating woman—all two hundred and fifty pounds of her.

"Come, come, Daniella. Don't lag," Louisa Merriweather said, trying to wave Dannie forward.

Gladys Colby's tiny eyes landed on Dannie and nailed her to the wall like a pin-board butterfly. Dannie gave the woman a weak smile and took hold of the windowsill behind her. "I'm fine here, ladies. You go on ahead."

"Goodness, Louisa, I believe Daniella is frightened."

"Nonsense, sister. A sweet young lady like Daniella Storm certainly has nothing to be afraid of."

"Oh, but I've heard the town is half-crazed with this gold business."

"Why, Maybelle! Are you saying that the good Christian people of Shady Gulch would condemn a young lady who has never missed a Sunday of church and has always given selflessly to her community?"

The three other customers in the bakery were overhearing the Merriweathers' conversation, as Dannie was sure they were meant to. She did her best to avoid their interested gazes, wondering why in the world she had agreed to this outing in the first place. And on today of all days. She'd barely slept an hour the night before. The feel and scent of Jake Kiley was still clinging to her skin, her confidence was running at an all time low, and she just plain wasn't in the proper state of mind to confront her persecutors.

What she needed was a strong shot of whiskey, a good nap, and then a solid dose of moral indignation. She'd actually considered speaking to Minister Stevens, confessing to her unscrupulous actions on the Merriweathers' porch the night before. But Dannie knew that easing her conscience wouldn't make up for her loss of life if the minister did what she feared: Make Marshal Kiley do right by her. She was sure that for the great honor of forcing him into a shotgun wedding, the marshal wouldn't think twice about shooting his blushing bride right between the eyes.

"Daniella!"

Dannie's attention returned to the sisters, who were both peering at her as if she'd lost her mind. "I'm sorry, what?"

"Daniella, do come up here and tell Mrs. Colby the flavor of pound cake you would prefer with your supper tonight."

Dannie knew everyone was still watching her, just as she knew she was on the brink of making an utter fool of herself. She took a few careful steps forward. "How about"—she cleared her throat—"how about banana walnut?"

"We don't have any walnuts," Gladys Colby responded in a voice that fell far short of friendly.

"How about lemon?"

"We don't have any lemons—"

"Gladys Colby, I can smell the lemons in this bakery halfway down the street," Louisa said.

Gladys crossed her arms over her ample chest. "We—don't—have—any—lemons."

"Well, this is just short of maddening. Wouldn't you say, Louisa?"

Louisa hadn't heard her sister, she was too busy wagging her finger at Gladys Colby. "I have half a mind to report you to the new marshal! He's a very good friend of ours, you know, and of Miss Storm!"

Dannie's eyes rounded. The last thing she needed was to come face-to-face with that devil of a lawman. She peeked out the front window, hoping that the mention of his name wouldn't call him forth.

"You go on ahead and report me!" Gladys was shouting back. "I reserve the right to refuse service to anybody I please!"

"Well, by the looks of you, madam, you can't be pleasing many," Louisa retorted, bringing a shocked gasp out of the onlookers.

"Oh, goodness, Louisa, that was a sharp one," Maybelle said, smiling. "But do you think it socially correct of you to insult the woman's appearance?"

Louisa's nose was now high in the air. "You may be right, sister. If I worked behind the counter of a bakery all day I imagine I would have a difficult time not eating everything in sight."

"You two old biddies get outta here before I get my gun!" Gladys Colby shrieked. "And take that piece of Storm trash with you!"

Dannie's heart clenched at the loathing in Gladys Colby's voice. She'd never been hated before, not directly to her face, anyway, and certainly not without good reason. She wanted to pick up her skirt and run from that store and never look back, but it seemed the Merriweather sisters hadn't finished yet.

"You remember, don't you, Louisa, that the last batch of tarts we bought here gave us the trots."

"Oh, yes." Louisa cast serious eyes to the woman standing next to her. "My sister and I spent three entire days wearing a rutted path back and forth to the necessary."

"Perhaps we should rethink our decision to buy goods here in the future, sister."

"My baked goods are made with the freshest ingredients!" Gladys cried defensively.

"Tell that to our offended bowels, Mrs. Colby. I'd watch out for those tarts, ladies," Louisa said. Then she and her sister spun on their heels, took Dannie by an arm each, and led her back out onto the crowded boardwalk.

They'd only gone a few steps before hearing a string of high-pitched curses. Dannie glanced back over her shoulder to see all three of Gladys Colby's customers filing out of the bakery, empty handed. Maybelle and Louisa gave into a fit of giggles.

Dannie was astounded at what had just happened. She wasn't sure whether to be upset or grateful. "You two are really very bad."

"Yes, but never boring, my dear."

"Oh, gracious no, never boring. Father always said, 'You either live or you die, there is no in between.'"

"Now what shall we do, sister?"

"There is that bit of lace you need for that shawl you're knitting . . ."

Dannie didn't mind being the Merriweathers' source of entertainment for the day. As a matter of fact, once they'd entered the seamstress shop with the NO STORM SYMPATHIZERS sign hanging in the window, she'd actually warmed up to the idea. Of course Maybelle didn't get her lace, but, by the time they left, the prospects of anyone else buying lace in that shop ever again were very thin.

The three of them had spent the entire afternoon weaving their way in and out of shops when Dannie looked up and found Marshal Kiley standing directly in front of them on the boardwalk.

"Hello, ladies. Just exactly what is it you're finding so funny?"

At the sight of the marshal, Dannie practically swallowed her tongue. Her laughter, needless to say, was cut short. "Why?" she found the courage to ask. "Is there some law against laughing?"

He gave her a look as dark as the night sky, but she kept her chin up and looked him directly in the eye. Nothing had changed. He may have acquired the unnerving ability to make her knees feel weak, but she wasn't about to let him intimidate her.

Surprisingly, *his* eyes were the first to waver, and Dannie felt a brief flash of triumph. Her victory was short-lived, however, as the marshal bit his bottom lip, unconsciously bringing her attention to that warm, plump curve of flesh. Dannie felt a stab of heat so strong that she almost fell at his feet.

As she stood there, fighting to regain control of herself, Maybelle was the first of the ladies to speak. "We were just having a lovely walk up and down the boardwalk, Marshal. Would you like to join us?"

"Thank you for the invitation, but, actually, I'd appreciate it if you would allow me a moment to speak with Miss Storm in private."

Dannie's heart leapt and began to pound a loud beat in her ears. There was a certain corrupt part of her that wanted desperately to know what he had to say, but the sensible side, which didn't trust him or the way he could make her feel, wanted nothing more than to turn and run.

Maybelle's gray eyebrows rose. "Sister, I do believe we are being dismissed."

"Oh, hush, Maybelle, and come along. Let the children have a moment alone."

Any thoughts Dannie might have had to detain the women were lost when the two of them turned and headed back in the direction they'd come, still chattering away.

"Louisa, I would think they would have plenty of moments alone at the house—"

"Hush, Maybelle!"

Dannie fidgeted with the flower buttons on the front of her blue gingham dress. She smiled at Rawlins Beekman, who waved as he walked by. She pulled her skirt aside as three small children darted past. She finally found the courage to look up at the marshal, thinking that for somebody who claimed he had something to say, he sure was quiet. She found him looking at her, just looking. She began to twiddle her thumbs.

"What is it you wanted to say?" she finally asked. She wished there was no such thing as memory. She wished she could snap her fingers and forget what it felt like to be held in his strong arms.

"I am continually amazed by you."

Despite the sudden flip of her stomach, not for one second did she think he was complimenting her. "What have I done now?"

"I just received a visit from Gladys Colby."

She rolled her eyes, knowing what was coming.

"She told me you brought the Merriweather ladies into the bakery this morning and proceeded to run off every customer she had."

"I did no such thing. If you must know, *they* brought *me.*"

People were pausing to stare, and the marshal took her by the arm and pulled her close beneath an awning. "You expect me to believe those two nice old women scared off not only the customers in the bakery but the seamstress shop as well? Come on, Daniella. Don't the Storms have enough followers? Did you really have to drag those kind-hearted women over to your side?"

Dannie attempted to shake his hold off her arm before she could blush and betray the way his touch made her feel, but she knew from experience that he wouldn't be letting go until he was darn good and ready. "I didn't drag anybody anywhere—*Let go of me!*"

"I know firsthand the kind of games you play, lady. The kind of interesting *moves* you make."

She read the meaning in the depths of his dark eyes and blushed clear to the roots of her red hair. Damn him! Why had she dared to hope that their incident last night would be forgotten? Why had she dared to hope he would deny their kiss, even to her face?

"I am going to warn you one time, Miss Storm, and one time only. If I catch you stirring up trouble, I'll charge the whole lot of them and stand them before a judge."

Dannie finally jerked her arm free and pulled back from his reach. "It must make you feel exceedingly happy, holding the lives of three helpless men over my head like that!"

"As a matter of fact, it does."

"Well, you can save your threats, Marshal. I don't have, nor have I ever had, any intention of stirring up trouble. But you've made your point. Now, if you don't mind, I'm expected for lunch."

Straightening her sleeve, she turned to go, her thoughts and feelings a riot in her head.

"I have a message for you from your father," he called, and she had no choice but to stop and look back over her shoulder at him.

"What's the message?"

"That you need to check on *it* again today."

"It" was, beyond a doubt, that stupid nugget. She sighed and glanced in the direction of the jail. Her family apparently hadn't taken any of her parting words to heart yesterday. It seemed that gold was still the most important thing in their lives.

"I take it this message means something to you?"

She avoided his eyes. "It does. Thank you for delivering it. Shall I give the ladies your regrets on lunch?"

She sensed that he was watching her again. She could practically feel the heat of his gaze on her back. "You do that, Miss Storm. I plan to be doing some hunting this afternoon."

She turned slightly and glanced at him. "A little late in the day for hunting, isn't it?" Would it be too much to hope that he might get lost in the woods and never find his way back?

His quick smile made her more wary than anything else he'd ever said or done. "Not for what I plan to bag."

10

A bucket, a nail, and a piece of light blue yarn.

Dannie smiled in satisfaction as she rode her father's horse out of town. It was midafternoon. The sun was high and bright, and a faint warm breeze rustled through her hair.

All through lunch she'd relieved her confrontation with the marshal. She couldn't explain her body's reaction to his nearness, but she knew that it had been nothing but spiteful of him to remind her of her inappropriate actions the night before. So, in return, Dannie Storm had conjured up some good old-fashioned spite of her own.

Still smiling, she pressed her heels into Diablo's flanks to move him at a faster clip and squinted at the sun. She was looking forward to winter, to the blankets of snow, sometimes five feet deep, that would cover the ground. Cold weather always reminded her of her mother—of hot spiced tea, of warm woolly sweaters, and of family stories around the fire. Of course there hadn't been any tea or stories since Colleen Storm had died four summers ago, but the memories were still there, locked deep inside Dannie's heart, waiting for the first snowfall to bring them to the surface.

Her mother wouldn't approve of what was happening. Family and friends had always been very important to Colleen Storm. If a person had family and friends, a person had everything. But since Colleen's death the Storms' greatest allies, the Potters, had become their enemies. And gold had become more important than friends.

Dannie's chin began to tremble and she stiffened her spine. Tears never amounted to anything but a waste of time and energy. She hadn't cried since her mother died, and she wasn't about to start now—not over something as paltry as a pesky nugget of gold, and not over something as senseless as her irrational feelings for a disagreeable lawman. She'd do as her father asked and check on his precious nugget, and then she'd bide her time until Marshal Kiley came to his senses and let her family out of jail. After that, he'd climb up on his horse and ride out of her life forever.

The idea brought a sudden frown to Dannie's face, but then a sound behind her caught her attention. She glanced over her shoulder and found the road bare except for a tiny swirl of pine needles spinning in the breeze. Wondering if the drip edges on the house were clogged with leaves, she turned her attention back to the road in front of her.

The sound came again, and this time she knew it wasn't pine needles. She reined Diablo to a halt and peered into the trees.

"Who's there?" she called out.

The hair on the back of her neck raised at the silence that answered her. Another sound came, the distinct sound of twigs snapping beneath heavy feet, and then William Potter walked out onto the road, leading his horse.

"William Potter, what are you doing sneaking around in the woods?" She thought of the nugget and of her father's warning about the Potters trying to steal it. "Were you spying on me?"

Handsome William, with a lock of pale blond hair hanging in his eyes, gave her a humble smile. "Yeah, I was."

"Would you mind telling me why?"

"I was hopin' we might get a chance to talk, Dannie. Pa told me he went to see you last night."

William was keeping his free hand stuffed down in his pocket and his eyes lowered, but Dannie wasn't fooled by this submissive posture. Beneath that boyish face and those sparkling eyes lurked the heart of a prowling mountain lion.

"And just exactly what do you feel we have to talk about?"

"Aw, come on, Dannie. You can't still be holdin' that kiss against me. That was almost a year ago."

"*That kiss,* William Potter, was nothing short of a drunken assault. Or do you still claim that I didn't resist?"

His smile would have been charming if Dannie hadn't understood the mischief behind it. He let loose of his horse and moved a step closer. She got a whiff of the alcohol on his breath. There was no time to escape as he reached out and took hold of the hem of her dress.

"You tore my shirt—"

"Trying to shove you off me," she said, trying to bat his hand away.

"It's not like I'd never kissed you before."

"When I had a mind to let you."

"Well, how's a fella supposed to know when a woman suddenly doesn't appreciate his attentions? One minute she's kissing you back and the next she's introducing your face to the stinging side of her palm."

"It's very simple, William. They say no."

She gave Diablo a nudge with her knees, anxious to get away from William before the alcohol he'd obviously been drinking gave him more courage than she knew how to deal with. He didn't release his hold on her skirt, however, and she was almost yanked from the saddle before she could stop the horse.

"What do you want?" she demanded.

"You know exactly what I want. Pa said he made our point crystal clear last night."

She tried to kick his hand away, but he only took a firmer grip, this time on her ankle. "So now you're here to force me into marrying you? Is that it, William?"

"Like I said, I'm here because I was hoping we could talk."

"And I say we don't have anything to talk about!"

His square jaw tightened, and a hard glint came up in

his eyes. "Somebody has to talk some sense into you, girl. And since your daddy is locked behind bars, where he belongs I might add, it appears that I am left with the obligation."

"The only obligation you have to me is to let go of my leg!"

"I will, just as soon as we get a few things straight. Number one: You will stop sassing me all the time. Number two: You will hand over that nugget your daddy stole from my creek. And number three: You will climb down off that horse and give your future husband a proper kiss!"

Dannie stared down at him in shock and then broke into laughter. "You always were a little too greedy, William."

"You get down off that horse, Dannie Storm, or I'm gonna pull you off."

She recognized his expression, the cold sound of his voice. He had used that same tone with her the day of the Simmons' party when he'd spent half the night at the punch bowl and then cornered her in the gazebo to finagle a kiss. When she'd resisted, he'd tried for a whole lot more.

"I am not afraid to hurt you this time, William Potter. And I don't care if you're drunk, either."

He smiled, and a foreboding chill crawled up Dannie's spine. "It was Donovan who came to your rescue that night, Dannie, sweetie. But good ol' Donovan ain't gonna be able to help you this time around."

With one hard yank he had her off the horse and sprawled on the ground at his feet. But, true to her word, Dannie wasted no time before she kicked him soundly in the knee.

As William cupped his leg and hollered, she climbed to her feet and dusted the dirt from the back of her skirt.

"You red-haired she-devil, you about broke my leg!"

"That isn't all I plan to do to you if you don't ride on and leave me alone!"

William took her by the hair, and she cried out in surprise and pain. Then he yanked her hard against his chest. "We're gettin' married, missy. And if I have to take my husbandly rights this very minute to make it so, I'll damn well do it!"

His hand closed around one of her breasts, and she let out an indignant scream. She lifted her foot and stomped on his toes, and he grunted in pain. But, instead of releasing her, he slapped her on the side of the head, making her ears ring. Her scalp burned where he gripped her hair, but no matter how hard she struggled she couldn't seem to break his hold on her.

The sound of a rider approaching brought a new burst of strength to her limbs. She pushed away with all her might, and at that same moment William released her. Thus Marshal Kiley rounded the bend in time to see her do a nosedive into the dusty road.

She pushed up from the ground, groaning, and looked back to see the marshal taking in the scene. William was standing there, looking as innocent as the day he was born. It was at that moment that Dannie decided she'd had about all she could take from the men of Shady Gulch. William Potter wasn't going to get away with manhandling her this time. She'd see to it personally.

She rushed to the marshal's side, ignoring the curious look he gave her, and yanked the heavy gun from his holster before he could stop her. Taking three steps back, with an angry twitch of her upper lip, she leveled the gun at William.

Dannie wasn't sure what she'd expected the marshal's reaction to be, but she was surprised when he merely stared at his gun in her hand and then turned his attention to William. "Interesting situation, Mr. Potter. Care to enlighten me?"

"Yes, William, do tell the marshal all the tiny details. It won't bother me to wait before shooting a hole clean through the front of your pants!"

William's hands crossed protectively over his crotch. "You best get that gun away from her, Marshal Kiley. She's a total looney bird! I wasn't doing nothing but minding my own business when all of a sudden she come tearing down the road behind me and knocked me clean off my horse!"

Dannie moved away from the marshal, just in case he got it into his head to believe William's story. "That's right. And then I threw myself to the ground, yanked out a fistful of my own hair, slapped myself, and squeezed my own . . . bruised my own self!"

William laughed nervously and shook his head. "Jesus, Marshal, you can see she's plumb lost her head."

Dannie raised her aim and narrowed her eyes down the sight of the gun. "In about five seconds you're going to know firsthand what it feels like to lose your head."

The marshal swung down off his horse, and Dannie shuffled nervously as he walked toward her. "You shoot him and I'll have to put you in jail, Daniella, no matter what I promised you before."

"I don't care. I'm not going to let him get away with attacking me again."

She gave the marshal a wary glance and saw his eyes narrow. He crossed his arms over his chest and leveled his gaze on William. "Potter, has Miss Storm complained about this type of behavior from you before?"

In response to the low, almost dangerous tone in the marshal's voice, William broke into one of his charming smiles. "Marshal, Miss Storm and I are gettin' married—"

"In your dreams—"

"You hush up!" William said to her, and then smiled again. "We have little tiffs like this every now and again. It's only natural, what with the tension between our two families and all."

"Did you attack her or not?"

William snorted. "Marshal, I can't believe you'd even ask me—"

"Answer the question, Potter—Daniella, you're going to have to hold the gun with both hands to steady it."

Dannie glanced up at him in surprise and then took the gun in both of her hands.

"Now straighten your arms. No, don't lock your elbows . . . I'm waiting for your answer, Potter."

William was starting to sweat, and he was glancing anxiously at his horse, which was too far away from him to use as a clean get away. "You can't let her shoot me, Marshal—my pa would see you hanged right alongside her!"

"Is this a forty-four?" Dannie asked casually.

"Army issue," the marshal responded.

"What kind of a hole do you think something like this might make at this distance."

The marshal leaned toward her and eyed the distance between her and William. He pursed his lips. "'Bout fist size."

Dannie smiled at William. "Did you hear that, William? From this distance I could knock your tiny brain right out of your head."

"All right! All right! I pulled the woman off her horse! But only because that sassy mouth of hers had pushed me too damn far!"

Dannie felt the blinding urge to cock the trigger, but she steadied her hand, willing to wait until the entire story had been dragged out of the drunken fool.

"And what were your intentions once you got Miss Storm off her horse?"

"To talk to her—I only wanted to talk to her!"

"About?"

"About the damn wedding!"

"She claims there isn't going to be a wedding, Potter, and I've heard the same said around town."

William pointed a finger at the marshal. "You're wrong, mister. That there is my woman. And frankly, you got no business interfering in our domestic squabbles!"

"He said he was going to force his husbandly rights on me in order to make me marry him," Dannie said. She hardly felt embarrassment at having to reveal that to the marshal, not if William got his just deserts for once.

There was a moment of silence, and then came the sound of the marshal letting out a long, slow breath. "Were you going to force yourself on Miss Storm?"

"W-well why the hell not? She's mine! My property! My red hair." He closed his eyes. "My soft . . . sweet lips."

Dannie didn't care whether Jake Kiley or Moses himself was standing beside her. And she didn't care if William Potter was so drunk he'd bounce. She was damn well going to shoot him!

She didn't even have time to cock the trigger, however, before the marshal closed the distance on William Potter and punched him square in the nose.

Dannie paced the parlor, from one gold satin wall to the other, wringing her hands in the folds of her skirt. She'd returned to the Merriweather house well over two hours ago, which seemed like plenty of time for the marshal to have locked up William Potter.

Dear God, he was locking up William. And he was doing it for her protection. She'd actually heard him say that—right after William had regained consciousness. "William Potter, you're going to jail. If not for my own satisfaction, then for the protection of Miss Storm."

He was protecting her.

She pressed her fingers to her lips to keep from smiling. She really shouldn't care at all that the marshal had taken her side over William's. The fact remained that he'd locked up her family for nothing but minor and easily explainable crimes. But if he was looking out for her safety, then that meant he must care something for her. And the idea of Marshal Jake Kiley feeling anything besides loathing for her gave her the sweetest little thrill.

"Sit down!"

She started and reached for the back of the wing chair. "Hush up, you stupid bird," she said. "You practically stopped my heart!"

"Stupid bird! Stupid bird!"

She smiled wickedly. "That's right. Stupid bird—"

The sound of the front door opening sent her into an instant panic. What was she going to say to the marshal? Should she thank him for tossing Willie in jail, or would that only make her sound callous? Her hands shook in agitation as she crept toward the parlor door.

He was hanging his long black coat on the coatrack in the foyer. Dannie stared at his broad back, watching the muscles flex in his shoulders as he reached for a curved branch. But as he turned toward her she lost her nerve and darted back into the parlor. She heard the sound of his heavy steps on the stairs.

Taking a deep breath, she decided it was for the best that she hadn't approached him just then. She was behaving like a silly child, peering around doorways to ogle him in such a simple act as hanging up a coat. The smart thing to do would be to wait until they'd both had some time to think about the afternoon's events. Maybe after supper—

A dull *thunk* and a heavy splash made her freeze in place. She shut her eyes and said a silent prayer that God would strike her down now and save her from the horrible death that was sure to come. The sound of her name being bellowed from the second floor echoed down the stairs and overcame any impulse she had to run. Certainly a man as angry as Jake Kiley would search the ends of the earth for her.

By the time she found the courage to open her eyes he was standing in front of her. She had to give herself credit; it had been a direct hit. He was drenched from the chest up. His hair was matted down; his shirt plastered to his shoulders. Streams of water were trailing through his heavy eyebrows and down into his deadly dark eyes.

She'd forgotten about the bucket, the nail, and the piece of lightblue yarn.

"Your little surprise, I presume?" he said through clenched teeth.

What could she say? Yes, she'd done it. Yes, she'd intended it for him. Yes, it was out of spite. There simply wasn't any defense. If this were a trail, she'd be sentenced to hang at dawn.

"Over the door." He wiped his hand across his damp face. "Very imaginative."

"I'm sorry—"

"Oh, please, don't be. I'm impressed."

The hard look in his eyes didn't match the calm, almost passive tone of his voice. Despite her earlier thoughts, she now found it hard to believe that he was impressed with a single thing about her.

"I never would have guessed your talents ran to these extremes. And, hell, I should be glad it was only water."

She tried again to apologize. "Really, Marshal Kiley, I didn't mean . . . that is to say, I didn't intend—"

"I oughta wring your scrawny neck, Miss Storm."

"Scrawny neck! Stupid bird! Two-bit lawman!"

"Marshal, I swear to you—"

"But I'm not going to, and do you know why?"

She swallowed thickly and shook her head.

"Because that would be too quick. No, I'm gonna get you back, honey." He smiled coldly as if savoring the moment in his mind. "And when I do, you're gonna be begging me to let you off the hook."

He strode out of the parlor, and she sank down into a nearby chair. So much for thank-yous. So much for being liked. If he hadn't hated her before, he surely did now. And that realization made Dannie's heart feel like a hundred-pound weight in her chest.

"Stupid bird!"

She hugged her shoulders. "Here's a new one, Harvey. Stupid Dannie, stupid Dannie, stupid Dannie . . ."

11

Dannie awoke late that night and sat straight up in bed. The room was dark except for the moonlight glowing against the far wall. She rubbed her eyes and wondered what had roused her. Then the sound of a gunshot brought her attention to the window. Gunfire had been the norm in town lately, but she'd never heard it so close to the Merriweathers' house. She climbed out of bed and, clad only in her nightgown, crept down the stairs toward the front door.

The house was dark, but she refrained from lighting a lamp. She pulled back the curtain on the sidelight and saw the shadow of Marshal Kiley standing on the porch. Frowning, she cracked open the door. "Well? Are you going to see what that shooting was about? Or are you just going to stand there, contemplating the end of your nose?"

He sighed. "Miss Storm, I've heard some men can sense a hurricane by the ache in their knees. So what do you suppose I should make of the sharp, knifing pain I get in my gut every time you turn up?"

She edged out onto the dark porch and stood in the shadows, wrapping her arms around her body to ward off a chill. "Guilt, I suppose."

"Guilt?" He turned his head toward her and she could tell by his rigid posture that he was still stewing over her earlier prank. "You mean about putting your noble family behind bars where they belong?"

Another gunshot sounded, and she jumped. "Are you going to do something about that or not?"

"What, no challenge? No, 'My family is innocent, Marshal?'"

"I'm tired of arguing that point. Now, you've proven a fondness for tossing people behind bars." She gestured up the street. "What are you waiting for?"

He turned his attention back to the stretch of road outside the wrought iron gate. "My deputy can handle things just fine."

"But I thought you always did the rounds."

"Well, tonight, it seems, I've made an exception."

She smiled. "Bean insisted, did he?"

Another sigh, and then he tucked his fingers into his front pockets. "He thought I could use a good night's sleep."

Was it her imagination or did he sound like a fretful father? "You're actually worried about him, aren't you?"

"I am concerned, Miss Storm—yes."

She had to fight down a laugh. It had obviously been difficult for him to admit that to her. "Bean is competent, isn't he?"

He gave her a sharp look. "Bean Toomey was upholding the law when you were still just a twinkle in your daddy's eye."

"Then why aren't you upstairs getting a good night's sleep?"

"Because I'm used to being awake! I haven't slept more than a few hours a night since I came to this town, lady, thanks to the Storms and the Potters!"

"How do you figure that your lack of rest is our fault?"

"Oh, maybe it's the way you've got this town so riled up that these people would shoot their grandmas for saying the wrong thing."

"*I've* got them riled up?"

"I spend half my time calming tempers and the other half throwing your family in jail. Not a second goes by when there isn't somebody stepping on somebody else's toes over that goddamned piece of gold!"

She took a step back, hating to admit that everything happening in town did involve either the Potters or the Storms. But it certainly wasn't her fault that he'd come to Shady Gulch in the first place. "Well, forgive me, Marshal, but if you're having such a difficult time of things maybe you're in the wrong profession?"

His eyes narrowed and he took a threatening step

toward her. "My professional services do not include baby-sitting a town of ignorant, half-crazed miners!"

She gasped. Normally she would have protested such an assessment of her town, but he actually looked as if he were about to strangle her. She took another step back and wisely kept her mouth shut.

"I have never, in my entire life, dealt with such a bunch of empty-headed fools. Is excitement in this town really so hard to come by, Miss Storm? Is it?"

He'd backed her up against the closed door, and she wondered if he had any idea of just how much he was frightening her. With his hands on either side of her head, staring savagely down into her eyes, he seemed to be waiting for her to answer his question. When she didn't, his expression changed to one she quickly recognized. He leaned a little closer, brushing up against her hips, and all at once Dannie began to tingle with a strange kind of excitement.

"Cat got your tongue again, Miss Storm?" he asked in a seductive whisper.

Somehow, she found her voice. "I . . . I keep myself amply entertained."

His eyes raked over the front of her thin nightgown. "Was that before, or after, I came along?"

Although Dannie still had her arms crossed over her chest, she felt vulnerable, naked to his gaze. Like a bee to honey, or a cat to cream, her attention was drawn to his mouth. She heard him pull in a slow breath and looked up in time to see his eyes darken.

"Do you have any idea what it does to me when you look at me like that?"

She shook her head mutely.

"Then let me show you."

He bent his mouth toward hers, but she quickly turned her head, longing for his kiss but fearing it even more. "You're . . . you're assuming a lot, Marshal."

His fingers traced the line of her jaw and slowly turned her back to him. "Am I?" he whispered.

When his mouth closed over hers, the passion of the night before returned to Dannie in a giant wave of sensation, preventing her from resisting. She moaned, parting her lips beneath his tongue, and he pressed closer.

She could feel her legs beginning to give way beneath her, and she clutched the front of his shirt, wishing she had the strength of will to push him away. This power he had over her was not only dangerous, it was terrifying.

When he began to undo the buttons on her nightgown and push the neckline down past her shoulders, she knew that if she didn't stop him soon, she'd be lost. His mouth left hers to burn a path from her ear to the top of her bared shoulder, and she whispered, "Wait."

His warm, wet lips against her fevered skin was the most incredible thing she'd ever felt, and she knew that if he suddenly decided to force himself on her she wouldn't have the will to fight him.

He paused, and then nipped her bared upper arm with his teeth. "Why put off the inevitable?"

He tugged her nightgown down another fraction of an inch, and Dannie held her breath as he ran his tongue over the tops of her breasts. "Be-because I want you to stop."

He lifted his head and looked into her eyes. "You don't want me to stop. You're just afraid of giving in."

She swallowed, hoping the heat of her blush wasn't as apparent as it felt. "I am not afraid of you or—or of anything. I'm just decent . . . moral. Two words you've probably never heard before."

His smile was quick but cold. "Not in connection with myself."

"Does that mean that you're not going to stop?" Dear God, was that excitement she felt at the idea?

"Depends."

"On . . . on what?"

"On whether or not you really want me to stop." He leaned closer until his lips were brushing her jaw. "Or are you just playing the timid maiden?"

She didn't think she was playing timid. Her body didn't want him to stop, that was evident—even to him—but her good sense was warning her not to give in to his raw, almost brutal, desires. She tugged her nightgown back up over her shoulders and answered him quickly, before she had a chance to think about it any longer. "I want you to stop."

There was a long, uncomfortable silence, and then he took a step backward. "Let me know when you change your mind."

She calmed her racing heart and crossed her arms back over her chest, not so much to protect herself from the cold but from his roving eyes. "Don't hold your breath. Despite what you obviously think, your particular brand of entertainment I can do without."

He smiled smugly. "For the moment anyway."

Another gunshot echoed, but Dannie ignored it. "Normally I wouldn't justify that remark with a reply, but since you're new in town allow me to enlighten you. I am not a tramp, a prostitute, a soiled dove— whatever the going term is at the moment. I do not sell, offer, or throw myself at men. Just because I am nineteen and unmarried does not make me needy, wanton, or lascivious in any way, shape, or form. And if you ever touch me again, lawman or not, *I will kill you!*"

She spun on her heel, threw open the door, and stomped into the house. Unfortunately, the marshal wasn't interested in letting her make an indignant exit and bounded after her, catching her by the arm before she could reach the first step on the staircase.

She let out a soft cry as he wrenched her around to face him. "Don't you *ever* threaten me, lady."

She tried to pull herself free but succeeded only in getting yanked hard against his chest. She glared up into his eyes, and his expression instantly turned hot.

"And as for touching you," he continued breathlessly, "If you don't appreciate my attentions, then I suggest you stop meeting me on darkened porches."

His mouth closed over hers again before she could think to stop him, and the now familiar spark quickly ignited, singeing her with hot flames of desire that stole away her reason. His hands skimmed down her back to mold her bottom, and she arched into him, raising her arms to push her fingers into his thick, silken hair. An ache rose up in her like never before, and she couldn't find the words to stop him as he lowered her to the stairs.

He ravaged her mouth and pressed her downward. The sharp edge of a step dug into her back, but she ignored it. He brought himself directly between her thighs and began pushing her nightgown up past her knees.

"Stop me, Daniella," he whispered. "Stop me now."

She couldn't tell if the words were a challenge or a plea, but it didn't matter either way. He'd completely stolen her strength, her will to resist him.

Her shoulders were bare yet again, and then she felt cool air brush over her breasts. The heat of his hands startled her at first, and then drew a long, low groan from her throat as he brushed his callused thumbs over the tender nubs of her nipples, teasing them to hardened peaks. When he lowered his head to touch her with his tongue she thought she would die with pleasure. But nothing compared to the torrid sensation of him closing his mouth over her. She groaned—almost sobbed—digging her fingers into his back. His other hand had found her naked hip, and he was curving his fingers around to lift her bottom when a shriek of surprise hit them both like a bucket of icy water.

"Oh, my heavens!"

Dannie tilted her head back to find Louisa Merriweather standing at the top of the stairs with her mouth hanging open, and she choked out a sob as shame flooded through her. She began to struggle, unintentionally thwarting the marshal's attempts to bring her nightgown back to some semblance of order.

After she returned her neckline back up around her neck, he helped her to her feet, and they faced the woman still gaping at them from the top of the stairs.

"What is it, Louisa?" Maybelle called from her bedroom.

"Nothing sister! Go back to sleep!"

The tone of Louisa's voice alone was enough to bring Maybelle out to investigate. "What are you two doing up?" she asked, rubbing her eyes.

"Don't ask, sister."

Dannie swallowed, and began, "Louisa." The word came out on a hoarse whisper, and she paused to clear her throat. "I'm sorry—"

The woman seemed to be regaining her composure—at least her color was returning. "No—no need to apologize, my dear. Might I suggest, however, that the next time you two put forth a much more rigorous effort to make it all the way up the stairs to your room?"

Dannie felt herself blush four shades of red. "There won't be a next time."

She heard the marshal shuffle behind her, and then Louisa gave her what could only be described as a tiny skeptical smile. "My dear, some may call indulgence a sin, but I believe it is a greater sin to deny the soul that which it craves the most."

"Indulgence in what, sister?" Maybelle asked.

"Oh, Maybelle, don't expect to enter in the fourth act and know what's happening onstage. I have better things to do with my time than bring you up to date."

Louisa turned for her room, but Maybelle lingered to give the two of them a bewildered scowl. "I don't suppose you two could bring me up—"

"Sisssterrr!" Louisa called. "Come along!"

Maybelle scurried off without a backward glance. The sound of their bedroom doors closing sent a flash of panic through Dannie. She was once again alone with the marshal. She spun around to face him and found a glimmer in his eyes that she didn't trust.

She began backing up the stairs with one hand on the banister to steady herself and one hand held out in front of her to restrain him. "Now, this is not a threat," she said, "but please, *please* don't touch me anymore."

He grinned, and she recognized the glimmer in his eyes as amusement. "It might be a sin not to indulge."

"I'll take my chances with hell, thank you very much."

He climbed up the first two steps, and she almost stumbled in her haste to get up to the landing.

"You'd choose hell over heaven?" he asked, his smile growing broader.

She was backing up to her room, and he was slowly climbing the stairs after her. "You choose and I'll take whichever one's left."

"But the ride to heaven is a lot more fun when it's shared, Daniella—"

"Don't call me that!" she blurted out. "You can call me lady, or Miss Storm." Anything else sounded too intimate coming from his lips.

By the time he reached the landing her fingers were closing around her door knob.

"Not Daniella? Then how about sweetheart? Darling? Honey-bunch? . . ."

She went into her room and slammed the door shut, then leaned back against it as if that might stop him if he chose to pursue her. Breathing hard, she listened to his footsteps on the carpet in the hallway as he moved past her door and into his own room. And then came the soft, deep sound of his laughter.

Dannie gritted her teeth. Her palms were damp and her heart was racing. No matter how hard she tried, she couldn't deny the excitement that was tingling her spine. It was true that she was doing her best to despise Marshal Jake Kiley, but her body wasn't interested in paying attention.

The next day was Sunday, and it was the first time Dannie would have to attend church without her family at her side. She visited them at the jail, glad that Marshal Kiley had left the office to Bean for the morning, as usual. After an hour of listening to her family rant and rave about the injustices of life, Dannie joined the Merriweather sisters for the ten-o'clock service.

Louisa didn't appear inclined to say a word about the night before, and Dannie was beginning to think that her morning was going pretty smoothly. It would have continued on that way if Mr. Potter hadn't been waiting for her in the courtyard after church.

"Well, little missy? What have you got to say for yourself!"

Dannie turned to find him staring at her with rage in his eyes. "I seem to get blamed for a lot of things lately, Mr. Potter. I'm afraid you're going to have to be more specific."

"You know what I'm talking about. You led him on—we all know that. You taunted and teased him just like you did the last time. And when he finally gave into the urge, like any normal man, you cried foul!"

"Mr. Potter!" Louisa Merriweather exclaimed, aghast. "Honestly, this is not the proper—"

"Louisa," Dannie interrupted, "you and Maybelle go on home. I'll be there shortly."

"Oh, but Daniella—"

"I can take care of this myself. Go on."

She waited until the two worried women were in their buggy and headed up the street before she lit into Mr. Sherman Potter. "You pompous, ignorant, old bag of wind! I did not lead William on, he came out of the woods at me and yanked me right off my horse!"

A crowd was beginning to gather around them, murmuring their own speculations.

"Ain't it funny," Mr. Potter said, his smile not quite reaching his eyes, "that you are the only woman in this town that has ever complained about my boy? Ain't it funny that you seem to be the only one who claims to have a problem with William?"

"Well, I'm certainly not laughing!"

His expression looked almost murderous. "My boy's in jail because of you, and either you're going to see that he's set free, or I'm going to make sure that you and your family pay for this for the rest of your miserable, no-good lives!"

Dannie couldn't help but feel a deep sense of despair that a man who had once meant so much to her and her family could threaten them so viciously.

"Did I just hear you intimidate my witness?"

Dannie heaved a sigh of relief as the marshal rode up and swung down from his horse. Her heart warmed at the sight of him, at the vision of the sun shining down on his thick black hair as he walked her way. He would see her out of this mess with Mr. Potter. She knew it as surely as she knew she was coming to count on him in a way that would open the gates of hell, should her family ever find out.

"This doesn't concern you, Marshal," Mr. Potter said. "So I recommend you stay out of it."

"I happen to be the one holding the key to your son's cell, Potter, so I'd say I have quite a bit to do with this. What's the problem? I thought we'd settled all this yesterday."

"Nothing was settled! My boy didn't do a damn thing to this girl. I don't know how she convinced you that he attacked her, but I want him set free!"

"You want this discussed out here in the open, Potter? Fine. William admitted to me, himself, that he pulled Miss Storm off her horse yesterday—"

"Says you!"

Dannie glanced up at Jake in time to see his jaw tighten. "Are you calling me a liar?"

Mr. Potter took a few steps closer to the two of them.

"That's right, Marshal. I can only wonder what favors this hussy did for you to win you over to her side."

Dannie opened her mouth to defend herself, but she refrained when the marshal lifted his hand, indicating for her to remain silent. "You're looking for a fight, aren't you, friend?" he said to Mr. Potter. "Well, you're not gonna be finding one with Miss Storm. You're gonna be finding one with me."

Mr. Potter laughed and glanced around at the gathered crowd. "Is that supposed to be a threat, Marshal?"

"That's a warning, Potter. When I threaten you, you'll know it."

"But all I'm asking is that my boy get a fair shake. That's what we all want after all, isn't it? Justice!"

"If he keeps his nose clean in my jail, I'll set him free when the surveyor passes through, along with the rest of them."

Mr. Potter's tiny dark eyes centered on Dannie and she flinched at the rancor she saw in them. "If she'd just admit to the truth, it would save us both a lot of trouble."

Dannie cleared her throat. "William is guilty, Mr. Potter—"

He took a threatening step toward her. "You take that back, you conniving little—"

Jake moved into his path. "Potter, you are testing the limits of my patience. I suggest you stop worrying about William and go on home before you get yourself into trouble."

"Here's what I think of your suggestion!"

Dannie watched in shock as Sherman Potter took a

swing at Jake. The marshal ducked just in time, but when he straightened back up she could see that he was angrier than a wounded bear.

"You stupid son of a bitch," he muttered. He caught hold of Mr. Potter's arm and twisted it up behind the man's back. "You've just earned yourself a bed right next to your son's!"

The crowd was in an uproar as the marshal led the enraged Mr. Potter away. Dannie stared after them both, astounded. They would all be in jail now, every male Storm and every male Potter.

"It's all her fault!" somebody shouted.

"Her fault? It's them Potters what have been causin' all the trouble!"

"I say it's them Storms and you're no better!"

Minister Stevens broke through the crowd and calmed the peaking tempers with a few calmly voiced religious sayings, and Dannie took that opportunity to slip away.

Every day it seemed to be something else. She glanced up at the clear sky, tears stinging her eyes, wishing for the hundredth time that it would rain. Maybe if the weather returned to normal, then so would the rest of life in Shady Creek. For now, the best she could hope for was that with both families in jail the town might forget about the gold for a while and get on with their lives.

And then there was the ever-changing marshal. She wiped her eyes as she walked blindly toward the Merriweathers' house. He had once again intervened on her behalf—had taken her side, protected her. She couldn't help but be wary of his motives, but if he kept up this kind of behavior she wasn't sure how much longer her heart could hold out.

12

Dannie paced the tiled foyer in the Merriweathers' house, wondering why it always took so long
for Jake to jail a Potter. It was past noon, she was half-
starved, and the Merriweathers had left for Sunday
lunch at the Applebys' over fifteen minutes ago. But
Dannie wasn't setting foot outside until she was sure the
enraged Sherman Potter no longer walked the streets.

When Jake finally arrived Dannie had worked herself
into a snit. "What always takes you so long!"

He paused, startled. Then he unbuckled his gunbelt
and hung it on the coatrack. "So long to do what?"

At the sound of his calm voice, she clasped her
shaking hands together in the folds of her skirt. "I have
been waiting here for almost two hours."

He shrugged and walked past her to the kitchen. "I
figured you'd be out having lunch with the Merriweathers."

She followed him and watched as he rummaged

through a cupboard. "They went on without me. I wanted to wait for you so I could be sure Mr. Potter didn't talk his way out of going to jail. He's very good at talking, you know. He is in jail, isn't he?"

"And the arrest reports, which always take up most of my time, are all filled out to the letter. Now, if I've eased your mind, I just saw the sisters turn the corner onto Hale Street. If you hurry, you can still make lunch."

"He didn't give you any problems? Didn't try to threaten you into letting him go?"

"I didn't say that. But he's in jail just the same."

"What did he say?"

"What difference does it make?" He sat down at the table and began slicing a wheel of cheese with his pocket knife.

"A lot, if it had anything to do with me. That's not all you're going to eat, is it?"

She went to the counter and took a fresh loaf of bread from the bread box. Then she sat down in the chair opposite him. "Could you make my slices a little thicker, please?"

He looked up and raised an eyebrow. "What about lunch?"

"I'm not all that hungry." She hoped he didn't hear her stomach giving evidence to the contrary. Somehow the last thing she wanted at the moment was to be apart from him.

"Suit yourself." He lowered his eyes back to the cheese wheel and began cutting thicker slices while she fidgeted with the lacy edge of a place mat.

"How is everything at the jail?" she asked.

"Noisy."

"I can imagine. How's Bean handling living in the room next to all the chaos?"

"With plenty of earplugs."

There was a long silence while his knife continued to *thunk* down onto the table, moments filled with tension and uncertainty.

"What did Daddy say when you brought in Mr. Potter?" she finally said.

"Your father laughed until he could barely breathe." He handed her a stack of slices.

Dannie smiled at the image. "I'll bet. And William? What did they do when you brought in William last night?"

Jake's expression hardened, and he appeared to ignore her as he began slicing the loaf of bread. Dannie felt a moment of trepidation.

"Marshal?"

"Hmmm?"

"I asked you how my family responded to William's arrest."

He put a piece of cheese between his teeth and leaned back in his chair to chew it. "You really want to know?"

He was hedging, and Dannie's misgivings grew. "I wouldn't ask if I didn't."

"All right. The left cell was full of saloon brawlers from the night before, so I put William in a cell with your family."

She blinked. "With all three of them?"

"A few minutes later I put him in with the drunks."

"But surely you didn't tell my family why William was there?"

He ate another piece of cheese. "I might have."

Dannie had visited the jail just that morning, and now the image of William, curled up on his cot and facing the far wall, flashed through her mind. William Potter certainly wasn't one of her favorite people, but the last thing he or anybody else deserved was to be abused while in jail.

"They could have killed him," she whispered, fear making her voice raspy.

"They only had him for a few minutes—"

"But that was a pretty stupid mistake," she said more forcefully.

His eyes locked with hers. "Who said it was a mistake?"

She was stunned. "What did they do to him?"

"The last I saw, he had two black eyes, a bloody nose, and he wasn't walking a very straight line. He'll survive."

She jumped up. "I can't believe this!"

"Neither can I," he said, with a short laugh. "Your family works pretty fast."

"You allowed them to beat William and that's all you have to say?"

His smile faded and his eyes narrowed. "They did exactly what you would've done to him if you'd been bigger and stronger—"

"But that doesn't matter—"

"Like hell it doesn't, lady! And don't think I was doing you a favor! A father deserves to know when his daughter has been mistreated so he can make sure it doesn't happen again. And believe me, Willie got the point."

"Oh, well thank you very much, Marshal! The next time I have an argument with one of my friends I'll be sure to hand them over into your impartial hands!"

His eyes darkened. "I wasn't aware that you counted William Potter as one of your friends."

"William deserves justice, just like anybody else."

"Did he attack you or not?"

"Yes, of course he did!"

"Then, as far as I'm concerned, justice was served."

She slammed her hands down onto the table. "My God, you are the most stubborn, pigheaded man I have ever met!"

"And you are the most impertinent, thankless woman *I* have ever met!"

"I am *not* thankless."

He stood slowly and loomed over the table at her. "From where I'm standing you sure the hell are. And not only that, you're scheming, deceitful, defiant, forward, and immodest. And if you don't get your shapely little fanny out of my sight, I'm gonna throw you to the floor and make love to you till you scream."

She backed up so fast she slammed into the wall. "You wouldn't dare."

He moved around the edge of the table toward her, a smile curving his lips. "You don't know me very well, do you?"

Suddenly, the front door banged open and Bean burst into the house. "Jake! Shit, Jake—beggin' yer pardon, ma'am—you gotta come quick! They're shootin' up every store in town, and they are bound ta turn on each other any second!"

"Who?" she and the marshal said at the same time.

"The whole damn town! That's who!"

The marshal went to the foyer to get his gun belt. Dannie followed while addressing Bean. "The whole town is shooting up saloons?"

"They're all hotter 'n hell about both families being in jail. One side's sayin' the other should be hung, and vicey-versy. If we don't do something quick ta cool 'em off, Jake, there's gonna be blood in the streets!"

Dannie reached for her shawl, but the marshal took hold of her wrist. "What do you think you're doing?"

"I'm getting my shawl."

"You won't need your shawl, Miss Storm. You're staying put."

"You can't force me to stay here. It's none of your business where I go or what I do!"

His jaw tightened, and he herded her backward into the kitchen where he saw her into a chair. "I'm making it my business, sweetheart. The last thing I need is you mucking things up even worse."

She bounded up. "And what makes you think I can't help?"

He pushed her back down. "Because where you go, trouble follows. Do the whole town a favor and don't get out of that chair."

The marshal and the deputy left and Dannie clenched her fists against the smooth pine surface of the kitchen table. She'd actually thought that with her family in jail she'd have a little more freedom, but it seemed the marshal had volunteered to step in as her keeper. Well, he wasn't one of her brothers, and he certainly wasn't her father. She could stand right up from this chair and he wouldn't be able to do a darn thing about it!

She leapt up from the chair, sending it skidding across the floor.

She stormed into the foyer. "And I can take this shawl"—which she yanked from the coatrack—"and I can leave this house any time I darn well please!"

But where was she going to go? She could hear shooting and shouting outside and now wondered if it was wise to ignore the marshal's warning. It sounded like the whole town was on the brink of a civil war. How had it come to this? The Potters and the Storms. Two families that had once been the best of friends.

And then she thought of Mary Ellen.

A lump caught in her throat. She hadn't seen Mary Ellen Potter for so long she could barely picture her face. After the two of them had been caught sneaking swims in the creek, Mr. Potter had started keeping Mary Ellen at home and out of "Storm reach."

They'd grown up together, she and Mary Ellen. They'd shared scraped knees, secret wishes, and even the losses of their mothers only three months apart. Then the family feud had come between their friendship. Just another casualty of war.

She pulled her shawl tightly around her shoulders and headed for the back door. It was time she assessed Mary Ellen's view on things now that the two of them were the only ones left free. Maybe without the men around to get angry over every little thing, the women might be able to come to some sort of agreement over Spangle Creek. And maybe if the two of them put their heads together, they could come up with a way to put an end to this senseless town war.

The Potter house sat on a rise about a mile down the road from Dannie's. It was a bit nicer than the Storm home, with two more rooms in an upstairs level. The barn was immense, with two hay lofts and a grain bin and had been a perfect place for hide and seek when they were children.

As she rode up the front drive, a flood of memories assailed her: She and Mary Ellen skipping through the meadow out back; the two of them holding foot races against their brothers and winning; long lazy afternoons of sitting beneath a tree, playing with rag dolls and day dreaming. It all seemed like a lifetime away.

She climbed down off her horse and, gathering her shawl and her courage around her, stepped up onto the neat white porch and pulled back the big brass knocker. Mary Ellen opened the door. Her eyes were just as blue and her hair was just as golden as Dannie remembered. They stared at each other for a moment, and then flew into each other's arms, both of them talking at once.

". . . I heard that Douglas was jailed, and then Donovan, and then your Daddy . . ."

". . . the gold, and with everything going on in town I wasn't sure what you were thinking . . ."

". . . forget the whole idea, and then yesterday William pulled another trick on you . . ."

". . . your Daddy was hauled off to jail this morning, and the whole town just sort of exploded—"

Mary Ellen stopped talking, her eyes flying wide. "Daddy was put in jail this morning? What—what for?"

"He tried to punch Jake in the nose."

"Jake?"

"Marshal Kiley."

"Oh . . . Well . . . Isn't this interesting? Now I suppose I'm just a poor helpless female living by herself, with no one to direct her every move?"

Dannie smiled carefully. "That's right, Mary Ellen. Just like me. And the marshal plans to keep them all in jail until the surveyor arrives."

Mary Ellen bit her lip and began to break into an ever-widening grin. "How awful. How simply dreadful! Why, I'm not sure what I should do first. Visit my poor incarcerated family? Or go for a swim in the creek!" She started skipping around the foyer, and Dannie laughed. "Or maybe I'll hitch up the buggy and see if the town has changed in the past six months!"

"Oh, it's changed. That's why I've come. You wouldn't believe how involved everybody has gotten in the gold find."

"Oh, I can imagine. That is all Daddy and William ever talk about. That and marrying you." She stopped skipping and grew serious. "I told them, Dannie. I told them you'd never agree to marry William. But my family never listens to a thing I say."

Dannie rolled her eyes. "Welcome to womanhood."

"So what has the town got to do with the gold?"

"In their minds, everything. But I'm beginning to get an idea that might just fix the problem."

Mary Ellen clapped her hands. "Oh, Dannie girl, how I've missed your ideas."

"You mean the ideas that always got our bottoms blistered?"

"They may not have always turned out the way we'd planned, but they were always loads of fun!"

Jake sat at his desk, writing an endless stack of arrest reports. He had over thirty people in his jail, all packed into two cells, and they were raising a ruckus to rival a stampeding herd of buffalo.

Bean stepped out of the cell room and shut the door on a combination of shouts and curses. "Got a Storm mixed up in the Potter cell. I took care of it, though."

"He survive the mistake?"

"Oh yeah. Had 'em all held off with the knife you overlooked in his boot."

"Shit."

"Yeah, you woulda been if he'd a stabbed any of them fellas. You ain't never been this careless before, boy-o. You got somethin' wrong with your brain today?"

"If I did, do you think they'd let me off this dog duty?"

"Doubt it. Seems to me the governor would be tickled pink to have this town drive you all the way to the looney bin. Maybe that's what he's had in mind all along?"

"He should just let them all kill each other. This town is nothing but trouble."

"Ohhh. I see."

Jake looked up from his papers to find Bean grinning like an idiot. "And what is it that you suddenly think you realize?"

"Nothin'. It just occurred to me that you've been spendin' a lot of your time in the past week savin' that cute little Storm gal from one disaster after another—"

"What did I tell you about calling her cute—"

"And it is true that I have never seen you so preoccupied." Bean hitched one of his boney legs over the edge of the desk. "Need ta bend my ear, son? Need a kind and understandin' shoulder ta lay your troubles on—"

"What I need is for you to get your ass off my reports."

Bean broke into a hoarse cackle, but he didn't move. "You're hooked, Jake. When are ya gonna face it? She had you dead to rights the day she came in here wavin' that shotgun under yer nose."

"I think maybe we better have somebody come and confiscate your brain, Bean. Sounds to me like you're getting too old to use it."

"I see it in yer eyes, plain as day."

"All right, Deputy, I'll admit that there is a definite attraction where the lady is concerned. But as for *hooking?* Daniella Storm is no different from every other young lady I have had the pleasure of acquainting myself with."

"Yes she is."

Jake closed his eyes and prayed for patience. He hated

it when Bean got that know-it-all tone in his voice.

"Every other woman you've ever *acquainted* yourself with has purty near fallen at yer feet and practically climbed yer legs to get the pants off ya. Daniella Storm has had you on the run since day one. And she don't take a minute of yer crap, neither. She goes toe-to-toe with ya, and damn, but it is a beautiful thing to witness."

"She's a shrew."

"She's a handful. There is a big difference, Jake. A shrew is cold and hateful. A handful is warm and spirited. What you gotcher self there is a handful."

Bean's reference brought Jake's thoughts careening back to the night before—for about the one hundredth time that day. Damn, but she was so warm and so soft. Her skin tasted like sweet, smooth cream. Her hair smelled like fresh milled cinnamon. And her breasts, God, her breasts. . . .

He dropped his quill pen and pushed a hand through his hair, realizing that Bean was right. There was something different about Daniella Storm. He wanted her more than he'd ever wanted any other woman. The thought of leaving town before feeling her naked body against his, having her long legs wrapped around his hips, and hearing her cry out his name made him ache with deep regret.

"And what about the nugget?"

Jake cleared his throat. "What about the nugget?"

"You heard the governor. If that thing isn't secured by the time the surveyor gits here our butts are gonna be hash. Until the property lines are decided, it don't belong to nobody."

"I sent her after it. I tried following her."

"Yeah, but then ol' Winsome Willie got in the way."

"Drunken bastard. Remind me to punch him again the next time I get the opportunity."

"Miz Storm was here visitin' her family this mornin'. I understand Willie didn't even lift his head to look at her. Appears he finally figured things out."

"So, unfortunately, did Miss Storm."

"Meaning?"

"I made the mistake of telling her that I let her family have him for a few minutes."

"Uh-oh. Tried tootin' yer own horn, did ya?"

"Yeah, well, she didn't exactly throw her arms around my neck and thank me for my assistance."

"Uh-huh. And would that account for the shocked look on her face this afternoon when I came bargin' into the kitchen?"

"No. I think my threatening to take her on the floor would account for that."

"Oh. And what if I hadn't come along?"

Jake shrugged. "That would have depended on the lady."

"Then I'm glad I didn't barge in five minutes later. You still plannin' on following her to the nugget?"

"Maybe." He flashed Bean a grin. "Or maybe I'll seduce it out from under her."

Bean gave him a warning look. "You try that and she's liable to shoot you between the eyes."

"What? Your cute, sweet, little Miss Storm shoot somebody? Admit it, Bean. Pretty or not, feisty or not, she's trouble. Just like the rest of her family. The upheaval in this town is proof enough for me, and it should be proof enough for you too."

Bean didn't respond. Jake glanced up from his paperwork, thinking that maybe he'd finally gotten through to the old man. But Bean's attention was focused on the open window. As a slow smile crept over the deputy's face, Jake rose and looked out into the street, searching for what could possibly be so interesting.

"Take a looky at yer troublemaker now, Jake."

And then Jake saw them. His eyes widened, and for the first time in a long while he was at a loss for words.

It wasn't natural. It went against everything he'd assumed. But sure enough, there, walking down the boardwalk arm and arm, were the supposed bitter enemies of the two warring clans: Daniella Storm and Mary Ellen Potter.

13

Dannie and Mary Ellen paused in the doorway of Potter's Mercantile. Dannie's heart was thundering despite Mary Ellen's constant words of encouragement. But Dannie had good reason to be nervous. It had been a long time since she'd been welcomed into the store, and by the stern look on the clerk's face she knew that today wasn't going to be any different.

Their plan was bound to end disastrously. Not an hour ago it had seemed faultless, but now that she was feeling the townsfolks' stares, her courage was faltering.

"I'm not so sure about this," she said. "Maybe we should spend more time strolling the boardwalk."

"Don't be silly," Mary Ellen replied. "I've practically worn out my shoes as it is. It is time to invade uncharted territory."

"Uncharted territory?"

"Yes. Like Christopher Columbus and Juan Ponce de León. We are two explorers forging ahead into the unknown."

"Mary Ellen, I hope you don't take this the wrong way, but I think six months of confinement has pickled your brain."

"And I think your confrontations with that new marshal have left you flighty. Now, stop worrying and let's get to it."

Dannie felt that this might be a good time to tell Mary Ellen that none of her plans had worked since Marshal Kiley had come to town, giving her good reason to be flighty, but before Dannie could say another word Mary Ellen had edged behind her and given her a good shove, sending her tripping into Potter's Mercantile.

She stumbled over her own feet and managed to right herself just before colliding with a display of toilet water. She gave Mary Ellen a glare. But Mary Ellen merely smiled and brushed past Dannie toward the far counter.

Dannie turned her attention to the four other customers in the store, all women. She steadied her nerves, knowing she had no choice but to wait for her cue as Mary Ellen began her performance across the room.

"Mr. Billabee? I have come to inform you that my brother and father are both in jail, and that I am now in charge."

The balding store clerk shook out his Denver newspaper and laid it on the counter. He glanced over at Dannie and grunted behind his wire-rimmed spectacles. "Does your father know that you're out wandering the streets with the likes of her?"

Faces turned her way, and Dannie wished that she could melt into the floor. She lifted her chin and silently dared anyone to condemn her.

Mary Ellen said loudly, "This is my very best friend, Mr. Billabee." The store broke into noisy murmurs. "And she would like a pound of our best sugar."

The man looked stunned for a moment and then cleared his throat. "I have my orders, young lady. No Storm, nor any of their friends, are to buy a single thing inside these four walls."

Mary Ellen gave Dannie a look of victory and Dannie sighed with relief. Their entire plan hinged on Mr. Billabee's resistance.

Mary Ellen, the consummate actress, sidled closer to the clerk. "Mr. Billabee? Do you enjoy your job?"

"Why, yes, Miss Potter, I do. I've been working here for over twenty years and your father has never had a single reason to complain."

"Good. Now, if you'd like to keep your job, sir, I suggest you fetch my friend a pound of sugar."

"I've got my orders—"

"*Now*, Mr. Billabee!"

His head snapped back so hard at Mary Ellen's shout that his spectacles bounced on his round nose. He pulled a hanky out of his pocket and dabbed at the sweat breaking out on his brow. "Miss Potter, your father will skin me alive if I don't do what he says. Now, it doesn't matter what I think about the situation one way or the other—"

"That's right, Mr. Billabee, it doesn't. My father is in jail. I am not. Therefore, I am in charge of this store." She smiled sweetly. "And you are fired."

When Dannie heard her cue her muscles tensed. Forcing her legs to move, she rushed toward the counter. "Mary Ellen, this man depends on his job to feed his family! You can't just fire him over a pound of sugar!"

Mary Ellen turned to her, blinking her wide blue eyes. "Why, of course I can, Dannie. I am his employer. The man has to do whatever I say. And I say, get out of my store, Mr. Billabee."

It took a conscious effort for Dannie not to mouth the words she and Mary Ellen had practiced so carefully earlier that afternoon. "What has come over you, Mary Ellen Potter? This man is only following orders from his employer."

"I am his employer. Mr. Billabee, why are you still here—"

Dannie threw herself in between her friend and the clerk. "You will not fire this man because of me!"

There was a moment of tense silence in the store while everyone waited for Mary Ellen's response. She and Dannie shared a subtle look that said the time was ripe for the crux of their plan.

Mary Ellen turned from the counter to the four women who were watching the scene with shocked interest. "Let's put it to a vote then, shall we? How many of you agree with me that this impertinent man should be fired?"

The four women in the store exchanged glances. Cornwall Billabee had been a valued citizen of the community for over thirty years. None of them was about to advocate his dismissal.

Mary Ellen's brows rose. "So then I'm to take it that you're all siding with Miss Storm?"

Tension filled the store and every face went pale. "I—I wouldn't exactly say that," Mrs. Johnson said.

"Oh? Then why didn't you raise your hand?"

"Well, because we don't want ol' Billabee to lose his job," Mrs. Hankner spoke up.

"But, if you don't want Mr. Billabee to be fired then you are agreeing with Miss Storm."

"Her opinion certainly seems to make the most sense," Mrs. Johnson reluctantly agreed.

"Goodness, then I've been misinformed. I thought you all despised the Storm family."

"Who says we despise 'em? We just don't care for 'em stealin' your gold."

"And who, Miss McGuire, invited you to care one way or the other about the gold?"

"Stan says—"

"Stan?"

Dannie leaned closer to Mary Ellen and whispered, "Stan is *Mrs.* Thompson's new husband."

"Oh, congratulations, Mrs. Thompson, and do go on. Tell us all what your Stan has told you to think."

The woman blinked. "Well, he didn't exactly tell me what to think—"

"Then what exactly did he tell you?"

"That I was to . . . that is to say, *we* was to stick by the Potters—'cause the Storms stole your gold!"

"Mrs. Thompson, you know as well as I do that that gold doesn't belong to anybody at the moment."

"Well, no, not yet, but—"

"So in that sense, nobody has stolen anything from anyone. Wouldn't you agree?"

"Well . . . I suppose."

"Then the question remains, Why have you taken my family's side?"

Old Mrs. Cragmore pushed forward to stand in front of the other three women. "Because her husband told her to, that's why! A husband knows best!"

Mrs. Cragmore was perhaps the most formidable woman in town, and Dannie wondered if Mary Ellen would be able to stand her ground. Surprisingly, Mary Ellen didn't miss a beat. "Well, forgive me, Mrs. Cragmore, for expecting these women to have minds of their own."

The old woman grunted. "We don't have to have minds of our own, we're married. As you should be!"

"If getting married means never again having a free thought, I believe I'll pass on the custom."

"The good Lord says woman shall cleave unto her husband!"

"Yes, but I don't recall the good Lord saying woman shall marry and then promptly toss her brain out the window. And what about the rest of you? Have your husbands told you what to do and what to think as well?"

Almost immediately the store broke into pandemonium as all four women started talking at once, voicing their opinions and comparing notes on their husbands' views. The three younger women didn't appear to appreciate the idea that they'd been instructed what to think, which was precisely what Dannie and Mary Ellen had hoped for.

When all was said and done, stubborn old Mrs. Cragmore stomped out of the store in a huff while Dannie was warmly embraced by the three other, very repentant, women. And Mr. Billabee's job was saved, although no one would buy a single thing from the store until Dannie had been sold the pound of sugar that she hadn't really needed in the first place.

Dannie and Mary Ellen left the mercantile, bursting with triumph, and strode across the street toward Storm's Gun Shop to put their plan into action there. It seemed that Mary Ellen Potter was badly in need of a bag of Winchester cartridges.

"Hello, Daniella."

Dannie and Mary Ellen had just come out of the gun shop when the smile promptly slipped from Dannie's face. The marshal was leaning back against the knot-holed wall of the barber shop. She tried to keep Mary Ellen moving past him at a steady pace, but the headstrong girl stopped the instant the marshal spoke.

"Well, hello. You must be the new marshal Dannie has told me so much about."

Dannie fought a blush, but it seemed to have a will of its own as it crept up her neck and flooded her cheeks. The marshal gave her an inquisitive look and she lowered her lashes, hoping to calm herself and hide the effect he had on her. "Marshal, this is my friend, Mary Ellen."

"Mary Ellen *Potter*," he clarified, as if she weren't aware of Mary Ellen's last name.

She looked up at him. "Mary Ellen *Imogene* Potter."

"Daughter of *Sherman* Potter—"

"Born 1842," Mary Ellen joined in. "Mother: one Mary Potter, originally from England . . . This is a very odd conversation."

"The marshal and I rarely have conversations at all, let alone normal ones."

"A pleasure to meet you, Miss Potter. Miss Storm, I believe I told you this afternoon to stay put at the Merriweather house."

Dannie shifted her bag of sugar to her other arm and replied "And I believe I told you to go to hell."

A faint smile curved his mouth. "No, not quite so colorfully as that, anyway."

"Oh, Marshal Kiley, don't be angry with her." Mary Ellen laid a gentle hand on his arm, and Dannie was struck with the strangest urge to take her bag of sugar and wallop her friend over the head with it. "She simply wanted to pay me a visit. I do hope you won't hold it against her."

The marshal turned his attention to Mary Ellen, and Dannie watched with growing irritation as his eyes traveled over her golden hair and pretty face and flickered over the front of her bodice. Then the man actually smiled! "For a pretty lady like yourself I might be able to make an exception just this once."

Dannie gritted her teeth. "What happened to not doing favors for people who aren't your friends?"

He looked back at her and his expression instantly darkened. "You should be thanking Miss Potter for saving your skin. I was determined to take you back to the house and lock you up in your room."

"You and what brigade!"

"Don't tempt me, lady. Be glad I'm in an agreeable mood."

"Agree—well, it's obvious you don't even know the meaning of that word!"

"By my estimates, neither do you."

She took a step toward him and glared up into his face. "At least I'm not overbearing."

He laughed. "Says who?"

"And I don't swagger around claiming to be a man of justice one minute and letting a man get beaten the next."

His eyes narrowed, and he took a threatening step closer to her. He bent down until his nose was practically touching hers. "One of these days you're going to push me too far, lady. Then we'll see who wins this thing once and for all."

The sound of Mary Ellen clearing her throat drew them apart. She was watching them with raised brows, and Dannie could only imagine how all this must appear to her.

Marshal Kiley crossed his arms and leaned back

against the wall. "I don't suppose either of you would like to tell me what you're doing wandering arm in arm through town?"

"That's none of your—"

"We're presenting a united front."

Dannie gave Mary Ellen an annoyed look and said, "Don't waste your time explaining anything to him. In his point of view, we're just as troublesome as the rest of our families."

Mary Ellen either didn't hear or chose to ignore her. "If Dannie and I can remain friends throughout all this, then certainly the rest of the town can come to terms and patch things up among themselves. Don't you agree, Marshal Kiley?"

The marshal nodded intently, as if what Mary Ellen had to say was the most interesting piece of information he'd ever heard. "And what about the gold?"

"You see there," Dannie said quickly. "I told you he'd miss the point. All the men of this town think about is that gold—"

"And what *is* the point?" he demanded.

"The point, Marshal," Dannie said tightly, "is that *we* don't care about the gold."

He started to laugh, and Dannie looked at Mary Ellen. "What did I tell you? The man is impossible."

"But Dannie is telling you the truth, Marshal Kiley. All the two of us want is for our town to be the same quiet happy home it used to be. If we had our way, that gold would never have been found."

The marshal quieted down and studied them for a moment. "All right, Miss Potter, let's say for a minute that that's the case, and you're out to soothe the frazzled nerves of your neighbors. You don't honestly think that parading around town holding hands is going to make them all fall to their knees with guilt and remorse?"

"Oh, we have more than this planned—"

"Don't you say another word, Mary Ellen. We agreed to keep this between ourselves, remember?"

The marshal gave Dannie a warning look. "Don't let me catch you causing trouble, lady. It's not like I don't have enough problems today."

Dannie frowned and looked up and down the street. "Everything seems quiet enough. As a matter of fact, more quiet than usual. Maybe our plan is already working better than you'd care to admit, Marshal."

He grunted derisively. "The reason the streets are so barren, Miss Storm, is because half the men in this town are in my jail for the night."

"Half?" Mary Ellen repeated.

"At least half."

"And just what have *they* done wrong?" Dannie asked.

She saw his jaw clench and found satisfaction in her ability to irritate him as much as he did her. "For starters, they were shooting out windows on Lane Street. And when the deputy and myself arrived and told them all to go home, they refused. One of the idiots even took a shot at me."

Dannie felt the color drain from her face. A vision of Jake Kiley laid out, bloody, in the street sent a panic through her like she'd never felt before. "Was anybody hurt?"

"No. But next time we might not be so lucky."

"Then things really have gotten out of hand," Mary Ellen said.

"And I doubt the two of you are going to be able to make a bit of difference. I suggest you go home and wait for things to quiet down—with your doors and windows locked."

Feeling strangely relieved that he was unharmed, Dannie went back to being annoyed with him. "You mean hide? Stick our heads in the sand like a couple of ostriches and hope that the world goes away?"

"That sounds like a smart move, yeah."

"Well, you can forget it, Marshal. We're in this thing up to our ears and we plan to do everything we can to fix it. Isn't that right, Mary Ellen?" She held out her hand to her friend.

Mary Ellen glanced down at Dannie's outstretched hand and then looked hesitantly at the marshal. "Do you think we'll be in any sort of danger?"

"Mary Ellen!"

"I'm only trying to get both sides of this!"

"That's good to hear, Miss Potter. *You've* got some sense."

Mary Ellen's smile could have blinded an eagle soaring three hundred feet above ground, and Dannie thought she might hit her with the bag of sugar after all.

"He wasn't complimenting you, Mary Ellen, he was insulting me." She handed her the sugar. "Take this and start heading for the Merriweathers'. I'll be along in a minute."

Reluctantly, Mary Ellen accepted the package. "It was nice meeting you, Marshal Kiley. I do hope we see each other again."

"I'm sure you can count on that, ma'am."

Mary Ellen turned to go and the marshal's hand lifted to his head as if he were reaching for a hat. Then his arm fell to his side and he gave Dannie a cold glare.

She waited until Mary Ellen was out of earshot before saying what was on her mind. "Found a new path to my bad side, have you?"

"Why Miss Storm, whatever do you mean?"

"You can smile and tip your invisible hat to every little thing she says, Marshal, but just realize that I happen to know exactly what you're doing."

"Do you, now?"

"You're trying to goad me by being nice to her, but it isn't going to work. She's not the naive thing you think she is. I'll wager that the next time you two meet she'll have you all figured out."

He leaned closer, and her pulse quickened. "And what, exactly, is there to figure out about me?"

She saw his lips move, but it took a moment for her to register what he'd said. "That—that you'll do anything to get my goat. Anything at all."

"I don't want your lousy goat. What I do want, however, I think you're gonna be pretty reluctant to give me."

She took a step back and glanced around to be sure no one was paying them any mind. "You just keep your lecherous intentions to yourself—along with everything else of yours!" she whispered. "You may be able to kiss me crazy, but you won't be able to coax me into your bed!"

He frowned, as if that hadn't been at all what he'd meant. "And what the hell makes you think I want you in my bed?"

"Because the stairs are mighty uncomfortable!"

Instantly his expression warmed. His eyes roamed across her face, bringing her blush out of hiding again. "You are quite a handful, Miss Storm."

Dannie blinked. His comment hadn't sounded the least bit condemning. "I am none of your concern."

He raised his hand toward her, and she didn't have the presence of mind to back away as he slowly wrapped a lock of her hair around his finger. "I wouldn't count on that."

His lashes were lowered in a seductive stare, and it was all she could do not to throw herself against him and kiss him right there in the center of town. She finally took a step back and his hand fell away. "Will—will you be home for supper?"

There was a pause, and then he answered, "Suppose so."

"I'll tell the sisters then."

She turned to go, but the sound of her name stopped her. She didn't turn around, knowing she might make a fool of herself if she looked into his warm dark eyes again.

"Do us both a favor, Miss Storm, and don't come out on the porch tonight."

His soft, smooth voice drifted into her ears and caressed her from deep within. She looked down at her threaded fingers and wondered if her legs would have the strength to carry her home. "And why not?"

"Because next time I won't let you go until the entire game is finished."

14

In the glow of starlight, Jake dragged his feet up the walk to the Merriweathers' house and climbed the porch to the front door. He paused, knowing he was late and hoping he wasn't going to catch any grief about it. It had been one hell of a long day, and he wasn't sure if he was up to the cheerful supper banter at the Merriweather table.

He leaned his head against the polished oak door, and then went inside to the foyer. He could hear voices coming from the dining room, along with the sound of silver scraping against plates. He unbuckled his gun belt and looped it over the coatrack.

The sound of Daniella's laughter reached his ears, and his mood took a sharp turn for the worse. God, how he hated the tingles that ran up and down his spine whenever she was near. He hated the way her scowls dug at his heart, and the way one of her smiles could make him forget what a troublemaker she was.

Most of all he hated his inability to resist touching her, no matter where they were. It didn't matter if they were standing on a wide open porch or in a freezing mountain creek; whether they were glaring at each other on a busy boardwalk or arguing on the stairs. It certainly didn't matter that he had no claim to her. As far as he was concerned, the powerful longing he felt when he held Daniella Storm in his arms was entitlement enough.

He'd warned her away from him, he reminded himself, and then he smiled, wondering whom he'd thought he was fooling at the time. Telling Daniella Storm to do anything only meant she'd do the exact opposite, and, damn, if the ache between his legs didn't make him hope this time wouldn't be the exception. In his experience the best way to end any kind of craving was to get your fill until you puked, so maybe holding back was the worst thing he could do. Maybe it would be better not only for him, but for Daniella as well, to just give in to this crazy attraction and let things ride.

The idea filled him with a strange sort of pleasant anticipation. He walked down the hallway to the dining room and was brought up short by what he found there. A blond man was sitting next to Daniella, attempting to feed her a piece of chocolate cake, while the sisters sat across the table, laughing like a couple of well-dressed hyenas.

"Sorry I'm late."

Daniella turned, and the offered piece of cake slammed against the side of her face. The sisters broke into another stream of giggles, and the blond man at the table looked so embarrassed that Jake thought the fellow might burst into flame.

"This is obviously much harder than I'd imagined," the man said.

Smiling, Daniella took up her napkin and wiped the frosting off her cheek. "I'm sorry, Oliver. It's my fault for being distracted."

"But children are constantly distracted," Louisa Merriweather stopped laughing long enough to say. "That's where the fine art of patience comes into play."

"Yes, and they are usually not so cooperative as our sweet Daniella when it comes to accepting what you're offering."

"I'll keep that in mind," Oliver muttered.

"So our point is proven?" Louisa asked, her brows arched.

"Your point, ma'am, is proven. Keeping a child clean while feeding it is next to impossible."

Maybelle clapped her hands. "Good. Marshal, you're late for supper, and you weren't here on time to accompany us for lunch this afternoon. I think we are going to have to start getting testy with you, wouldn't you say, Louisa?"

"Perhaps the marshal has a good excuse, sister. Give the man a chance to sit before you start harping on him."

Jake sat down across from Daniella, trying to keep his eyes off the smudge of dark frosting she'd missed on her cheek. He wondered what the other three at the table would do if he went over to her and licked it right off her face. Then the blond man moistened his thumb, and Jake could only watch with growing irritation as he rubbed the smudge away.

Jake yanked his napkin off the table and tossed it down onto his lap while Daniella thanked Oliver for pointing out her oversight. The man was obviously making advances, and she was too busy batting her eyelashes to notice.

"Marshal?" Maybelle said. "Have you met Oliver Treemont? He's come to call on Daniella this evening."

Jake turned back to the man across from him. Oliver Treemont smiled, and a dimple, of all things, appeared on his smooth cheek. Surely Daniella wasn't interested in this boyish, peach-faced, moron. The man stretched his hand across the table, but Jake pretended not to notice it while he stabbed a slice of cold roast beef and slapped it down onto his plate.

Mr. Treemont pulled back his hand. "So, Marshal. I hear you locked up half the town in your jail today."

Jake didn't spare him a glance as he spread a healthy amount of preserves on a fresh-baked muffin. If the man was interested in conversation he could take it up with the sweet, cute Daniella.

"I do hope you don't intend to keep them there overnight," Treemont continued. Jake felt a muscle in his jaw begin to twitch. "The men were only having a little sport, keeping themselves occupied."

"Keeping themselves occupied?"

Jake glanced up at the sound of Daniella's voice and was surprised to find her staring disbelievingly at Treemont. "Oliver, you don't have any idea what you're talking about. Those men could have killed somebody."

"I understand your sensitivity to this subject, Dannie, but honestly, locking men up for blowing off a little steam? I find that ridiculous, and more than a little"—he looked back at Jake—"petty?"

Jake was in just the mood to reach across the table and take the man by the throat, but he quickly discovered that he wouldn't have to. A familiar glint came into Daniella's eyes, and Jake took a bite of muffin to hide his smile.

"You call shooting up an entire street blowing off a little steam? I call it barbaric, bordering on the deranged."

"Oh, Dannie, it was only a few windows—"

"I doubt the shopkeepers feel that way."

Oliver Treemont paused, and then he made a disastrous mistake: He gave Daniella a patronizing look, the kind a parent would give a silly child. "I'm sorry, Dannie. Here I sit squabbling with you, when you must be frightened to death with your whole family behind bars. But rest assured that you needn't worry over this situation, my dear. You are perfectly safe." He patted her hand, and Jake wanted to give the man a different kind of pat—a punch in the nose.

Jake set down his fork and leaned back in his chair. He'd always heard that hiding behind a woman's skirt was cowardly, but if Daniella was insistent on draping the thing over him, who was he to refuse?

She took a sip of water, and then gave Oliver Treemont a tight smile. "Frightened? Worry myself? Why, Oliver,

I'd rather die than crease my perfect forehead with a frown of apprehension."

"That's the spirit, Dannie. Let the marshal worry about all of this. It is his job, after all."

Treemont was turning out to be even slower than Jake had originally thought. And damn the bastard for bringing *him* into this. Daniella looked across the table at him, her brows arched in question, and Jake shrugged. As far as he was concerned, he was only there for decoration.

"Tell me something, Oliver. If you were marshal— which is a vast stretch of the imagination, I know—but if you were, what would you have done this afternoon?"

"Well, I, uh, probably would have told them all to run along home." Treemont laughed, then sent a smile around the table, as if this particular solution had never been thought of before.

"Really? And what if their response was to shoot at you?"

Treemont snorted. "I think that's stretching things a bit far, don't you think, Dan—"

"They shot at Marshal Kiley."

The man's mouth snapped shut and he cast a questioning look across the table. Jake gave him a quick grin, thinking that it hadn't taken a whole lot of rope to hang Mr. Oliver Treemont.

Treemont went still and then said, "I suppose I owe you an apology, Marshal."

"Well, I should think so," Maybelle remarked, followed by a sharp shushing sound from Louisa.

"I meant no real offense."

Yeah, like a rattler means no real offense, Jake thought. He locked eyes with Daniella, wondering if she had anything to say about Mr. Treemont's apology. He was still finding it hard to believe that she'd stood up for him.

After a long pause, Treemont cleared his throat. "Well, that certainly was a lovely supper, ladies."

The two older women nodded briskly but didn't say another word—which had to be another first for the record book. Then Oliver turned to say something to Daniella, but she glanced away from him to stare down at her plate. It seemed that he had been dismissed.

The man cleared his throat again and stood. "And now, if you'll excuse me, I really must be going. Dannie?" He reached for her hand, but Daniella didn't offer it. "It's been a—a pleasure." He barely spared Jake a glance as he scampered from the room.

After they heard the front door close Maybelle was the first to speak. "That certainly was . . . interesting, wasn't it, sister?"

"Imagine the nerve of that man, attacking a guest in my home. And mind you, Marshal, that was an attack if I've ever seen one."

Maybelle sighed. "Oh, but Daniella stood up for our brave lawman so wonderfully—"

"Don't you ever invite Oliver Treemont for supper again, sister. He's always been such a snob, anyway. What could you possibly have been thinking?"

"But, sister, you said having him to supper might be just the thing to move things along between—"

Louisa cut her off with a loud laugh. "Oh, sister, your mind is getting as dull as mine. More roast beef, Marshal?"

Jake shook his head and considered the two of them, suddenly getting the impression that they had more to do with this little scenario than they were letting on.

"Come along, Maybelle. Let's get started on those dishes."

Jake was just beginning to anticipate being alone with Daniella when she pushed back her chair. "I'll help—"

"No, you won't, dear." And with that, both sisters exited through the swinging door and into the kitchen.

Daniella settled back down in her chair. Jake leaned his elbows on the table and rested his chin on one fist. As silence fell over the room he found himself staring at her. Although making her uncomfortable and watching her blush was quickly becoming one of his favorite pastimes, in this instance he simply didn't know what to say. The last thing in the world he'd expected was for her to defend him.

"Don't think I did you any favors," she finally said.

He nodded in agreement, not in the mood to fight with her. Had her hair always sparkled like that in the lamplight?

"It's just that I'm tense lately, and I'm bound to jump down anybody's throat who irritates me. Besides," she added with a flick of her wrist, "Oliver's a moron."

He had to press his knuckles against his lips to keep from smiling.

"I can't figure out why he called on me tonight. He's one of William's friends. You do remember William Potter, don't you?"

Ah, the subject of William. Jake knew exactly what she was trying to do by mentioning the sorry bastard. She hoped to divert his attention to more familiar ground by baiting him into an argument. Well, he wasn't going to let her do it. Not this time.

He stood up and came around the table toward her. She watched him warily, rising only when he stood directly beside her. He was impressed that she didn't back away from him, even though she had no idea what he intended.

"What you said to Mr. Treemont was a very considerate thing to do, Miss Storm. And, whatever your motivation, I appreciate the gesture."

He could tell, just by the way she was looking at him, that she was trying to decide if he was being sincere or mocking. So, just to reassure her, he gave her a broad smile, and she jumped back from him as if he'd suddenly dropped his pants.

It took a conscious effort for him not to laugh. "A little edgy tonight?"

"I . . . I don't trust you."

"I'd say that's plain enough." He held out his hand. "Come back here and let me change your mind."

She stared at his hand and then shook her head. Instead of moving forward she backed up a step, and Jake somehow managed to stay where he was against the table edge, despite his impulse to pursue her. If he was going to have her, and he'd already decided that he was, then he'd need to build a bridge over the mistrust he could see in her eyes.

"Daniella. Come here and let me show you that you can trust me. Come on. Let me show you."

She looked back down at his outstretched hand and took a step toward him. Then she paused and picked up a heavy skillet from the sideboard. "Just for insurance," she said, smiling.

Damn, she was full of fire, just like the glorious mass of red hair tumbling over her shoulders. Once he had her naked in his arms, it was going to take every ounce of willpower he had not to turn into a wild animal. But he'd be taking something precious from her, and he swore to himself that she'd be getting plenty of pleasure in return.

Her fingers finally reached out and touched his, and he took hold of her hand. With a slow, gentle tug, he eased her closer to him. "That wasn't so hard, now, was it?" He could see her steady pulse thrumming at her throat and wondered if it was beating for him.

She rested the skillet on the table but kept her hand closed tightly around the handle. "Is . . . is there a point to this?"

He brought her hand to his mouth and fought the incredible wave of desire he felt as he tasted her skin. He caressed her knuckles with his lips, and watched the sparks ignite in her brilliant green eyes. She'd admitted to him earlier that day that he had the ability to "kiss her crazy," and he wondered if that pertained to the rest of her body as well as her lips.

"I want to thank you," he said hoarsely. He somehow

managed to move his hand past her inviting breasts and up to the side of her face. Before his overwhelming longing could overcome him he tipped her head down and gave her a light kiss on the forehead. "So . . . thank you."

She looked completely bewildered—and, he hoped, a little disappointed. He gave her one last smile, gathered up his undeniable cravings, and left the room as calmly as he could.

Dannie refolded the covers below her chin. She glanced at the clock on her night table and groaned. It was nearly midnight. At this rate, she wasn't going to get any sleep before the sun rose. And it was all Marshal Kiley's fault.

First he'd warned her that afternoon to stay off the porch and away from him, and then at supper he'd practically had her hand for dessert. One minute she hated the man and the very next she wanted him pressing her down onto the hard steps again. He was driving her out of her mind!

Where was that damn surveyor, anyway? Once he arrived, things could get back to normal, and Marshal Jake Kiley could ride back to Denver and take that darn mouth of his with him!

She slapped her arms down to her sides and molded the heavy blanket around her. Her mind was running in five different directions, and she knew she was fooling herself if she thought she was going to fall asleep any time soon. She glanced toward her window, where the moonlight poured in through the open lace curtains. She had the greatest temptation to go down to that porch and show Marshal Jake Kiley that he couldn't push her around, that she could go anywhere she darn well pleased and there wasn't a thing he could do about it.

What could he possible do to her? Throw her to the ground and rape her out in the open night air? No, Jake Kiley might be arrogant and domineering, but he wasn't violent. That much she was sure of. So why not? Why didn't she just give in to the impulse and go down there and show him who was boss?

"Because you're scared, that's why," she whispered into the darkness. But it wasn't him she was afraid of, it was herself. Of the way she felt in his arms. She knew that no matter how strong her self-control, if he was determined to have his way with her, after one kiss she'd give in without lifting a finger to stop him. No, despite her pride, she couldn't take the risk. She wasn't moving from her bed, and that was final.

A chinking sound came from the window, and she looked over just in time to see a shower of pebbles hit the glass. Perplexed, she got out of bed and peered down to the street. The night was decidedly quiet with half the town in jail, and the yard below was empty as far as she could see. Then the shower of rocks came again. She pressed her face against the cool glass, straining to see if there was someone directly below her, but the shadows were too dark for her to make anything out. Her curiosity peaked, she threw caution to the wind and slipped on her wrapper.

Then she tiptoed out of the room and down the stairs.

The house was dark except for one lamp burning low on the sidelight ledge by the front door. Instinct told her that Jake Kiley was out there, waiting for her, and she made a sharp turn toward the back door, hoping to uncover whoever was throwing rocks at her window without having to meet up with the marshal.

She slipped out the back door, grimacing when it creaked, and edged her way around to the side of the house. There were footprints in the dirt below her window, but the yard was empty. She stood below the window and looked up, wondering who had thrown the rocks and why. Then she heard his voice and was almost torn in two with feelings of dread and excitement.

"Good evening, Daniella. I don't suppose I should ask you what you're doing out here in the middle of the night."

She turned and saw the marshal leaning over the porch rail, watching her, and wondered how long he'd been standing there. Then she decided it didn't matter. What mattered was her getting back into the house and safely to her room. She took off at a dead run, not caring how cowardly her actions were. She wasn't even sure she'd closed the back door tightly as she dashed down the hallway, past the dining room, and on toward the staircase.

Then she came to a halt. The lamplight illuminated his tall body as he stood, leaning an elbow on the banister at the bottom of the staircase.

He'd beaten her there by coming in through the front door. Out of breath, Dannie looked for some other place to run, some other place to hide. But the smile that crept over the marshal's face told her that, whatever her next move, it would be as futile as her dash to get away from him. She was ensnared. And now the best that she could hope for was that what she saw burning in his eyes was anger and nothing more.

15

"Should I take this as a bona fide offer?"

He was guarding the stairs like a dark sentinel. She crossed her arms over her breasts to shield herself from the intensity of his stare.

"You should—you should take yourself out of my way, Marshal. I am going back to my room."

He didn't move, and despite her intent, Dannie couldn't find the courage to skirt around him. She'd never been looked at so thoroughly before. He was caressing her with his gaze, touching every inch of her, making her burn with shameless longing.

"Marshal Kiley—"

"Call me Jake." He stepped closer, reaching out to trace a finger along her jawline. "It's a simple word, like look . . . touch . . . kiss."

With his finger under her chin he brought her toward him until she could feel the heat of his body just a breath away. He was going to consume her, burn her to a cinder with the fire in his eyes.

"Really, I . . . I should be getting back to my room."

"So you can lie in your bed and think about me?"

She blinked at his insight and tried not to notice that he kept staring at her mouth. "Once again, you're letting your arrogance show, Marshal—"

"Jake."

She arched a brow. "If you don't want me to scream my head off, *Marshal,* then I suggest you let me pass."

He ran his thumb over her bottom lip and a shiver raced up her spine. "I'm not stopping you from leaving."

"You . . . you are standing directly in my way."

"So go around."

She moved back and he followed, slowly.

"Has there ever been something you wanted, Daniella? Something you wanted so badly you'd do just about anything to get it?"

Searching his face, she tried to discern whether he really expected her to answer. She bumped into the dining room door, and a shock of fear raced through her as he raised his hands to trap her there. Desperate to escape, she ducked beneath his arm.

"There's been a mistake," she said. "I didn't come down here for this."

"Why did you come down here then?"

"Because . . ." She stole a glance at the unguarded stairway, and it took her a moment to remember the answer. "Because somebody was throwing rocks at my window."

He smiled faintly. "Curiosity killed the cat."

He moved toward the stairs, and she knew she'd never make the first step before he had her in his arms again. She decided the parlor would be her next safe bet. At least there she could put a couch or a chair in between them—anything to keep him from touching her with those gently coaxing hands of his. If only she hadn't come downstairs, if only . . . Something dawned on her and her eyes narrowed with suspicion. "I don't suppose you saw someone standing below my window?"

He shrugged. "Not a soul."

She doubted he was as blameless as he was acting, but before she could say another word he was approaching her again and she was backing toward the parlor. It was all so ridiculous. She hadn't come down to tryst with him, and yet by the look in his eyes she could see that he intended just that. And with each step he took in her direction she found it harder and harder to deny the quickening of her heart.

She planted her feet on the threshold, determined to stand her ground with him and the strange feelings he provoked in her. "Would you please stop prowling after me like that!"

He stopped, directly in front of her, and smiled. "Is there another way you'd prefer me to prowl?"

"What I would prefer is that you stop for a moment and give me half a chance to catch my breath!"

"I told you earlier what would happen if you met me on the porch again—"

"But we aren't on the porch, we are in the foyer!"

He reached up and fingered a tendril of her hair, and she had to fight not to turn her cheek into his hand. "Merely a technicality," he whispered.

"Really, Marshal, I . . . I think we should stop for a minute, and—and—" The irony of the situation hit her and she smiled, almost laughed in fact. "Think about what we're doing."

Her humor only seemed to intensify the look in his eyes. "I like your smile. Especially when it's pressed against mine."

He bent his head toward her, and in one last effort to help them both regain control, she pressed her hands against his hard chest. "We can't do this."

"Oh, I think you'll be amazed at the things we can do."

His mouth covered hers and she couldn't hold back a low moan of pent up desire. He pushed his hands into her hair to hold her to him, but the action was unnecessary. The warmth of his embrace flooded through her quickly and, like a soothing tide, drowned her meager resistance and washed away her doubts. Almost instantly the familiar ache and longing returned, and she knew that she could no longer deny the obvious: She wanted this man. When he held her in his arms, nothing else seemed to matter.

She clutched his shoulders as his tongue swept into her mouth. The stubble on his chin scratched her cheek, but she felt only the strength of his arms as he wound them around her and bent her to his will. His mouth was incredible. It could laugh and sneer, scowl and shout. But then it could search and devour, making her helpless with desire.

His hand lowered from her hair, to her shoulder, to her breast, and she arched against the gratifying pressure. He moaned like a man getting his first taste of something wonderful, and feeling reckless, she nipped at his mouth.

He took her bottom lip between his teeth and teased it with his tongue, and she closed her eyes, having to grab his shirt to keep from falling like a wilted flower at his feet.

The clock in the parlor chimed one o'clock, and he pulled away from her as if their time together was up. She took advantage of the moment to catch her breath. "We—we need to control ourselves."

He took a handful of her hair and tipped her head back so he could look into her eyes. "That's not possible anymore."

His mouth claimed hers again, and she slid her arms around his neck to pull him closer. This time his kisses gave instead of took, and her heart skipped at the sweet, savage way he could beguile her.

He loosened the tie on her wrapper. The garment slipped off her shoulders, leaving only her thin cotton nightgown to cover her aching breasts. He pulled back to look at her, to caress her with his eyes, and their gazes met.

"What I want more than my next breath is to make love to you, Daniella Storm."

She gasped as his candor sent a burst of sparks shooting through her. He bent to kiss her neck and began to work his way down to the peaks of her breasts. She found herself holding him tighter, a plea for him never to stop resting on the tip of her tongue.

His hands slipped to her waist, and she felt the cool air of the night touch her calves, her thighs, her bottom, as he raised her nightgown to her hips. Then he swept her into his arms and lowered her to the floor of the parlor.

He was gone for a moment, and she missed his heat, but he soon returned to press her down onto the soft oriental carpet. And he was kissing her again, distracting her from the fact that he was easing himself between her thighs. When their sexes came in contact with each other she arched against him, instinctively seeking the hard part of him that was pressing at her very core.

"Christ, Daniella," he said with a gasp. "You're going to undo me before we've even started."

He slipped one of his hands beneath her bottom, lifting her hips, and Dannie opened her eyes, awed to find his big, muscular body poised above her own. "Marshal?" she whispered.

"Jake. That's the name I want to hear you moan, Daniella." He entered her, just the smallest amount, and his jaw clenched. "That's the name I want to hear you cry out in my arms."

He pressed in a little farther and Dannie gripped his bulging arms. A heat was beginning to grow deep inside her, spreading tiny, fiery fingers up through her stomach and down through her legs, filling her with an incredible hunger.

Jake moaned, tensing above her. Though he'd hardly moved, he was breathing hard as he rested his forehead against hers. "I want it all, Daniella," he rasped. "All of you."

His mouth covered hers, and with one deep, powerful thrust, he broke through her maidenhead and claimed her very soul.

The pain was sharp but quick, and when Dannie opened her eyes again, it was to find him staring down at her while buried so far inside that their hips were melded to each other. His jaw was still clenched, and his eyes were burning like never before. "Ready?" he asked hoarsely.

She wasn't sure what he meant, but she nodded just the same. When he tried to withdraw from her, however, she felt a slice of pain and clamped her hands down onto his backside to keep him in place.

He met her eyes again. "I'd be flattered, sweetheart, but I have a feeling that you're not doing that just to map the shape of my ass."

The man was buried in her to the hilt and yet she still had the ability to blush. "I—I'm sorry. It hurt a little, and—"

He kissed her, warm and hard. "Movement will ease the pain, Daniella. I promise." Resisting the pressure of her hands, he eased back a bit, and the pain was quickly taken over by a deep throbbing sensation that drew a gasp from her throat. Watching her carefully, he pulled all the way back, then pressed forward again, and Dannie let out a long, low groan.

He repeated the motion, again and again, and a sensation like nothing she'd ever felt before began to thrum inside her. Instead of using her hands to hinder his progress, she helped him move faster. He whispered things in her ear—sweet, seductive things that set her on fire and made her twist beneath him.

And then it happened. A thousand tiny moonbeams came down around her and burst across her body with the intensity of a bolt of lightning. She arched, every muscle in her body tensing with an explosion of sensation so great she thought surely she would die.

And he was there, coaxing her, commanding her.

"Jake!" she cried. "Oh, yes, Jake, yes!"

He thrust deeply: once, twice, three times, then fell over her in completion. Catching his hand up in her hair, he kissed her deeply again and again, murmuring her name, and telling her how amazing she was. She lay wrapped in his arms for a while, basking in the afterglow, and then suddenly everything stopped: the touching, the caressing, the kissing.

Her body was still tingling when he rolled off her and stood to pull on his pants. Still slick with his sweat, she shuddered from the chill. He was buttoning his fly, and she found she needed him to say something to reassure her. But he didn't. Instead, he ran his hand through his hair, seeming so calm compared to her riotous feelings.

He swallowed and looked down at her, his gaze roaming over her still-exposed body. She pushed her nightgown down past her thighs, although knowing it was a bit late to hide herself from him, and waited for his words of comfort.

"I'll take you back to your room."

Tears stung her eyes. Unsteadily, she climbed to her feet. "I can find the way there myself."

She tried to brush past him, but he caught her by the arm. "I said I'd take you to your room."

"And I said—"

He swept her up into his arms, and she didn't have the strength to stop him as he carried her through the foyer and up the stairs. Turning the knob on her door, he elbowed his way inside her room where he deposited her on the bed. As he turned to leave, a sob caught in Dannie's throat. He paused to look back at her, his expression cold and distant. She refused to let him see the tears in her eyes.

"You're expecting too much," he muttered.

"Am I?" she managed to choke out.

"Just take it for what it was, Daniella—"

"And just what was it, Marshal? A fling? A mistake? A *game?*"

He came back to her and leaned over the bed. "It was sex, Miss Storm. Pure, animal, lust. We both wanted it. We both got it. Now shut your goddamned eyes and go to sleep."

He left her there, stunned. And once he'd closed the door, she rolled over in her bed and broke into tears.

Jake paced his room like a caged tiger. He'd done it. He'd had the little minx, so why the hell was the craving for her still twisting at his gut like a bad case of the grippe? She'd cried out his name, and the sound kept ringing through his head, making him ache with longing all over again.

He slammed his hand down onto the dresser. It was apparent that he hadn't gotten rid of his craving for Miss Storm, that he was going to need a few more strong doses. After the way he'd just left her, he wondered how she would feel about the idea.

A soft cough drew his attention to the wall that divided their rooms. The sight of her naked and moaning beneath him flashed through his mind and he squeezed his eyes shut, willing the image away. He'd kissed her and held her afterward, that had been his mistake. In the past, when he finished with a woman, he gathered his things and left. But for some unknown reason, this time he'd stuck around long enough to hold Daniella, to whisper things to her that now he could hardly believe he'd said. Thank God he'd caught himself and ended the situation, for both of their sakes. He certainly didn't need her getting any silly ideas about commitment.

Another sound drew him closer to the wall and what he heard nearly tore him in two. She was crying. He could hear her muffled sobs and sniffles, and pictured her curled up in a ball of despair on her bed. He swore beneath his breath. This was the last thing he needed. What the hell was her problem? She'd wanted it as badly as he had!

Forgetting that he was wearing nothing but his drawers, he left his room, intent on setting Miss Storm straight on a few things so he could get a good night's sleep.

He paused outside her door, suddenly hesitant, and then carefully tested the knob. It turned easily in his hand and he cracked open the door. He wasn't sure what he hoped to accomplish. An apology certainly wasn't going to fix anything. Chances were she'd say something that would only irritate him, and then he'd end up hurting her even more. But he couldn't ignore the sound of her quiet sobs any longer. He stepped into the room and closed the door.

It took a moment for his eyes to adjust to the meager light, and then he saw her, huddled on the bed. Her crying had stopped, and he assumed she knew he was there.

"I . . . I know you'd probably like to shoot me right now, Daniella, and I don't know if this will make you feel any better, but, I'm sorry. Okay?"

There was a long moment of silence before she rolled over in the bed and looked at him. "You're sorry? I happen to wander downstairs, and you corner me in the parlor and steal my honor, and you're *sorry?*"

"Now, hold on there. I didn't steal anything. I took what you offered me, plain and simple."

She sat straight up on the bed. "Because you're a silver tongued, seductive bastard!"

He strode toward her. "There were two people moaning and groaning down there, lady, and they sure as hell *both* weren't me!"

She looked up at him and he could see tears glistening on her lashes in the moonlight. "How could I have let you?"

Her worn, defeated voice tugged at his conscience and he pushed a hand through his hair. "Sometimes desire wins out over common sense."

"And a smooth-talking man doesn't help matters."

"Dammit, stop trying to blame this all on me! You're lying in here, wailing like a child, for God's sake. Grow up and take some responsibility!"

The minute the hasty words had left his mouth he knew he'd said the wrong thing. She stood up from the bed to face him, and the moonlight caught her furious expression, at the same time highlighting her incredible body through her thin nightgown. He fought down a new burst of desire.

"How dare you come in here and demand that I act responsible! And for your information, Marshal, I was not wailing! I was lamenting my decline into madness! Surely I had to have been crazy to let you touch me!"

"The pleasure was mine, lady."

"That was obvious!"

He grit his teeth, inwardly berating himself for even bothering to come to her room. She wasn't losing her mind, he was losing his. His next actions proved that. He took her by the arm and hauled her up against him. "Would you like me to demonstrate just how much pleasure you had, Miss Storm?"

Instead of fighting him as he'd expected her to do, her eyes wavered and her breath quickened. She looked like a frightened doe, and it was all he could do to keep from kissing her. "What, no quick retort? No demand for your release?"

Her eyes searched his, and then she whispered, "Please let go of me."

With that one plea, his anger dissipated, but for all the money in the world he couldn't have done as she asked. "Come here." He slipped his arms around her waist and eased her closer. Her hands pressed against his chest, but he knew from experience that her protests would be faint and brief, and after a moment of squirming, she relaxed against him, even resting her cheek against his chest.

"I've never done anything like this before," she whispered, sniffing.

"I should hope not."

"Am I . . . am I soiled now?"

He tucked his hand into her hair and pulled her head back so that he could look into her glistening green eyes. "Not from where I'm standing."

Her expression softened and her gaze drifted over his face. She had the ability to stare him into hardness, especially when she looked at him as she did now.

"Marshal—"

"If you don't start calling me Jake, I'm gonna turn you over my knee."

Surprisingly, she smiled, and his groin became painfully tight. "Have you kissed a lot of women?"

"There's an odd question to be asking me right now."

"It's just that you're, well, you're very good at it, and I . . . I suppose I need more practice."

"Practice?" He caressed the smooth slope of her neck down to her shoulder and tried not to laugh.

"Anything you want to be good at takes practice," she said.

"And you want to be good at kissing?"

"Well . . . just so I can measure up."

"For me?"

She scowled. "For anybody."

He gently squeezed her neck. "For me?"

"For whomever I care to gift with a kiss."

"Miss Storm, I catch you gifting anybody with

anything, and I'll lock you in your room so fast you'll forget what day it is."

Her smile broadened and he kissed her, long and hard, deciding that if anybody was going to give her practice it was damn straight going to be him. Her slender arms twined around his neck, and she opened her mouth to him. She was warm and sweet, and his stomach clenched when she touched his tongue with her own. Any more practice on her part was bound to kill him.

He reached for the edge of her nightgown and lifted it up over her head. They stood there in the moonlight, their bare chests pressed together. He kissed and touched, tasted and explored, until he burned with a passion hotter than anything he'd ever felt before.

Then, tentatively, she touched him, skimming her gentle fingers down his bare shoulders and over the muscles in his arms, smoothing her palms across his chest and hips. She pushed his drawers down to the floor and then began to explore his thighs. He moaned, catching her hands before she could undo him.

He kissed her again, bringing his hands beneath her arms to flick the hard nubs of her nipples with his thumbs until she said his name with a gasp. Then he eased her down to the bed and filled her body.

Her nails dug into his back, and he groaned, determined this time to purge her from his soul forever. Each of her tiny cries pushed him closer to the edge. Each of her sweet, warm kisses delighted him, as did every tempting touch of her hands.

They climaxed together, with her crying out his name. Afterward he stayed in her bed and held her, kissing her and stroking her silky hair, in awe that they could share something so unimaginable, not once but twice in the same night.

She fell asleep in his arms, and no matter how hard he tried he couldn't bring himself to leave. He was, plainly, in trouble. Though he hated to admit it, after making love to her twice his hunger for Daniella Storm had only increased.

16

A soft gasp woke Dannie the next morning, and she lifted her head in time to see her door being pulled shut. The sun was beaming in through the window, and she squinted at the room around her. Something was different. Then she felt the aches, the tightness, that even now were wrapping like a vise around her inner thighs. Dear God, she'd given herself to him. Not once, but twice!

A gentle snore came from behind her and her eyes widened. She froze, hoping the sound had been only in her imagination. But when it came again, she couldn't ignore the obvious. Not only had she made love to Jake Kiley last night, he was still in her bed. And one of the sisters had come to wake her for breakfast only to find him snoring beneath her covers.

"Oh, my God," she whispered, scrambling to her feet.

Jake groaned and shielded his eyes with his arm. His

hair was tousled, he needed a shave, and except for the blanket at his hips he was completely bare. Dannie snatched up a quilt to hide her own nudity.

"What time is it?" he mumbled.

She glanced at the clock. "Eight—eight thirty."

"Damn."

"Why are you in my bed?"

He lifted his arm and looked at her, and the sleepy droop to his eyes made her pulse race. "If you don't know the answer to that, Daniella, then you do need more practice."

"But I didn't expect that you would . . . would . . ."

He frowned and glanced around the room. "Neither did I."

"Well." She pulled back her shoulders and tried very hard not to stare at his broad expanse of chest, at the black hair that had rubbed enticingly against her breasts the night before. "I suppose I should be getting dressed."

Instead of politely turning his back, or even better, getting up to leave, he tucked his hands beneath his head and watched her, as if her discomfort was the most interesting thing in the world. "Don't let me stop you."

"I'd rather you left."

"I'd rather I stayed."

"I'm not getting dressed in front of you, Marshal, so you can put that leering grin back in your dreams where it belongs."

"My, my. And who was it that once said I was a bear in the morning? Do you actually think you have something I didn't get a good look at last night?"

"Don't you have rounds to make?"

"Bean's done them by now. I dare you to drop the quilt."

She blinked. "You dare me?"

"Yeah. I dare you."

A short laugh rose up in her chest. "You must think I'm hideously stupid."

He sat up higher in the bed, and the thin blanket slipped lower on his hips. "No. But I do think you lack the nerve to drop that quilt."

It took Dannie a moment to respond, so completely baffled was she by this playful side of him. "I've changed my mind, Marshal. You're not a bear in the morning, you're a two-year-old."

A smug look crossed his face. "Guess I win."

"Win?"

"The contest."

"What contest? There was no contest, Marshal Kiley, just you annoying me. As usual," she added.

"Christ, Daniella, you really are a sore loser."

He was clearly mocking her, and Dannie took a deep breath, but it didn't seem to help her frazzled nerves. "Would you *please* leave my room?"

He shrugged and lifted the blanket in order to slide out of the bed. She caught sight of one bare hip and quickly averted her eyes. "Wait—wait, a minute. You don't have any clothes on."

"And who's fault is that?"

She cracked open her eyes to see him sitting back down on the bed and re-draping himself with the blanket. "Would you please just put something on and leave?"

"Fine. Where are my drawers?"

"How in the world should I know?"

"You're the one who took them off me."

A blush raced up Dannie's neck, and she shut her eyes in mortification. "Please, Marshal, please get out."

She waited, listening for the creak of the bed that would tell her he was getting up. It didn't come.

"Sounds to me like you forgot my name again."

Sighing, she opened her eyes. "That's not all I'd like to forget."

"Ah, regrets. The true price of sin."

She moved closer to him. "I don't think you understand the situation here. I think one of the sisters knows you're in my room."

"One of them? Believe me, Daniella, if one of them knows anything, then they both do."

"Well?"

"Well what?"

"Well, what are we going to do? I can only imagine what they're thinking right now."

"Oh, I'm sure they're thinking we finally succumbed to the hot urges racing through our ripe, young bodies."

Dannie gritted her teeth. "That's not funny! How am I going to face them after this?"

His gaze drifted over the quilt she was wearing. "Hopefully with more on than that."

"That's it." She glanced at the window. "I'm jumping."

"And knowing this town, they'd all claim I'd pushed you and then hang me for murder. So, for my own sake, I'm afraid I can't let you do that."

"Your concern is touching."

"Daniella, what is the problem? The Merriweathers adore you. They're not going to banter your name around town. If anybody should be concerned, it's me."

"*You?* Men are never held to blame for things like this. It's laughed off as just another notch on their belts."

He let out a long breath. "Tell you what. You protect me from the Merriweathers, and if anybody dares to refer to you as a notch I'll shoot 'em. Deal?"

She bit her lip. "Deal."

"Good. Now turn your back or get an eyeful."

He stood up and she quickly closed her eyes.

"You know something, Marshal? There are a few, although very rare, times when you're actually easy to get along with."

"You can look now."

She opened her eyes. He'd only raised his drawers to his knees, and he was grinning back at her, affording her a very nice view of the hard curves of his bottom. She slammed her eyes shut and he laughed.

"Sorry. Guess I can't stand the idea of being easy to get along with. Now you can look."

She carefully opened one eye and found him standing in front of her in his faded red drawers. The broad plains of his chest were so enticing that, in her opinion, he didn't look a whole lot more decent than he had a moment ago. "That was a mean trick."

He reached out and tucked her hair behind her ear. "And you are, beyond a doubt, the queen of those. I have a favor to ask you."

She was about to tell him exactly what he could do

with his favor when he brought his hand under her chin and rubbed his thumb over her bottom lip, just as he had the night before. A vivid image of his body pressing down on top of hers sent a surge of desire through her, and her lips parted with a gasp. Closing her eyes, she lifted her face and waited for his kiss. It never came.

"I want you to give me the nugget."

Her eyes snapped open. "You what?"

"I need it."

"You . . . you need it." She shoved him away as if he were the devil himself, and dread seized her by the throat. All morning she'd been asking herself why? Why had he made love to her when only a couple of days ago he hadn't even liked her.

"My God," she whispered. "I *am* a idiot."

"After last night, I hope you understand—"

"After last night? This is your revenge, isn't it?"

"My revenge?"

His look was so innocent it was insulting, and she wasn't sure whom she hated more, him or herself. "The revenge you swore you'd exact on me until I was begging you to let me off the hook. Well, you certainly had me begging last night, didn't you?" she choked out. "You figured you'd get me into your bed and then sweet-talk yourself into a chunk of gold! Didn't you! You filthy, lying—"

"What the hell are you raving about!"

She brought her hand back and slapped him harder than she ever had before. His head snapped to the side and when he turned back to her his eyes were hard, as cold as the day they'd met.

"You're no different from the rest!" she shouted at him. "All anybody ever thinks about is that gold! That goddamned gold! Get out of my room!"

He left the room without saying a word, and she stood in her doorway watching him stride toward his door. Her eyes were blurry with tears. "I don't ever want to speak to you—or set eyes on you again! I wouldn't give you that nugget if your very life depended on it!"

She slammed her door and covered her mouth to muffle a sob. How could she have been so stupid? He hadn't wanted her, the sharp-tongued, inexperienced daughter of a man he'd thrown in jail. He'd wanted the gold. Well he wasn't going to get it!

A few minutes later she heard heavy footsteps in the hall, then on the stairs. Then came the loud slamming of the front door. It seemed he was pretty upset that his plan hadn't worked.

A soft knock came at her bedroom door, and she sniffed and wiped her eyes. It was the Merriweather sisters, she knew. Her time of reckoning was at hand.

The door opened a crack. "Daniella?" Louisa called. "Are you all right, dear?"

Both women came into the room, and Dannie took one look at their sympathetic faces and burst into tears. "He—he just wanted the gold," she wailed.

"Oh, my dear," Louisa said soothingly. She came forward to sit on the bed next to her.

"Men!" Maybelle said. "They're all alike. Get what they can, and then skedaddle. Why, I remember when Horace Higgin—"

"Sister, I hardly think this is the time to reminisce.

Daniella is obviously distraught. Now you go down and warm some milk for chocolate. Daniella and I will be down shortly."

Maybelle hesitated, looking hurt that she wasn't going to be included in the comforting. "All right, sister. But you be sure to tell that young lady how happy we've been for fifty years without a man. A man isn't the be-all and end-all—"

"Shoo, Maybelle!"

With one final glance, Maybelle swished out of the room.

"Now," Louisa said, handing Dannie a silk handkerchief. "You get comfortable and you tell me all about it."

Dannie wiped at her nose. "I can't stand to imagine what you must think of me."

"Nonsense, my dear. It doesn't matter what other people think. What matters is what you think."

"But we were right here," she whispered, shame creeping through her. "In your house."

"That's certainly better than out on the front lawn, I should think."

"You mean you . . . you really aren't angry with me?"

"Daniella, what happened between you and the marshal last night Maybelle and I have seen coming for a while. There's a spark between the two of you, the kind of spark that simply can't be denied."

"Just the same, I should have resisted his advances."

The woman nodded. "Some might say that. But sometimes a woman meets a man that she can't do without. And don't you listen to Maybelle. She thinks just because she had one, lone relationship with Horace

Higginbothum over thirty years ago that she's an expert on men. The truth is, Daniella, and don't you tell a single soul that I told you this, the truth is, Maybelle's just a lonely old woman who sticks her nose in other people's business for fun." Louisa laughed faintly. "She doesn't know a darn thing about men. Wouldn't recognize love if it was crawling up her leg."

"Love?"

Louisa's gray brows raised. "That is what we are talking about here, isn't it?"

Dannie busied herself by folding the handkerchief into a tiny square. "Love is the last thing going on between me and Marshal Kiley. He's overbearing, and lecherous, and all I am to him is a ticket to Easy Street. . . . I wouldn't trust that deputy of his, either."

"Mr. Toomey? Why, he's the kindest, most considerate gentleman I have ever met." Louisa smiled whimsically. "Just between us girls, I think that man has a crush on me."

Dannie had thought for quite some time that Bean Toomey had a crush on both Merriweather sisters, but she didn't think right now would be a good time to discuss it.

"Tell me something, Daniella. Why do you think the marshal wants your nugget?"

"The same reason anybody would want it, I suppose. To get rich."

"Then why, if he wants to be rich, doesn't he just go down to the creek, that he alone guards, and pan for all the gold he wants?"

Dannie frowned. She hadn't thought of that. Then

she shrugged. "Why pan for gold when he can seduce it right out of my gullible hands?"

"Bah! The last thing in the world anybody anywhere thinks you are, Daniella, is gullible. I think maybe you're being too hard on the mar—"

"You're taking his side?"

"I didn't say that. Personally, I think he's gone about this thing all wrong. He should have explained himself to you, thoroughly. I think I'll have to box his ears for that."

Dannie smirked. "He made me promise to protect him from you. And in return he promised to shoot anybody who called me just another notch on his belt."

"That, my dear, sounds like a man who cares."

Tears clogged Dannie's throat again. "Or a man who's covering his tracks."

Louisa sighed and stood. "I can see that my point of view isn't doing a whole lot of good. Let's go down to the kitchen and try a cup of chocolate."

Dannie wiped her nose one last time and followed Louisa downstairs. The woman had brought up some good points, but the risks were too great. Dannie just couldn't take the chance of trusting Jake Kiley again.

"Blew it all to hell, didn'cha?"

Jake set his empty whiskey glass down on the table. He'd come to this empty corner of the saloon to find some peace and quiet, but now he had his spouting deputy to contend with. "Bean, I am not in the mood for one of your bullshit sermons."

"Oh, I see. You break Miz Storm's heart, and *you're* not in the mood." Bean leaned over the table at him. "Well, let me tell you something, boy-o, I got two, sweet little women hoppin' mad at me this mornin'."

"Why's that?"

"Well, it sure as hell ain't because I tracked mud through their house! I happen to be friendly with *you!* And right now that ain't the wisest thing to be in this town."

"Old man, make your point and then leave me to my bottle."

Bean took the chair opposite him. "Goddamn, Jake, what the hell is wrong with you? Son, I know you. I know you didn't use that little lady just to get the nugget. Even though you joked about it, I know you really wouldn't do it."

"Your confidence in me has made my day." He tipped the whiskey bottle to his glass. "Now, if you'll excuse me, I am in the process of getting drunk."

Bean grabbed the bottle and slammed it back down on the table. "This ain't some bar floozie, or some philanderin' wife we're talkin' about here, Jake. This is a young innocent girl. Where the hell is your conscience?"

"In my pants, Bean. In my pants."

"Well, goddamn, you ain't the first man to fall in love against his will, but you sure as hell are the sorriest."

"Love? You're the one who's out of his mind. She doesn't mean any more to me than all the others."

"Is that right?"

"That's right."

"Then how come you're drowning yourself in that bottle? You just walked away with a laugh and a smile after all them other women. As a matter of fact, I ain't seen you get drunk since your ma died back in '51."

Jake lifted the bottle and gave his deputy a silent salute before taking a long swig of the burning alcohol. "Sometimes a man just needs to cut loose."

"Why didn't you tell her the truth? That the nugget was just part of the job, nothing else?"

"She didn't give me a chance."

"Sounds to me like *you* didn't give *her* a chance."

Jake took another tug on the bottle. "You ever been slapped by a woman, Bean? I don't mean smacked, I mean really and truly slapped, with all the rage and all the hate in their eyes burning a hole straight through you?"

"She don't hate ya, Jake. A woman like that one don't do what she did last night with hate in her heart."

"Yeah? Well, maybe she didn't hate me then, but she sure as hell hates me now."

"And it's all because of a simple misunderstanding."

"No, it's all because she can't help but think the worst of me. I imagine that's my fault, though, for thinking nothing but the worst of her for so long."

"But you don't anymore?"

"She and Mary Ellen Potter are doing everything they can to set this town straight. You were right, Bean. She's got some mettle, that woman." He rubbed his still aching jaw and laughed. "And I think most of it's in her right hook."

"Speaking of Mary Ellen Potter, she was down at the jail this morning, visiting her family."

"That right?"

"Yup. And you wouldn't believe what I saw."

"Do tell."

"The young Miz Potter making googly eyes at none other than Mr. Donovan Storm."

Jake paused and looked at his deputy over the lip of the bottle. "You're kidding me."

"Nope. And Donovan was all quiet and gushin' in the corner." Bean snorted. "Ya know, I heard this whole feud was started back about two years ago when Daniella refused to marry Willie Potter. Wouldn't it be ironic if the thing were all patched up by the same idear?"

"Mary Ellen Potter and Donovan Storm?"

"Sorta like a dove matin' with a buzzard, wouldn't you say?"

Jake stared at the bottle and then set it down on the table. "What are tempers like at the jail this morning?"

"Vile, like the rest of the town's. I'm telling ya, Jake. If something ain't done quick, Shady Gulch is gonna explode. And it's gonna take the both of us with it."

"And, uh, what's Daniella up to?"

Bean pursed his lips. "Haven't seen her. But I did catch a glimpse of Mary Ellen Potter headed for the Merriweathers' house not ten minutes ago. 'Spose there's gonna be some commiseratin'."

"'Spose so."

"It's you Miz Storm should be talkin' to, ya know?"

Jake grunted. "If I get within ten feet of her she's liable to rip my heart out."

"Kinda like you did to her last night?"

Jake locked eyes with his deputy. "Having you around is worse than having an angel sitting on my shoulder, nagging me day and night."

Bean smiled. "You're an upstanding kinda feller, boy-o. I know you'll do what's right eventually. I just hate to think that when you finally come around it might be too late."

17

Dannie opened the front door and pulled Mary Ellen inside. "You were supposed to meet me here at nine o'clock sharp! Where have you been?"

Mary Ellen gave her a surprised look but didn't resist when Dannie ushered her into the parlor. "I spent some time with Daddy and William at the jail."

"At the jail? Was the marshal there?"

"No, just the deputy—what has gotten into you? You look half-scared out of your mind."

"Stupid Dannie, stupid Dannie!"

Mary Ellen peered at the bird in the cage. "What in heaven's name is that?"

"It's a bird."

"Did it just call you stupid?"

"Believe me"—Dannie let out a sigh and dropped down into the wing chair—"Harvey's well informed."

Mary Ellen sat on the settee, arranged her skirt around her legs, and then set her reticule beside her. "Now. Tell me what is going on."

Dannie wanted to tell Mary Ellen. Lord only knew how badly she needed to purge her soul, but she just couldn't get the words past the shame that had been choking her all morning.

Mary Ellen leaned forward. "You know you can tell me anything, Dannie. And you know that I am going to die from curiosity if you don't spit it out!"

"I slept with the marshal."

"You—" Mary Ellen's response was cut short when her hand flew to her cover her mouth. "You slept with the marshal?" she whispered.

Dannie could only nod and sink lower into the chair. "I—I didn't mean to." As if that explained everything. "Oh, Mary Ellen, don't hate me! I know I'm supposed to despise him because of everything he's done to our families, and, well, now I do despise him—he's the lowest of the low—but last night I just couldn't resist him, he's got the warmest, softest mouth, and he can say the most incredible things—"

"Stop babbling and tell me what happened!"

"Well, I—I came downstairs last night because somebody was throwing pebbles at my window."

"Who?"

Dannie gave her a direct look. "I have my suspicions. Anyway, I assumed he'd be on the porch, lurking in the shadows like he always does, so I thought I'd just sneak out the back door to find the culprit, avoiding the marshal all together."

"And?"

"And . . . it didn't work out that way. He saw me from around the corner of the house and when I tried to hurry back upstairs he was waiting for me in the foyer."

"That scoundrel lured you out there, didn't he? Oh, Dannie, he didn't . . . you know?" Mary Ellen widened her eyes to make her point clear.

Dannie's chin started to tremble, and she shook her head. "I was a little hesitant at first, but then I went into his arms willingly. Oh, Mary Ellen, what am I going to do?"

"Does he plan to marry you?"

Tears pooled in Dannie's eyes. "That's the worst part. I found out this morning that he only seduced me so that he could get the nugget."

"He said that to you?"

Dannie sniffed and wiped at her eyes. "No, but he asked me for it, straight out. The smug, despicable low-life—"

"You're in love with him."

"I am not!"

"Dannie Storm, I haven't seen you cry since your mama died. And here you sit, sniffling away in front of me. There is no way you are going to convince me that you aren't head over heels for this man."

Dannie covered her face with her hands. "Oh, Mary Ellen. What am I going to do?"

"I'll tell you what you're going to do." Mary Ellen stood up and pulled Dannie to her feet. "You're going to come shopping with me again today, just like we planned. You're going to act carefree and happy, and show that heartless lawman just exactly how little his deception matters to you."

"I don't know if I can manage it."

"Of course you can." Mary Ellen bent down and

shook out Dannie's green muslin skirt. "And the first person to throw either one of us a slur, you can knock right onto their patooty."

Taking a deep breath, Dannie lifted her chin. Mary Ellen was right. No matter how bad she hurt on the inside, she had to keep up appearances. If not for the sake of the town, then for the sake of her own pride.

"Hello, Jake."

The marshal had had another long, frustrating day in Shady Gulch, and the sun had just begun to set when he glanced up from the paperwork on his desk. "Well. Duff McBride. I suppose it would be kind of stupid for me to ask what you're doing here, wouldn't it?"

Duff McBride's leathered face wrinkled as he smiled. He twirled a piece of straw in his mouth. "Ah, gold. It draws me like a bee to honey."

"Yeah. Like a fat fly to manure," Jake added.

"Now, don't tell me you're still mad about that situation in Pueblo. I told ya, ol' pal, it wasn't nothin' but business."

"Yeah, Duff. Business. Unfortunately that vaquero wasn't the man we were after, and by the time that small point was discovered, you, surprisingly, were long gone, and so, I might add, was the dead vaquero's bag of gold dust."

Duff snorted, as if the whole thing were a big joke. "I hear you and Bean ended up on probation, under the watchful eye of the governor." He sat on the edge of Jake's desk and shook his head. "I told ya you should've come with me."

"I would have considered it, but your kind of life-style gives me the dry heaves."

"Takes a certain type of man, I guess. Tell me about this nugget I've been hearing tales about since Denver."

Duff was doing his best to look only mildly interested, but Jake wasn't fooled. Gold was all Marshal Duff McBride ever thought about, which at times could make him even worse than the criminals he hunted.

"There is no nugget. Just the workings of an old miner's imagination."

"Really? Then what's all the hoopla around town about gold being discovered in the creek?"

"This is Colorado. Gold's being discovered every three seconds."

Jake went back to filling out his arrest reports, hoping that ignoring Duff would make him go away, or better yet, disappear off the face of the earth.

"I hear it's in the hands of a gal by the name of Storm."

Jake's hand froze, midsentence. He looked up at the man he'd come to despise. "You're hearing wrong, so it looks as though this little gold expedition was a waste of your time."

"Passed a surveyor on the way up here. Claims he's headed for this very town to settle a dispute about gold found in a creek. Says a nugget the size of a chicken egg was pulled out of the thing."

"It sounds to me like the good surveyor's been sampling the strong end of a bottle."

Duff smiled knowingly and slipped off the desk. "You haven't secured that thing yet, have you, Kiley?"

Jake clenched his teeth. He set down his quill pen and stood. "You've been in my office less than two minutes, Duff, and already you're beginning to rub me wrong. Let's say I give you a day to get out of town."

Duff laughed around the straw dangling from his cracked lips. "A day? You can do better than that, Jake buddy. How 'bout an hour, or better yet, a shoot-out at high noon."

"Don't tempt me."

"Ah, come on, Jake ol' pal. What's a little gold nugget between friends? You tell me where to find the girl, close your eyes just one second while I divest her of the little gem, and I'll split the pot with ya. Right down the middle."

"What's say, you get out of my office before I split you right down the middle?"

Duff McBride shrugged and slipped off the desk. He paused at the door. "Ya know I'm gonna get it, Kiley. With or without ya."

Through the window Jake watched Duff climb up on his horse and ride off. The bastard was right. That nugget was fair game as long as it was in Daniella's possession.

"Dammit, Daniella! This is one time when you're stubbornness is more than inconvenient."

In Jake's mind securing the nugget had just gone from a hope to a necessity, and just that morning he'd made the task close to impossible. Why in the hell had he opened his big mouth? Couldn't he have waited, maybe asked Daniella later in the day, when she wasn't standing half naked in front of him with her lips still puffy from his kisses?

The thought of going into the back room and demanding that Dreyfuss Storm tell him the hiding place, even if he had to beat it out of him, crossed his mind. But he knew the only way to get the nugget without Daniella hating him for the rest of her life was to somehow convince her to give it to him herself.

He looked up at the ceiling, wondering when Daniella Storm's opinion of him had come to matter so much, and when just the thought of her could make his heart pound.

"Bean's right, Jake ol' pal," he muttered. "You're in this thing deep."

Dannie ate supper in her room, refusing to take the slightest chance of running into Jake. She and Mary Ellen had made more progress that afternoon, presenting a united front to the town, and she didn't need a confrontation with the marshal to spoil that.

When a soft knock came at her door just after six o'clock, she assumed it was Maybelle or Louisa checking up on her and invited them to come in.

By the time she turned to find Jake standing in her room, it was too late.

At first he didn't say a word. He just stood there, looking at her, and she hated herself for the sudden heat that raced through her. His appearance was haggard, worn-out. He'd apparently had another exhausting day, and the impulse to soothe him was strong. But she stayed in her place by the window and waited to hear what he'd come to say, hoping that whatever it was might take away the pain of what he'd said to her that morning.

"I need that nugget, Daniella."

She felt her heart squeeze tight and turned her attention to the trees blowing in the night breeze outside. "I think I've heard this song before."

The creak of his gun belt told her that he was coming toward her, and she stiffened, vowing that no matter what she had to do, no matter what she had to say, he would not touch her. "You've given it one more pathetic try, Marshal. Now please leave."

"How can I make you understand—"

She spun toward him, just in time to see him reaching for her, and darted to the other side of the room. "Don't you *dare* come near me! And I understand a lot more than you give me credit for!"

"Dammit, Daniella, listen to me!"

"And don't you shout at me either! I'm the one who deserves to be angry here, not you!"

"You're the—I'll be angry if I damn well please! And if you'd be quiet for half a second, maybe I could clear this whole mess up!"

"Meaning, 'Shut up, Daniella, so I can talk you into seeing things my way.'"

"That is not what I am trying to do. I am trying to help you—"

"Oh, thank you, Marshal. But the nugget isn't so heavy that I need your help carrying it!"

"There's a man in town. Duff, Duff McBride. He wants it."

"What? A man? Who wants a big chunk of gold? Imagine that!"

"He'll do anything to get it!"

She arched her brows. "What a rat."

Clenching his jaw, he took three strides toward her, making her back up to the dresser. "Is that thing so important to you that you'd die for it?"

Dannie paused. This man McBride would actually kill her for the nugget?

"Because that's what it's coming down to," he continued more softly. "If you'd just give it to me—"

"No!" Her pride simply wouldn't let her do that, no matter if the devil himself was after it. Jake had shattered her heart for that chunk of gold, and nothing and no one in the world could convince her to give it to him.

He leaned forward and spoke directly into her face. "It's either me or him. The easy way or the hard way."

Dannie assumed that Jake thought *he* was the easy way, but he couldn't have been more wrong. She lifted her chin and responded, "Then maybe I'll save myself the trouble and give it to Mr. McBride as soon as possible."

He actually flinched, almost making her regret her words. But then he took her by the chin and said softly, "Don't do this, Daniella."

Then he kissed her, deep and lingeringly, and sure enough her resistance began to wane. But just as she was about to succumb, to offer him anything he wanted, a niggling thought entered her mind. He'd known that kissing her would break down her resistance. That's why he was doing it. Not because he cared, even the smallest bit, about her, but because he wanted his way.

She shoved him back and dragged her hand across

her mouth. "Nice try, Marshal. Fortunately, the effect of your practiced kisses has finally worn off."

He looked as if she'd slapped him again, and rage filled his dark eyes. "Fine! Keep the goddamned thing!"

Dannie was fighting tears. "I plan to!"

"Just do me one favor lady."

"Only if it will get you out of here!" she shouted.

"When Duff comes after you, and he will come after you, just give the damn thing to him. Don't put up a fight you can't win."

18

Dannie ate breakfast in her room the next morning and left the house by nine, knowing that the marshal would be in the midst of his morning rounds by that time and Bean would be keeping watch at the jail. The day was bright but chilly, and she pulled her shawl tighter around her shoulders as she walked past the doctor's office and the barbershop, keeping her head down to avoid the brisk wind.

She was turning over in her mind the things she'd need to say to her family and to the Potters when she pushed open the jailhouse door and stepped into the office. She expected to see Deputy Bean at his usual place behind the desk, but instead she found Jake Kiley. Her heart started to pound, and her palms started to sweat, and all her determination to put on a neutral face fell away.

Jake stopped writing and looked up at her. "'Morning."

She wanted to turn and run and never look back, but somehow she found the nerve to stand her ground. "I assumed you would be out on rounds."

"Yeah, well, I have some paperwork to catch up on today. Bean's taking care of things." A moment of tension hung between them, and then he said, "Surprisingly cold morning, wouldn't you say?"

She avoided his gaze. "Surprisingly. I, uh"—she took a deep breath—"I'm here to visit my family."

He set down his quill and stood, and Dannie cringed inwardly. He would demand to search her, unlike Bean, who always had the decency to take her at her word when she said she wasn't carrying any weapons.

She was filled with indecision. On today of all days she had to see her family, but she wasn't sure she'd be able to stand having Jake's hands on her without flinging herself into his arms and dissolving into tears.

He came out from behind his desk toward her and then surprised her by going straight to the cell door with the large key ring in his hand. He unlocked the door and opened it for her. "Take as long as you need."

She was stunned. "You're—you're not going to search me?"

"Would you like me to search you?"

"No . . . no, of course not. But you once told me that it was a rule. No one visits without being searched."

"Are you carrying any weapons?"

She gave him an imperious look. "None at all."

"Then go on in."

She was so shocked that she actually found herself

getting angry. He wasn't supposed to be gracious. He was supposed to be mean and demanding, and completely unaccommodating! "But what if I'm lying?"

"You're not."

"What if I am?"

"Daniella, when you lie your eyes dart around in your head like twin bumble bees. You're not lying."

She crossed the room toward him, hating the fact that he'd come to know her so well. "What if I've mastered the art?"

"Look, if you're that anxious to be searched put your hands on the wall."

"I am not anxious! You should be grateful that I'm reminding you of your duties. A slip like this with the wrong person could end up getting you killed!" She arched a brow. "You're obviously getting soft in the head."

"For which I have you to thank," he replied. "Now, you'd better get yourself into that back room before I change my mind."

"And revoke my visiting rights?" She rolled her eyes. "What a surprise that would be."

A familiar glimmer rose up in his eyes, and his gaze traveled over the front of her dress. "No, before I change my mind and strip-search you. You do know what that would entail"—he leaned closer—"don't you?"

His warm breath caressed Dannie's face, and she swallowed. "I—I'll only be a few minutes," she said in a hoarse whisper. Then she slid past him and into the back room.

Once out of the marshal's presence, she paused to

catch her breath, knowing she had to put him out of her mind if she had any hope of keeping her thoughts straight during the visit. She approached her family's cell. "Hello, Daddy. Donovan. Douglas."

"Hey, Dannie," Douglas called. He stood up from his cot. "You got any tobacco on ya? William said he'd give me a hard candy for some tobacco."

Dannie stole a quick glance at William in the far cell and grimaced at his bruised face.

"Douglas!" Donovan said. "What in the hell would she be doing with a pouch of tobacco, huh?"

"Geez, Donovan. It don't hurt to ask."

"It hurts me!"

Dannie leaned back against the wall and crossed her arms. "I can see your mood's improving, Donovan."

"Well, golly, Dannie, I wonder what I have to be happy about? I'm locked up in this stinking cell with Idiot, the talking boy, a trillion dollars worth of gold is probably washing right out of my hands and down the Rio Grande by now, and my loving sister doesn't appear inclined to lift a finger to set me free! Forgive me if I come off a little testy!"

"Hey, Dreyfuss," Sherman Potter called from the next cell. "Your eldest can't seem to keep from running off at the mouth. Care to use my boot to shut him up?"

"Shut up yourself, old man!" Donovan snapped.

"Don't you tell my pa to shut up, you backwards street rat!"

"Awful brave words, Willie, now that you're on the other side of those bars! It won't be that way forever, though."

"Yeah, and the next time it'll be just you and me, Donovan Storm! You and me!"

"Dannie, you sure you don't got any toba—"

"You ask her that one more time," Donovan growled, "and I'll grind *you* into tobacco!"

"Well," Dannie finally said. "Isn't this a pretty sight? The Potters and the Storms, locked up in jail, side by side for days on end, and still arguing. You just can't manage to come to some kind of agreement—"

Donovan charged the bars toward her. "Agreement!"

"Oh, we've come to an agreement, Dannie," William replied. He strolled toward the front bars a bit more civilly than Donovan. "We agree that you're playin' footsie with that marshal."

Dannie went pale, and her father and younger brother joined Donovan at the barred door. "I don't know what you're talking about," she responded.

"Ya see there, Daddy," Douglas said. "Her eyes do jump around in her head, just like the marshal said."

Donovan grunted. "We heard you out there, talking all soft and breathy to him—"

"I was not talking soft and breathy!"

"Don't you wanna search me, Marshal?" Douglas said in a high-pitched voice.

"How 'bout a strip search, sweetie," William joined in.

"What's been goin' on between the two of you, Daniella?" her father asked.

"Nothing is going—"

"There go her eyes again."

Dannie gave Douglas a frosty glare. "Nothing is going on between us."

"It sure doesn't look like nothin' to me."

"A snail crossing the road would look like something to you, William," she retorted.

"Yeah," Douglas said, laughing. "Lunch."

"Shut up, toad face!"

"Daddy, he called me toad face again. Can I whiz in his cell?"

"Good Lord!" Dannie exclaimed. "I'd hoped, I'd *honestly* hoped, that after sharing the same room for three days the five of you would come to some kind of understanding—at least between you and Sherman, Daddy, two supposed adults."

Her father lowered his eyes. "Well, now, Daniella—"

"And don't give me any excuses. I am as tired of this feud as I am of your reasons for perpetuating it. It's no longer a problem of our family and the Potters. It's destroying the whole darn town!"

Donovan rolled his eyes. "You always were a bit on the dramatic side, Dannie."

"I hardly think a few healthy fights would constitute the ruination of our town," William added with a laugh.

"Healthy? Let's just say that when you get out, there might—just might—be a town left to greet you!"

A proud smile broke over Donovan's face, a smile he shared with Douglas. "It's good to know that our cause has not been forgotten. Right, little brother?"

"No, Donovan," Dannie said, "it hasn't been forgotten. Just yesterday little Tommy Tyler broke his brother's nose for calling him 'a Storm.'"

The Potters burst into laughter.

"Oh, and William? The Simmons' sow gave birth

two days ago. To the single ugliest piglet this side of mud . . . They named it Potter."

Now the Storms joined in on the laughter. "No, your cause hasn't been forgotten. This town has lived and breathed your cause every waking moment for the past two weeks. They've argued and fought, teased and gossiped, even started pulling guns on each other. But if you think for one second that it really has anything to do with any of us, you're bigger fools than I thought."

"Whadaya mean?" William demanded.

"It has everything to do with us," Donovan added.

"Oh, really? Then why haven't they come in here, demanding your release? Where are all your staunch supporters? The only reason this town is up in arms is because it has been one hell of a long, hot summer and a little excitement is definitely welcomed. That, combined with the hope that if they choose the winning side, a little gold dust might show up in their Christmas stockings this year."

There was a long moment of silence, and then William said, "Ah, she doesn't know what she's talkin' about."

Dannie smiled. "You didn't actually believe they were siding with you out of the goodness of their hearts."

"I don't care what you say," he snapped. "The only thing that matters is that they are rooting for us."

She shook her head and laughed. "William, I'm afraid the only ones they're rooting for are themselves. If it turns out that you don't own the gold, I guarantee that every Potter sympathizer in Shady Gulch will be

knocking on the Storm front door, begging our for-
giveness."

William pointed a finger at her. "Well, that ain't
gonna happen!"

Donovan grunted. "Like hell it ain't."

"And if it turns out the other way, Donovan, every
Storm sympathizer will be knocking on the Potters'
door. Suddenly you won't have a single friend to your
name. Storm will be written up right alongside moron
and idiot."

"You shut your mouth, Dannie Storm," Donovan
said. "I had friends before all this started, and I'll have
'em when it's finished!"

"If I recall, the best friend you ever had was a young
man named William Potter."

Sherman Potter grunted from his cell. "Thanks to
you, missy, many fine friendships fell by the wayside a
few years back."

"Don't you go blamin' her again, Sherman!" Dreyfuss
Storm shouted. "I told you then and I'll tell ya now. She
made her choice! I'll not force her into something that
would only make her miserable."

Sherman Potter rose from his cot. "And I told you
my son wouldn't make the girl miserable! He claims he
loves her! Right, William?"

Amazed, Dannie looked over at William. She'd never
heard the word *love* pass his lips before, not that it
would have made any difference anyway.

William looked flustered. "W—well, I . . ."

"Get a grip on your tongue, boy, and spit it out. Tell
the girl you love her!"

"Well, love. I don't know——"

"This is beside the point, Mr. Potter," Dannie interrupted, not to help William but to spare herself. "Whether he loves me or not, I don't love him. The marriage would be nothing but a way to appease you and Daddy."

"What the devil is wrong with that?" Sherman Potter demanded. "In my day, a daughter did what her father said, not the other way around. Remember that, Dreyfuss, or have you gone soft in the head as well as soft in the spine?"

"At least I haven't locked my daughter up in the house for the past half year!"

"That is for her own good!"

"And I'm sure Mary Ellen will thank you for it someday," Dreyfuss said dryly.

"Thief!" Sherman Potter accused him.

"Cheat!" Dreyfuss Storm hollered back.

"Yellow belly!"

"Cold heart!"

"Gentlemen, please!" Dannie shouted. "I suppose I should just tell you why I've come and then leave you to your own private hells."

"Gee, Dannie," Douglas said. "I figured you'd just come to visit us, plain and simple, like you always do. By the way, you got any tobacco?"

Donovan actually growled, and Douglas paled. "Oh yeah. I already asked ya that, didn't I."

"I have come to inform you that until the five of you can come to some kind of civilized agreement, like civilized human beings, you will be cut off."

A hush fell over the room.

"She couldn't mean—"

"Naw," Douglas interrupted Donovan. "She don't mean that. She wouldn't do that to her own family. Would ya, Dannie?"

She broke into a slow smile, giving her brothers their answer.

"Oh my God!" Douglas suddenly wailed. "Our food! Our sweet, tasty meals!"

"Not a single plate, not a single drop or crumb of Merriweather fare will cross your lips until you can prove to me and Mary Ellen that you will put an end to this gold war and this ridiculous feud."

"What does my Mary Ellen have to do with any of this!"

"Mary Ellen and I are friends, Mr. Potter, despite your wishes and efforts to the contrary."

"Good God, Dreyfuss! Your spawn has gone and corrupted my beautiful little girl!"

"Well," Donovan said, "she's finally sold us out, fellow Storms. And I bet that sneaky low-down marshal is the one who put her up to this."

Dannie gave her older brother a false smile. "Believe it or not, Donovan, I have a mind of my own. And it can be just as stubborn, just as scheming, and just as diabolical as yours."

Without another word, she turned and left the room, closing the door behind her. She saw that Jake was seated at his desk, scribbling furiously with a quill pen, and wondered if he'd overheard any of the conversation in the cell room. Since he wasn't sparing her a glance or jumping down her throat about keeping out of trouble, she assumed he hadn't.

"Thank you, Marshal." She reached for the front door.

"I'll tell Joshua Christy at the Spur that he's in charge of meals again."

She froze and then slowly looked back over her shoulder at him. The angry expression she expected to find glaring back at her was absent. Instead she found only a soft, strange glow in his dark eyes.

"But I'll understand if you want to tell Mr. Christy yourself," he added.

"No. No, you go ahead."

He returned to his paperwork, and she stood there in the silence, staring at the top of his head. Finally, he looked back up at her. "Was there something else?"

"No—yes. Umm . . . will you be having lunch at the Merriweathers'?"

"Maybe."

"Could you . . . could you give them my regrets?"

He raised a dark eyebrow and asked softly, "Should I take that personally?"

If she hadn't made previous plans it was true that she would have avoided him at lunch, but she didn't have it in her to say as much. "I have an errand to run."

"Did you have an errand to run this morning?"

"No. This morning I ate in my room."

Instead of baiting her, as he would have normally done, he bowed his head and went back to his work, giving her the distinct impression that she'd hurt his feelings. She stood there a moment longer, teetering between walking out of the office and apologizing.

His head came back up, and this time his eyes were as dark and unfriendly as a stormy night. "You know, for someone who's trying to avoid me, Miss Storm, you sure the hell are having a hard time leaving."

She straightened her shoulders, amazed that she'd even considered apologizing to him, and quickly left the office, vowing to put the marshal and his unpredictable moods out of her head.

Dannie sat in the middle of her kitchen floor, holding the heavy gold nugget in the palm of her hand and staring at it with intense curiosity. She couldn't believe that something so small could have caused so much trouble. It seemed there wasn't a man alive who didn't want it: the Potters, the Storms, Jake Kiley, and now Duff McBride. She wondered what it was that made them value money over love and friendship.

She stood and slipped it into her pocket. There its bulk would be hidden by her skirt folds, and she would know that it hadn't fallen into the wrong hands. She was determined that nobody, not even her father, would have it until the surveyor decided exactly whom it belonged to.

She almost hoped it would be given to the Potters. *Let them worry about it for a change,* she thought.

Suddenly the front door burst open, and she let out a startled shriek. Standing in her doorway was a broad-shouldered man with dirty-blond hair and cold, squinting eyes. "Marshal Duff McBride at your service, ma'am."

Dannie's blood went cold as Jake's words of warning came back to her. *Give the damn thing to him. You can't win.*

The large man came toward her, his smile curving around a piece of straw that was hanging out of his mouth. "Well, now. Nobody told me you was so gal-darn purty, Miss Storm." His eyes raked over her, and a shiver crawled up her spine. "Maybe you and I can come to some sort of understanding."

As he approached her she realized that she'd misjudged his reach. Before she could back away his massive hand shot out and his fingers closed around her neck. The only thing Dannie could think to do was scream, but the sound died, muted, at the back of her throat.

She clawed at his fingers, expecting him to snap her neck at any moment. With her vision blurring, she prayed that her death would be quick and hoped that her father and brothers would finally come to their senses and patch things up with the Potters. Then she silently swore to haunt Jake Kiley for the rest of his life.

The man's cold, wet mouth closed over hers, his lips thick and slimy, and she struggled for a breath of air. His free hand traveled down her back and then grabbed her bottom, digging in with his fingers. Her body felt like it was turning into lead as bile rose up in her throat.

When he finally pulled away from her, grinning and laughing, she felt bruised and nauseated. "You're a sweet one, honey," he murmured as he held her pressed against his soft belly. "What's say old Duff initiates you into the joys of womanhood, and then we'll get down to doin' a little business?"

To Dannie, death was preferable to rape. She managed to find the strength to kick him and then somehow twist free. She stumbled backward, but the man only licked his lips and advanced on her.

"I like a woman with fire, Miss Storm. Let's you and me rub naughties. Whadaya say? Oh-ho, you'll like it, sugar. I promise."

He reached for her again, and Dannie darted behind the horsehair chair. With the heavy piece of furniture in between them she paused to take a deep breath. Then she let out a scream that could have raised the hairs on a jackal.

Duff McBride laughed all the more. "Go on and scream! There ain't nobody out here's gonna hear ya!"

But somebody had heard Dannie. And the breath caught in her throat as he stepped into the doorway, tall, brave, and competent. His dark eyes were glittering with rage, and she felt a burst of pride shoot through her.

Not noticing Dannie's sudden fascination with the doorway behind him, Duff McBride reached out for her, but Jake had crossed the room by then. He grabbed the man by the shoulder and threw him against the far wall.

"I thought I told you to get the hell out of my town, McBride! Looks to me like you don't listen too well!"

Dannie bit her lip as Jake punched the man, hard, in the stomach. Duff doubled over and fell to his knees.

"Damn, Jake ol' pal, your fists are still as . . . as hard as rocks. I'm sorry, buddy, I'm sorry. Is the woman yours? I had no idea. I swear—"

The man dove for Jake's legs, and Dannie let out a cry of alarm as Jake crashed to the floor with Duff McBride on top of him. The two of them went rolling across the planks and hit the small wooden side table her father had built, splintering it and knocking over the lamp. She grimaced as Jake's fist connected with Duff McBride's solid jaw and groaned for Jake as his head was slammed against the floor a time or two.

Then, as suddenly as it had begun, it was over. Jake was climbing to his feet, leaving the unconscious Duff McBride on the floor with his mouth bleeding and his eyes already swelling closed.

"Are you all right?" she asked.

He was breathing hard as he looked over at her. "I could have used some help, Miss Storm."

"I'm—I'm sorry. I suppose I should have gotten a gun or something. It just never occurred to me—"

"Did locking your *door* ever occur to you?"

Out of breath or not, having defended her or not, she didn't appreciate his tone. "Not in the middle of the day, no, Marshal, it didn't."

"Well, then, the next time you come to gaze at your priceless piece of rock, consider it!"

"I did not come to—how did you know it was here?" she demanded.

"Half the damn town knows it's out here somewhere, Daniella! Use your head, for Christ's sake!"

"Don't you yell at me! And I'm sorry if I lack the cunning it takes to hoard gold!"

Duff groaned and Jake gave him a kick to shut him up. "That man could have killed you!"

"Or worse!"

"There *is* nothing worse."

She grunted. "Maybe for a man."

Jake's expression darkened, and his eyes narrowed.

He looked down at the motionless man at his feet and gave him another kick.

"What are you doing out here, anyway?" she demanded.

"I followed you."

"Why?"

"Because I figured you'd be coming out here for the nugget. I gave you a five-minute head start."

"Dammit, why will I never learn? For one fleeting moment I actually thought you might have been concerned about me!"

"I was concerned!"

"Oh, save it, Marshal! You were concerned all right, concerned that Marshal McBride here would steal the nugget you've put so much effort into swindling from me!"

He dabbed the cut on his lip. "You are one piece of work. I charge in and save your sorry hide, and all you can do is accuse me of trying to take your lousy gold."

"And I have nothing to base that assumption on, do I!"

"I told you last night that the thing was yours to do with as you please!"

"Well, I certainly didn't need your permission!"

Duff groaned. "Could you two shut the hell up. You're making my head hurt. Aren't you supposed to put me in jail or somethin'?"

"Marshal Kiley would be happy to do that, Marshal McBride. It's his favorite pastime!"

She spun on her heel and stomped across the floor and out of the house.

"That's right, Daniella, run!" Jake yelled. "But a million miles between us will never make you forget that night!"

She continued on through the picket gate, her chin trembling. No, she would never forget. But maybe, with time and a little luck, it would stop hurting so damn much.

19

The weather took a turn for the worse that night. Dannie sat alone in the parlor in front of a fire, listening as the wind howled through the trees and crept in through the nooks and crannies of the old house. She'd survived her confrontation with Duff McBride that afternoon—and her confrontation with Jake, for that matter—and the nugget was still safely tucked away in her skirt pocket. Even now she could feel its weight pressing hard against her thigh.

The clock on the wall chimed ten times, and she glanced at the parlor doorway, wondering when Jake was going to come home. She wasn't waiting up for him, she kept telling herself, she just liked the idea of knowing where he was at all times so that she could better avoid him.

Since he had needed to fill out reports on Duff McBride's arrest, she hadn't been too surprised when he didn't come home for supper. The sisters hadn't been very pleased, however. In fact, they had been uncharacteristically quiet during the meal, and Dannie had gotten the distinct impression that they were disappointed because they'd planned on overseeing a reconcilliation between her and Jake.

If that was the case, then Dannie was relieved that he hadn't made it for supper. Any attempt at a truce between them would have ended in complete disaster. There was no middle ground for them. He wanted the nugget, and she wasn't going to give it to him. It was that simple.

She heard the front door open and quickly immersed herself in staring at the fire, hoping that Jake would head straight for his room and leave her in peace in the parlor. She didn't get her wish. He strode into the room and turned his back to the fire, acting as though she weren't even in the room. He warmed himself for a while, keeping his eyes pinned to the floor, and then he took off his long dark coat and draped it over the wing chair.

The silence that hung between them was disquieting, but Dannie wasn't about to get up and leave just because of him.

"Quiet day?" she asked pleasantly.

He acted as if he hadn't heard her as he shifted positions in front of the fire. At one point she thought she heard him grumble something but then supposed it had been just the wind.

"Now who's acting like a child?" she asked.

"Don't bother talking to me, lady."

"Well, I'm certainly not going to sit here in silence, and try to figure out what you're thinking."

He grunted. "You don't want to know what I'm thinking."

"Is that supposed to frighten me? Are you thinking about throwing me in jail on a lark? Or better yet, putting me in the Potter cell and letting them beat the tar out of me? Or maybe you're just wishing you'd let Duff McBride finish the job this afternoon. Is that it, Marshal?"

He gave her a cold smile. "You don't know when to quit."

"I don't quit. I just change direction."

"Then I suggest you be careful, Miss Storm, because everybody's got their own personal brick wall."

"I suppose I have yet to find mine."

He paused, then said, "You're looking at him."

She laughed, giving him a slow once-over with her eyes. "Nothing a good sledge hammer couldn't take care of."

"If you've got the desire to use it. Some people like brick walls. They claim the challenge is an inconvenience, but every now and then you catch them giving the grooves and the mortar a quick little caress."

She looked away. "I asked you if you'd had a quiet day."

His laugh was soft, almost inaudible against the howling wind outside. "A quiet day? After I got my face pounded this afternoon, yeah, I suppose I had about as quiet a day as a man can have in this town."

He sat down in the chair opposite her and put his feet up on the stool. Dannie looked back at the fire, never hating silence as much as she did at the moment.

"Stupid Dannie! Stupid Dannie!"

She shot a glare at Harvey's cage then glanced at Jake and found him watching her intently.

She cleared her throat, determined to ignore the bird. "What did my family get for breakfast?"

"Oatmeal . . . at least I think it was oatmeal."

She grimaced as she imagined how angry at her her father and brothers must be. "I really hate to do this to them. If they'd only see reason. I am so tired of this feud!" she burst out.

There was a moment of silence and then Jake said, "Care to hear an interesting idea?"

She looked at him wondering if he was serious or just had something disagreeable to say.

"How long have you known Mary Ellen Potter?" he asked when she said nothing.

She gave him an impatient look. "What does Mary Ellen have to do with—"

"Does she have her eye on any particular man?"

"Her father has always kept her very sheltered, Marshal. And if you're considering catching her eye, I can tell you right now that you're not her type."

"And what is her type?"

"Mannered, reserved, principled."

"Well, I've got news for you, sweetheart, her type is none of the above."

That sounded like a condemnation if Dannie had ever heard one. "Mary Ellen Potter is one of the kindest, most morally upright young women in—"

"What about Donovan?"

"Would you kindly tell me what you're getting at?"

"Just answer the question, Daniella."

"I've told you not to call me that."

"Has Donovan ever been in love?"

"You mean with someone besides himself? I doubt it. Although he claims that untold females have fallen helplessly under his spell, I have yet to see it cast with any adequate results. Would you please tell me what this is all about?"

He stood up and once again turned his back to the fire. "Mary Ellen is in love with Donovan."

Dannie was stunned for a moment, and then she started to laugh. "Marshal, I assure you, Mary Ellen is not in love with Donovan."

"She visited her family at the jail this morning. Bean said she was making googly eyes at Donovan the whole time."

"I heard you say yourself once that Bean and Maybelle could share a pair of spectacles."

"How about this then: Donovan never said a single word while Mary Ellen was there."

Dannie's laughter was cut short. In her experience, a quiet Donovan was either a sick Donovan or a dead Donovan.

"Bean claims your brother sat quietly on his cot, didn't even lift his eyes until after Mary Ellen had left."

"Are you sure about this? Mary Ellen and Donovan? The notion is pretty farfetched."

"I was just as skeptical as you are, but Bean tends to be pretty perceptive about things like this." He gave her a direct look and then shrugged. "Sometimes love can be found in the strangest places."

Dannie paused, then she turned away. "So, what does Bean suggest we do?"

"The feud started when a Storm refused to marry a Potter. He thinks maybe it can be solved by rectifying that matter."

"You mean, Mary Ellen and Donovan? Married?"

"As odd as it sounds—"

"No, this is actually good. Very, very good." She turned toward him. "Do you know what this could mean? No matter who gets the gold it will be in both families. Everybody would end up happy!"

"Hopefully."

"Undoubtedly! The next time I see Bean Toomey I'm going to give him a big fat kiss!"

"Big fat kiss! Yes, Jake, yes!"

This time Jake gave the bird a disparaging look. "You're forgetting two very important things, Daniella. Mary Ellen and Donovan. What if they don't agree that this is such a wonderful idea?"

She frowned, her mind already starting to work out all the details. "I'll cross that bridge when I come to it. First I have to get the two of them to admit their feelings for each other. Then, hopefully, love will simply guide the way."

He still seemed skeptical. "If it were that simple, I don't think we would have ever heard of Romeo and Juliet."

"Donovan and Mary Ellen will be married. And the Potters and the Storms will once again be the best of friends. It has to work. It has to!" She took a deep breath. "Now. I have a lot of thinking to do. Thank you for relaying Bean's idea to me. I'll see you in the morning."

She turned to leave.

"Daniella?"

"What?"

"I'm not trying to burst your bubble."

She turned back to him, her heart leaping at the tenderness in his voice. "I'm starting to get used to people doing that."

"About tomorrow . . . I'll help you any way I can."

"Two-bit lawman! Big fat kiss!"

Dannie ignored the bird. Jake's offer warmed her even more than the fire had. "Thank you."

She heard his murmured "Good night" as she walked toward the stairs, and then she heard him curse Harvey up one side and down the other.

The next day was dark and dreary. Thick, gray clouds hung over the mountains surrounding the gulch, and the burgeoning rumbles of thunder could be heard in the distance.

Dannie rolled out of bed, refusing to let the threatening weather change her plans. She pulled on her dress with the blue flower buttons, ran a brush through her hair, and went down to breakfast.

Jake was finishing his flapjacks when she entered the kitchen, and she faltered in the doorway.

"Good morning, Daniella," Maybelle sang. "Isn't it a wonderfully dreadful day?"

Dannie leaned over a chair to pick up a slice of ham. "Don't get your hopes up too soon, Maybelle. Rain has proved to be nothing if not fickle this past summer."

Maybelle shook her head. "I'll trust what my knees are telling me, my dear."

Louisa set a towering plate of flapjacks down on the table. "Sister, your knees couldn't predict a monsoon, let alone a simple rain shower. Sit down and eat, Daniella. You know how I feel about standing and food picking."

Dannie finished off the slice of ham and licked her fingers. "Actually, I'm not very hungry. I've got some things to do this morning, so if you'll excuse me—"

"Oh, but, Daniella," Louisa called before Dannie could leave the room, "we thought we'd make you and the marshal a basket and send you off in the buggy."

Judging by the look on Jake's face, Dannie could tell that he was just as surprised by the sister's plans as she was. "That's very kind of you two," she said, "but I really have some very important things to see to this morning—"

"Then how 'bout this afternoon?" Jake asked.

She blinked. "This afternoon?"

"Yeah."

"But it's cold, and windy, and—"

"The buggy has a roof."

He was waiting for her to say something, and it looked as if he actually expected it to be yes. "Can we talk about this later? I need to ride over to the Potters' before Mary Ellen goes calling."

"Meet you in my office around ten?"

"I plan to have Mary Ellen there by that time, yes."

"Excellent," Maybelle cried. "Then we shall send the basket along with the marshal. Oh, Louisa, aren't they adorable?"

Louisa gave her sister a sharp poke with her elbow. "I swear, sister, a hammer and nail could be more subtle than you."

"Ouch! And a nail would be a fine spot duller than that elbow of yours."

Dannie gave the sisters a warning look. "I will see you two later."

They exchanged anxious glances. "What do you suppose she means by that, Louisa?"

"Probably that once again you've been sticking your nose in where it doesn't belong."

"*I've* been sticking *my* nose in . . ."

Dannie left the kitchen and headed for the barn, her step lighter than she cared for it to be. She couldn't understand why the marshal was inviting her on a picnic and she desperately didn't want to get her hopes up about it, but once again her heart was beginning to overrule her head.

Jake was at his office by ten minutes to ten. He informed Bean about Dannie's plans for Donovan and Mary Ellen and then sent his deputy on a little errand. One that he hoped would help Daniella.

She arrived with Mary Ellen at precisely ten o'clock. There was a bright flush to her cheeks from the cold and probably from the excitement, and he had to fight down the impulse to pull her close and use his special technique of warming her up.

"Hello, Marshal," Mary Ellen said sweetly.

Miss Mary Ellen Potter was a pretty woman, with a gentle disposition. The kind of woman that would have turned Jake's head a couple of weeks back, but he'd recently discovered that he preferred a certain spitfire with hair like molten lava and a temper to match.

He came out from behind his desk to greet them at the door. "Good morning, Miss Storm, Miss Potter. What brings you two ladies out on this chilly morning?"

Mary Ellen tugged off her white kid gloves. "Dannie says you wanted to speak to me about something."

He gave Daniella a questioning look.

"Well, if I'd told her that *I* needed to speak with her," Dannie whispered furiously, "she would have demanded that I speak right there at her house. Then she probably would have refused to come with me. And what good would that have done? Besides, you said last night that you would help me in any way you could."

Mary Ellen was giving them both a very suspicious look. "Marshal, do you or do you not wish to speak with me?"

Daniella gave him a glare that clearly suggested that she expected him to answer the young woman. So Jake took Mary Ellen's arm and led her across the room to the warm potbellied stove.

"Mary Ellen—may I call you Mary Ellen?"

"Yes, yes of course."

"Mary Ellen, to put it straight, Daniella and I have uncovered your secret."

The young woman let out a startled gasp, and Jake thought for sure he was going to have a full-blown faint on his hands. He shot Daniella an irritated look.

"Good heavens! Oh, Dannie I—I am so mortified." She groaned and covered her face with her hands. "Oh, the two of you must think so little of me!"

"Well . . ."

Daniella cut Jake off as she placed her arm over Mary Ellen's shoulders. "Of course we don't think little of you, Mary Ellen. Things like this are a natural part of life, and, well, sometimes opposites do attract."

"So . . . so you understand?"

"Oh," Jake said, "absolutely."

Mary Ellen gave a deep sigh. "Good. Because I'm afraid it's spreading through town. I was really afraid you would hear about it from someone else—"

"I was a little stunned when the marshal told me about this last night, Mary Ellen. I thought we'd agreed a long time ago never to keep secrets from each other."

"Oh, Dannie, please understand. I just couldn't tell you. I was so afraid you'd never speak to me again!"

Dannie shook her head and laughed. "Mary Ellen, I fail to see how your attraction to my brother would make me—"

"My what!"

"Your attraction to Donovan. How could you

think I'd be anything but . . . pleased—are you all right?"

Mary Ellen's face had gone from ivory to a bright, fuchsia red. "Who told you about that?" she asked almost murderously.

"Well, I—I understand it was obvious when you visited the jail yesterday morning."

After a few deep breaths, the woman seemed to regain her composure. "Well, I suppose you, of all people, can understand how disconcerting it is to be attracted to the wrong sort of man, Dannie. I mean, who in their right mind would hold this against me? Besides my father of course. He'd hold it against me— he'd lock me in my room until I was sixty! Oh, Dannie, you have to help me! We can't let my father find out. I'm so sorry that I told Betty Mae Baxter about you and the marshal. She was going on and on about how he had all the Storms in jail and that you were going to be next. I just couldn't help my—"

"You did what!"

Jake's attention was caught by Daniella's tone, as it usually was whenever a woman's voice rose three entire octaves beyond the normal speaking range.

"How could you!" Daniella shouted. "And to Betty Mae Baxter, the fastest mouth in the west!"

Mary Ellen grew flustered again and stamped her foot. "I told you! She was saying terrible things about you and the marshal. I was only standing up for you!"

"Standing up for me? Damn, Mary Ellen, next time just sit the hell down!"

"Well, there's gratitude for you!"

"Gratitude! I could snatch you bald for this!"

Jake cleared his throat. "I don't imagine anyone would like to tell me what the devil the two of you are talking about, even though it sounds as though it has something to do with me?"

"Noth—"

"I accidentally told Betty Mae Baxter about you and Dannie being together," Mary Ellen whispered.

"Accidentally," Daniella scoffed. "And a chicken accidentally lays eggs!"

"Are you saying I did it on purpose! Because I didn't, Daniella Collette Storm—"

"Don't you middle-name me, Mary Ellen Imogene Potter—"

"Ladies, ladies," Jake said. Both women's mouths clamped shut. Their faces were redder than sun-ripened beets. "Let me understand this. When I said we'd uncovered your secret you assumed that we'd found out about you talking to Miss Baxter about me and Daniella?"

Mary Ellen nodded, and he smiled. "Then I guess the joke's on us."

"The joke *is* us!" Daniella replied angrily. "Thanks to her big mouth."

"I said I was sorry!"

"What I want to know, Daniella," Jake said, "is that, after all the worrying you did, what drove you to share this with anyone?"

"She was confused—"

"I can answer him by myself, thank you very

much!" Dannie turned to him, and he was entranced by the stubborn tilt of her chin. She seemed determined not to be daunted by this very touchy subject, one she'd avoided and agonized over for days. "I was confused. The Merriweathers seemed to think that I was being too hard on you, and I needed an unbiased ear."

"In my opinion she's in—"

"Shut up, Mary Ellen! We do not want or need your opinion! Now get in there and propose to my brother!"

"I will do no such thing!"

"Then this feud will go on for the rest of our lives, and our children's lives, and their children's lives! And all because Mary Ellen Potter couldn't swallow her pride just long enough to get married!"

This odd threat seemed to take Mary Ellen by the scruff of the neck. Her bottom lip jutted out and she looked as if she was about to burst into tears. "That's not fair, Dannie Storm! I don't even know if he loves me back! And if you holler in my face one more time I'm going to wallop you with my reticule!"

"Oh, for God's sake, Mary Ellen. Does Donovan speak to you—ever?"

"No!" she wailed. "Never!"

"Then trust me, he loves you back. Donovan Storm doesn't shut his mouth for just anybody."

"Oh, Dannie, do you really think so? I've worried about this for so long now."

"Why don't you go in there and ask him then, and put us all out of our misery?"

The young woman took a deep breath. "All right. Even though it may mean abject humiliation for the rest of my life, for the sake of the Storms and the Potters, I will give it my very best try!"

Jake retrieved the keys and opened the cell-room door. Once Mary Ellen had gone in, he turned his attention to Daniella. "Interesting—"

She held up her hand. "Not one word, Kiley. Not—one—single—word."

20

When Dannie entered the cell room, she found Mary Ellen already trading pleasantries with Sherman and William. Duff McBride was sitting on his cot in the farthest corner of the cell, eyeing the Potters and their pretty guest.

In the next cell, Donovan was staring at the floor and not uttering a sound. Douglas, however, seemed to have quite a bit to say. "Looky, Daddy. Dannie's come back to torment us some more. Did ya bring a knife this time, sister dear, so's you could cut out our hearts for real?"

Giving her little brother a bothersome look, she decided to try her hand at drawing Donovan out. "Donovan, how was your oatmeal yesterday morning?"

"It was about as tasty as muck on a pond," Douglas replied.

Ignoring Douglas, she tried again with her older brother. "What did you have for lunch, Donovan?"

"Some dried-up bile with pieces of dirt—"

"Douglas, have you forgotten your own name? If you hadn't noticed, I am not speaking to you!"

"Well, gosh, Dannie you don't gotta yell at me. Besides, Donovan ain't about to answer ya."

Her older brother finally graced her with his direct attention but said nothing.

"And why not?" she asked.

"'Cause Mary Ellen is—"

"Shut up, you idiot!" Donovan hissed. "You get on outta here, Dannie Storm. You've caused us enough trouble."

"I've done nothing but try to set to rights the mess you men have caused!"

Donovan only grunted and went back to looking at the dusty stone floor. Dannie had hoped to get a better reaction from him than that. She glanced at Mary Ellen and found her still immersed in conversation with her family. She decided to try the direct approach. "Donovan, why are you so quiet when Mary Ellen is in the room?"

He stole a glance at Mary Ellen and then shot Dannie a dark look. "I'm no such thing."

"Yes, you—" Donovan's glare shut Douglas up.

"You seem to love baiting the Potters, Donovan. I would think any member of the family would be fair game in your book."

"She's a woman. I don't . . . I don't fight women."

Dannie rolled her eyes, and Douglas moved closer to the cell door. "I think he likes her. Ya know, got a burnin' ache for her in the vicinity of his drawers? She is a pretty little—"

Dannie jumped back as Donovan leapt to his feet and spun Douglas around to face him. "I'm not gonna tell you again to shut your mouth, little brother. And you—" he pointed to where Dannie was standing—"you, get! We don't need or want you visiting us anymore!"

Mary Ellen looked their way. "I'd say that has to be one of the most ungrateful things I've ever heard, Donovan Storm. Your sister could have forsaken every one of you, you know, when you were locked up in here, but instead she has chosen to stand by you and comfort you."

Dannie cringed, knowing the worst thing you could do to Donovan was contradict him. But then she almost fell to her knees in astonishment when Mary Ellen walked toward the bars of Donovan's cell and his hard stare actually wavered.

"Mary Ellen!" Sherman Potter hollered. "You get yourself away from there. You don't need to be talking to that kind of trash."

For once in her life, Mary Ellen ignored her father. "Dannie's done nothing but worry about the three of you lately."

"But sh—she's cut off our good meals, and—and taken up with that marshal!"

"That marshal has spent the past two weeks looking out for her because you didn't have the good sense to keep yourself out of jail."

"Hey, now," Dannie's father spoke up. "Don't you stand there callin' my boy stupid."

"What's a matter with you, Donovan?" Douglas said. "Don't let that woman talk down to ya like that."

"I didn't call him stupid, I called him senseless. There's a big difference in my opinion."

"Not in mine," William said.

"And you hush up, William Potter. You have more to be ashamed of than anyone here. Attacking Dannie on the road like that—and don't you try to deny it. Our father might be refusing to see you for what you really are—a spoiled, drunken, hooligan—but I am not so blind!"

"Did you hear what she just called me, Pa?"

"Don't pay her any mind, son. She's been spending too much time with that Storm girl."

"The very girl you were so anxious to marry your son to that you started a feud over it," Mary Ellen pointed out. "Personally, I think the whole lot of you have fallen off the front porch!"

"See what you've done, Sherman," Dreyfuss Storm said. "Lockin' Mary Ellen up like that has turned her downright shrewish!"

"Mary Ellen ain't no shrew!" Donovan said heatedly.

"Don't tell me you're standin' up for one of them, Donovan?"

"She ain't one of them, Daddy. She—she's just plain old Mary Ellen."

"Did you hear that, Pa?" William joined in. "That Storm just called our glorious Mary Ellen plain and old! Get back to this side of the room where you belong, girl!"

"Oh, hush up, William!" Mary Ellen retorted. "He didn't mean it like that and you know it. Frankly, I think that's one of the sweetest compliments I've ever had."

Dannie about choked on her tongue as Donovan gave Mary Ellen the brightest smile she'd ever seen. "I would never have believed this if I hadn't seen it with my own two eyes," Dannie whispered as Jake came up beside her.

"I'm having a hard time keeping down my flapjacks," he responded.

Dannie stepped forward. "It appears to me that we could have an answer to our problems here."

"Look out," William said. "She's coming up with another plan."

Mary Ellen cleared her throat. "I know exactly what you're thinking, Dannie. And I think it's a splendid idea."

"Well, would the two of you care to share this splendid idea with the rest of us?" Dreyfuss Storm asked.

"Certainly," Dannie replied. "For starters I think it's clear that William and I will never be married." Mumbles and nods of agreement came from the Potter cell. "But I think . . . I think we might have before us another, more suitable, match."

Just then Bean burst into the room. "I got the preacher, Jake! He was a hell of a fella to find, but—"

Bean stopped short and glanced around the room as it suddenly fell silent. Every person behind bars was staring at the deputy with their mouths hanging open— even Duff McBride.

"You can't mean—" Dreyfuss Storm began.

"Not on your life!" William Potter exclaimed.

"Her ta him?" Duff asked.

"Never in a million years!" Sherman Potter bellowed.

"But Dannie," Douglas said. "I'm too young to be gettin' married."

"Not you, you imbecile!" Sherman shouted. "Him!"

Dannie refused to be daunted by their initial reaction. "I think you are all forgetting two very important opinions," she said. "Donovan's and Mary Ellen's."

"My opinion *is* Mary Ellen's! We don't run our home like you Storms! The men are the only ones who wear pants in my family!"

Dannie ignored Sherman Potter's remark. "What do you say, Donovan? In the interest of both families would you be willing to wed Mary Ellen?"

The tenderness in Donovan's expression grew more noticeable as he stared into Mary Ellen's eyes, and Dannie's hopes began to soar. But then Donovan glanced over his shoulder at his brother and father who were both shaking their heads. When he looked back at Mary Ellen his eyes were filled with regret.

"'Course—'course not," he finally said in a hoarse whisper. He backed up to stand by his family, his eyes on the floor once again. "She—she's a Potter."

Mary Ellen spun toward Dannie. "You see there? I told you. I told you." Dannie reached out to comfort her, but Mary Ellen ran toward her father's cell.

Indignation filled Dannie, and she took a step toward her family's cell. "She's a Potter, Donovan? What kind of an excuse is that! She's a beautiful, sweet woman, and if you think for one second that you'll ever find somebody like that to love you again then you are pure, sheer nuts! And you're going to give her up, just because they"—she pointed angrily at her father and brother—"they want you to?"

"*They* are my family."

"Maybe so, but they sure the heck aren't going to keep you very warm at night!"

"Daniella Storm!" her father exclaimed. "What the dickens are you thinkin' talkin' like that!"

"Appears to me, Dreyfuss, that the good marshal has been doing more with your daughter than watching out for her," Sherman Potter said with a short laugh.

Jake spoke up. "Potter, you open your mouth one more time, and I'm gonna reach in there and come out with a few teeth."

Dannie refused to give up on her brother. "Donovan, you love her! You know you do!"

Donovan shook his head slowly. "That's ridiculous. I could no more love her than I could a . . . a"—he looked down and drove the toe of his boot against the floor—"a boil on my big toe."

Mary Ellen began to cry, and Dannie felt tears of shame burn her own eyes. She reached out a hand to her friend. "Come on, Mary Ellen. Donovan, I hope your hate and your spite are enough to keep you company for the rest of your miserable life!"

Mary Ellen took her hand, despite Sherman Potter's protests, and Dannie led her to the door. She gave her older brother and the rest of her family one final glare. She'd done her best, but somehow that just hadn't been enough.

"Wait."

Both Dannie and Mary Ellen turned toward Donovan, but it hadn't been he who'd spoken. It had been Jake. He was standing by the Potter cell, his arms crossed, his expression disbelieving.

"Damn, if you people aren't the most stubborn . . . I'll make you a deal. Donovan weds Mary Ellen, right here, right now, and—Christ, I can't believe I'm doing this—I'll set every one of you free. Except you, Duff. You're staying right the hell where you are."

Dannie stared at Jake in shock as grumbles and murmurs filled the room. Mary Ellen sagged against her, and she noticed that even Bean had to steady himself against the door.

"Boy-o, you sure you know what yer doin'?"

"Hell, no, but that seems to be the way of things lately, so I figure why not be consistent."

"Marshal, you have got yourself a deal!" Dreyfuss Storm shouted above all the other voices.

"You mean we can go?" Douglas said, obviously stunned. Then he whooped like a saddle tramp back from a year on the range.

Sherman Potter was proving harder to convince. "I don't like the idea of my daughter marrying the likes of him."

"Look at it this way, Potter," Jake said. "Chances are, when Donovan gets out of here he'll eventually come to his senses and marry her anyway. This way, you can say they had your blessing and save yourself some embarrassment."

"Come on, Pa. I don't know if I can stand another night in here on Rolling Spur fare," William said.

"Well, now wait a minute, wait just a minute," Donovan spoke up. "Nobody is botherin' to ask me my opinion on this."

"Oh, Donovan, we all know you're too cow-eyed by Daddy to make up your own mind," Dannie said. She got precisely the response she wanted.

"I have never in my life been cow-eyed, Dannie Storm! Daddy!" he shouted. "I have changed my mind. I want Mary Ellen Potter to be my lawful wife! And, dammit, like it or not, that is the way it's gonna be!"

Everybody looked at Mary Ellen. Her jaw was set, and Dannie groaned. "Come on, Mary Ellen. Don't turn stubborn on me. He said he wanted to marry you."

"Yes, but does he love me? I won't be married just so he can get out of jail."

"Ah, Mary Ellen," Donovan said, looking toward the floor again. "I love ya. The marshal's right. I would've come to my senses eventually."

Again all eyes rested on Mary Ellen, waiting, tenuously, until she broke into a beaming smile. "All right, Donovan Storm. I suppose I could find it in my heart to forgive you for your pride. Just this once, though," she added.

In contradiction to earlier sentiment, the room errupted in cheers, and Dannie's eyes met Jake's in the midst of the uproar. She knew just how much pride it had cost him to do what he'd just done, and she felt her heart swell with gratitude.

"Preacher!" Bean shouted. "Get on back here. You got a weddin' to perform!"

Dannie stood alone on the boardwalk, listening to the rumble of thunder as dark clouds rolled in over the hills surrounding the gulch. She was waiting for the wedding couple to come outside. She and Jake had decided to let them use the buggy and the picnic basket for a private celebration. And then the new couple planned to join both families for supper at the Potter house. Relations between the Storms and the Potters were strained but calm so far, and Dannie could only hope that with time all the broken ties would mend.

She looked up to find Jake coming out of the office. "Everything's working out okay so far," he said.

She squeezed her fingers into the folds of her skirt, still not able to get over what he'd done. "I . . . I know you probably have some practical reason for doing what you did, in there, Marshal. But—but still, I'd like to thank you."

"What I did, Miss Storm, was a favor."

She looked up into his dark eyes. They were soft and warm, and her heart skipped a beat. "After everything, you did me a favor?"

He looked down at his boots. "Look, can we just—"

A loud crack of thunder boomed and she jumped toward him. He reached out to steady her, and their eyes met for one, brief moment. She muttered an apology, glanced up at the sky, and took a step back from him.

"Can we just start over?" he continued. "Try and forget everything up till today?"

If only she could. She'd been trying to convince herself for days that Jake had maliciously set out to seduce her, but if she were totally honest she'd have to admit that she'd wanted him to make love to her, probably from the first moment she'd seen him. So how could she go on placing blame at his feet without laying some at her own?

She met his eyes. "I don't think I want to forget everything."

He gave her an intimate smile, and Dannie knew what she had to do. She took a deep breath and pulled the nugget out of her pocket. "Here."

He looked down at it but made no move to take it. "If I accepted that, then what I did wouldn't be counted as a favor, now, would it?"

Dannie was a little surprised herself at what she was doing. Her family would likely throw a fit. "It's not a reward. It's . . . it's a long overdue gesture. Just take it, Jake." She opened his hand and set the heavy piece of gold in his palm. Her throat tightened, and she blinked away the tears that clouded her vision. "I know how much it means to you and I want you to have it. Besides, there's probably a lot more where that came from."

"Dammit, Daniella," he said softly, "this nugget doesn't mean anything to me. It never has. It's just part of my—"

Deputy Bean stepped out onto the boardwalk. "They're in your office, gettin' all the papers signed . . . under the watchful eyes of both papas." He looked up at the stormy sky and scratched his bristly chin. "Kinda romantic, this unexpected happenin'. Makes a man's mind take flights a fancy, eh, boy-o? Love and honor, all that kinda crap."

Jake's responding smile looked more like a grimace. "If you can get your head out of the clouds for a minute, Bean, I've got an errand for you." He handed him the nugget.

Bean's eyebrows shot up to his hairline. "Woo-wee," he said, his eyes wide as he stared at the gold. "She *is* about the size of a hen's egg. I wanna thank you, Miz Storm, for finally giving her to us."

Dannie smiled through a veil of tears. "Now you're a rich man, Mister Toomey."

The deputy blinked, and then he gave Jake a scowl. "You haven't told her the truth yet? Well, dag blarnit, if you ain't the sorriest son-of-a—"

"What truth?" Dannie asked.

"I was about to tell her when you came sauntering out here, spouting on about romance and flights of fancy," Jake snapped.

"What truth?"

Bean was starting to laugh. "So she gave ya the thing thinking you was keepin' it? Well, if that don't get it inta yer head how she really feels abou'cha, then yer a great big waste a air, Jake Jedediah Kiley. And when your mama gets you up to heaven, she's gonna beat you ugly."

"Excuse me? What truth?"

"The nugget, Miz Storm," Bean said. "We ain't keepin' it for ourselves."

She glanced from Bean's grin to Jake's assessing eyes. "But you . . . then you really . . ."

"Ya see, our job—"

"If you don't mind," Jake interrupted him. He

turned to Dannie. "Our job here is to secure the gold in Shady Gulch—all of the gold—so that when the surveyor hits town it can be given to the rightful owner."

Dannie felt shame shrink her from inside. If what he was telling her was true—and certainly not a soul alive could doubt the honest expression on Bean Toomey's face—then she had completely misjudged Jake. She'd actually accused him of sleeping with her to get rich, and she felt about three inches tall, standing there in front of him, wishing she could come up with something intelligent to say. She wanted to stamp her foot, get angry that he hadn't told her the truth before now. But she knew that she probably wouldn't have listened.

Bean cleared his throat. "I think it's time I locked this honey up in a safe where it belongs." He tugged the wide brim of his hat. "Miz Storm. Be seein' ya, I'm sure." He sauntered down the street toward the bank.

"I guess I should have told you from the very beginning," Jake said. "Daniella?"

Dannie couldn't find the courage to look him in the eye. She felt his hand touch her cheek, and her throat tightened with emotion. "I . . . I feel like such a fool."

He smoothed his fingers along her jaw to her lips, and took a step closer. "No, I've been the fool."

She raised her eyes to his. He bent his head until his warm breath was caressing her lips, and she waited, with breathless anticipation, for his mouth to claim hers.

Then the shouting began.

"Fire! Fiiirrre!"

They jumped apart as Josiah McIntire rode up to the jailhouse on his horse and reined up in a swirl of dust. "Marshal! Lightning's struck a tree in the thicket! The fire's burning toward the dry meadow! It's headed straight for town!"

21

"Let's hitch up the water wagon!" Jake shouted.

Josiah McIntire looked to Dannie for help. She shook her head despondently. Her father had been one of the few members of the town council who had voted for purchase of a water wagon last year, but the acquisition had been voted down. "We don't have a water wagon."

Jake turned back to her and then looked toward the southern horizon, where a plume of dark gray smoke was rising to mix with the heavy lid of storm clouds gathered against the hills. "Get as many men as you can, as many shovels, picks, and axes, as you can, and meet me at the northern edge of the meadow. Hurry!"

Dazed, Josiah McIntire jumped to attention. He leaped back onto his horse and charged down the street toward the residential part of town.

Jake went into the office and Dannie followed him.
"I'm coming with you."

"Stay out of the way, Daniella."

She took him by the arm and pulled him around to
face her. "I *am* coming with you!"

"Where ya goin'?" Douglas asked.

Jake opened the door to the utility closet and began
taking out shovels and picks. "Fire's broken out in the
southern thicket."

"Fire?" Dreyfuss Storm repeated, going pale.

"It's headed for town," Jake added.

Sherman Potter's eyes grew round with concern and
dread. "The whole town could go up in smoke!"

"That's right, Mr. Potter," Jake replied, grunting
beneath his heavy load as he carried it to the door.
"Care to do something about it?"

"Do what?" Dreyfuss demanded. "The damn water
wagon was voted down last year!"

"Fire line."

The room grew silent and full of confusion. "Fire
what?" Donovan asked from his place beside Mary
Ellen.

Jake sighed. "Would you like me to take the time to
explain this to you, or would you rather learn as we
go?"

They all grabbed tools and charged out the door to
pile into the Merriweathers' buggy. Dannie helped Jake
carry an armful of the digging tools outside. "I'm
coming with you," she repeated.

They put the picks and shovels into the back beneath
Douglas's feet.

"Daniella, I don't have time to argue with you. I want you to stay here, with Mary Ellen."

She glanced over her shoulder at her friend, who was standing in the office doorway, looking pale. "You're right, we don't have time to argue about this. And you certainly don't have time to deny an extra pair of strong hands. I don't know what you're planning on doing, Jake, but I can use a shovel and swing a pick just like anybody else with two good arms."

He sighed and looked away in irritation. "Get in."

Dannie sat in between her father and Jake, gripping the splashboard in front of her to keep from lurching from side to side every time the buggy hit a pothole. Her eyes were fixed on the horizon, on the swirling smoke that grew more dense and dark the closer they came to the meadow. And then she began to smell it. Thick and acrid, it stung her nose and burned her throat. She wiped her watery eyes and peered at the flames leaping up in the distance.

They reached the northern edge of the meadow, but as everyone else scrambled to the ground, Dannie stood in the buggy transfixed by what she saw. The fire was like a giant red monster with a mind of its own. Its spiny fingers reached out to everything in its path, wrapping its flaming arms around its prey and smothering the very life from it.

There was a loud bang and Dannie fell back on to the seat behind her as the thick trunk of a pine tree exploded from the heat, showering its neighbors with deadly sparks and sending a burst of flames and ash thirty feet in the air. The flames bounded from treetop to treetop as if playing a wild game of leap frog that inevitably would spread the fire to untouched sections of the thicket.

The most frightening thing of all was the heat. Dannie could feel it rubbing against her skin, even though she had to be at least a hundred yards from the fire itself. It was a dry, eye-watering heat, one that made her feel stifled and itchy. And if the heat could be this intense now, she could only imagine what it would feel like when it started racing toward them through the dry meadow.

She climbed down from the buggy. The men were already at work, digging up clumps of grass, weeds, saplings, anything they could get their hands on. She hurried over to Jake, who was digging a line from the creek with the shovel. "What do you need me to do?"

Before he could answer, they heard the sound of harnesses and watched as what had to be the entire male population of the town leaped out of six wagons, carrying shovels and picks in their hands. "Go tell them that I want a three-foot-wide strip of this meadow torn out from here to that ridge over there. Everything goes. Grass, weeds, flowers—anything that will burn."

Dannie looked at the rocky ridge that stood thirty yards away. Jake had chosen to take a stand where the creek and western ridge narrowed the gulch. She turned north and stared at the steeple of the town church that suddenly seemed so close. Too close.

"I know," Jake said. "If we don't stop it here there won't be any stopping it before it reaches town.

There's no wind, so, God willing, we'll have the time."

Dannie looked back at the blazing wall of destruction. It had reached the edge of the meadow and was igniting the dry grass. Great columns of flame shot up into the air as sage brush caught fire and fed the inferno that was moving ever closer.

She picked up a shovel and started toward the forty or so men gathered by the wagons. They were staring at the fire as though it were the devil himself come to take them to hell.

"All right, you men!" she shouted. "The marshal wants a fire line dug from the creek bed to that ridge over there!"

"A fire line?" somebody shouted back.

"That's right! Three feet wide. Everything that will burn has to be removed!"

"I say we do a bucket brigade from the creek!" somebody else called out.

"You kiddin' me, Franklin? That wall of heat ain't gonna slow for no sprinklin' of water. Look at it!"

"Well, what the hell's a fire line gonna do?"

"With nothing to burn, I'd assume that it would blow the hell out."

"That's right!" Dannie shouted. "Now get your tools and start working!"

"I don't know if I appreciate taking orders from a woman!"

Dannie pushed her way into the crowd. "Look, if you don't want your town to burn, gentlemen, you will start bending your backs to this task, now! Or would you rather start bending them tomorrow to build new homes for your families?"

There wasn't another moment of hesitation. They converged on the meadow and began plunging shovels and swinging picks. Dannie joined in, digging up pile after pile of sod and weeds, until she thought her arms would wither and fall from her shoulders. Trickles of sweat ran down her back from exertion and from the heat that was growing nearer and nearer as the minutes passed.

Finally, after what felt like hours, the weight of the shovel was taken from her. She leaned her hands on her knees, breathing hard, and looked up to find Jake holding her shovel.

"The line's finished, Daniella. We've done everything we can." He jerked his head in the direction of the others. "And maybe even a little more."

Dannie was amazed at what she saw. Everyone was working together, Potter and Storm sympathizer fighting side by side to save their town. She searched out her father and smiled when she saw him with Sherman Potter, working on one stubborn sapling that refused to give way. They were yanking with all their might and when it finally came loose they both rolled on to their backs and laughed.

Donovan, William, and Douglas were working in rhythm with their picks, digging up the last portion of fire line. The rest of the men had formed lines to dispose of ignitable material a safe distance away from the fire. It was the most beautiful sight Dannie had ever seen.

She smiled at Jake. "Even if the fire isn't stopped, I think this town is saved."

"And that's all you've ever really wanted, isn't it?"

She gave him a warm look.

"Here she comes!" somebody shouted.

They turned to find the fire sweeping toward them. Jake took her hand and pulled her back from the fire line. "Keep your shovels handy!" he shouted. "Watch for jumpers!"

Despite the threatening clouds, they'd been spared from any kind of a breeze so far that day. But Dannie soon discovered that fire, like the living thing it seemed to be, could create its own wind. Her hair fluttered back from her face, and the searing heat chapped her skin and dried out her throat. She squeezed Jake's hand and he took her back another step.

It pushed closer and closer to the fire line and they all held their breath, praying for themselves, each other, their town. Then, little by little it started to go out. With nothing else to consume, the flames began to die, vanishing in an instant as if someone had reached out and snuffed them with moistened fingers.

Murmurs began to come up from the crowd, sounds of triumph. An evil foe had threatened their homes and they'd beaten it back with intelligence and teamwork. It was truly a glorious moment.

And then, out of nowhere, a wind drew down on them. Within an instant the flames, which were a moment ago withering away not only came back to life but leaped across the fire line in search of further sustenance.

Jake dropped Dannie's hand and grabbed his shovel, darting for a spot fire to their left, while all around her chaos broke out as men scrambled to fight down the fire's last-ditch effort at life. Sparks flew on the rising wind, thunder boomed, and lightning split the sky. Dannie covered her face with her sore hands and prayed harder than she ever had in her life. "Please, God, please let it rain."

She was knocked to the ground by some unseen force and opened her eyes to find Jake lying over her legs, beating the singed hem of her skirt. "Christ, Daniella, pay attention!" He pulled her to her feet. "I don't want to have to worry about putting *you* out!"

She looked at the turmoil surrounding them. Spot fires were popping up left and right. It was going to take a miracle now to stop the fire from building again and heading for town.

"When are you going to learn that I can take care of myself!" she shouted at him above the thunder and the yelling. Her chin began to tremble at the hopelessness of it all. "I don't need your help! You or anybody else's!"

"Goddammit!" He threw back his head and shouted at the sky. "I'm in love with a mule! A damn mule!"

He marched away from her to pick up his shovel and she stared after him, her mouth agape. "What did you say?" He couldn't hear her above the noise, so she went after him and spun him around to face her. "What did you say!" she demanded again.

"I said, you're a mule, Miss Storm! Does it come as such a great surprise?"

"You said something else!"

His eyes flared, as though he'd just realized what it was he'd said, and he tried to walk away. She held fast to his arm. "You said you loved me!"

He looked down into her face. "Then let me also add that I am a lunatic!"

She searched his eyes. "You—you love me?"

"Enough to want to wring your neck for chasing me out here!"

"But this is . . . this is impossible," she said, not able to contain a laugh of astonishment and delight.

"Yeah? Well, sometimes miracles happen!"

Lightning crashed across the sky, and then, without warning, the clouds opened up with a deluge of rain. They both glanced up, and heavy rain drops splattered against their faces. One by one the threatening spot fires sizzled out in puffs of gray smoke that drifted toward them and then rose up into the sky.

The men let out loud whoops of joy and began splashing like little boys in the rapidly forming puddles. Hands were clasped and backs were slapped, as the rain continued to pour like an endless bottle of sweet wine. Someone picked Dannie up from behind, and she heard Donovan's soft voice in her ear above the pattering of raindrops. "Remind me not to blister you too bad when we get home, Dannie."

She turned around and saw that he was smiling. "Well, remind me not to hit you over the head with a skillet, Donovan. I suppose I should now leave that honor to your wife."

He broke into gleeful laughter and Dannie gave him a huge smile, enjoying the streams of water that were pouring down her face. "I'm invitin' everybody over to the Potters' for a weddin' reception of sorts, Marshal. Care to join us?"

Jake pushed his soaked hair back out of his eyes. "I appreciate the invite. But I think I'll stay and make sure nothing decides to spark up again."

Donovan looked at Dannie, and she shook her head. "I'll meet you there in a little while. The marshal might need some help."

Donovan gave her a knowing grin and a nudge with his elbow. "Don't you two start up that fire again, ya hear?"

Dannie helped Jake and the men load all the shovels and picks into the wagons. As the hitched horses pulled the heavy wagons out of the meadow and down the muddy road, she lifted her face to the rain.

"You should have gone with them."

Jake was standing beside her, his shirt plastered to his shoulders and chest, water dripping from the tip of his nose. She lifted her heavy skirt away from her ankles and shook the mud from the hem. Her hair was a heavy mass of wet tangles, and it was dripping water down her back, which she could feel soaking through to her underclothes.

"You're going to catch your death out here," he added.

She sauntered toward him and slipped her arms around his neck. "I'm not cold," she whispered into his face.

He made no move to embrace her in return. "Nobody could ever accuse you of that."

"Leastwise you."

His mouth turned up in a wry smile. "You like playing with fire, don't you Daniella?"

"I want you to call me Dannie."

He raised his hands to her hips and then slid them slowly down to the curves of her bottom. "No." He bent his head and tasted the moisture on her neck.

Her pulse pounded to the rhythm of the rain. "And why not?"

"Because the last name a man wants to shout out in the throes of passion is Dannie."

She broke into laughter, which soon turned to a sigh as he licked the water running down her jaw. Their mouths brushed, came apart, and then blended in an irrationally needful kiss. Like the hungry fire to the helpless pine tree, their passion began to consume them.

He drew back. "You know, you really should be getting out of those wet things." She gazed into his eyes, and his smile turned wicked.

She arched a brow. "The same could be said of you."

Without further prompting he stripped off his sodden shirt, wadded it into a tight ball, and tossed it in the direction of the buggy.

She was mesmerized by the water running over his powerful shoulders, down his chest and stomach, and beneath the waist line of his pants. He reached for her and pulled her back to his hungry mouth.

She let her hands slip over his wet skin, feeling every curve and every bulge of hard muscle. She tasted the rain as it splattered against their faces and mingled with their kiss. The feel of her damp clothes clinging to her body only heightened the experience.

He began to undo the buttons on the front of her dress, and she could feel the pattering of rain drops on her shoulders as he pushed the sodden gingham to her waist. Her back arched of its own volition as he licked a scorching path from her throat to her breasts. The rain beat on her forehead and slid between her parted lips while he raised her high off the ground.

She swallowed a cry of longing. The storm raged on, within and without, and she lifted her legs, locking them around his hips, and instinctively searched out that hard part of him.

He groaned as she rubbed against him. Then he glanced at the buggy and began carrying her toward it, nuzzling the side of her neck with every step. They reached it easily enough, but climbing into its shelter was another feat in itself. Once they'd accomplished it, he sat down on the leather seat with her still straddling his hips.

He kissed her long and hard and whispered, "Did you miss me, Daniella?"

The look in her eyes was all the answer he needed. What followed was a mad shoving aside of clothing and an explosive joining of bodies that put the previous fire to shame. He held her hips and coaxed her, guided her, whispered to her the things that she should do. And she revelled in it all, filling herself with him, body and soul.

She found her own release first, and shouted Jake's

name to the storm as the rain continued to patter on the buggy's roof. Once she'd stilled he took her face in his hands.

"Tell me how you feel about me, Daniella," he whispered hoarsely. "Tell me . . . tell me the truth."

She rested her forehead against his and looked deeply into his dark, passion-filled eyes. "I love you, Jake Kiley. The truth is that I love you."

He threw back his head and growled her name as fulfillment overtook him. Holding her to him, tightly, he rocked her with his hands and the subtle lift of his thighs, until, depleted, he rested his head on her shoulder.

They listened to the sounds of the storm as it passed over them, and once the rain had stopped Jake drew back, seeming content to simply sit and stare at her.

For want of something to say, Dannie whispered, "Some storm, huh?"

A smile started at the corner of his mouth and spread until his gleaming white teeth were flashing in the buggy's dim interior. "And she's all mine."

22

The hawk screeched as it soared through the sky and dipped its wings to catch the updraft. Then it glided gracefully toward the clear blue horizon.

Dannie picked up a rock from the bank and skipped it across the top of the water. The storm two days ago had passed, leaving the autumn sky bright and Spangle Creek near to overflowing.

The entire town was gathered around her. They sat in wagons, in buggies, or on chairs they'd brought from home. Some were even sitting on the rain-soaked ground. They were waiting for the surveyor, Mr. Mortimer Greenswaith. He'd arrived just that morning and for the past three hours had been ensconced in Jake's office. Everyone else had been instructed to wait for word by the creek.

Another rock joined Dannie's in the water and she glanced over to find William Potter standing beside her. "Dannie? I'd like to take this opportunity to apologize to you."

She looked up in surprise. His somber eyes met hers and she realized he was entirely serious. "While you're sober?" she asked dubiously.

He gave her a boyish smile and ducked his head. "My new brother-in-law has persuaded me to avoid the evils of fermented grain."

"Which means he'll lay you out flat if you even lick the spigot of a beer keg."

He pursed his lips and nodded. "Exactly."

"And how do you feel about the wedding?"

"It seems to have made Pa pretty happy."

Dannie squinted against the bright sun and lifted her eyes to where her father and Sherman Potter sat in rickety wooden chairs on the other side of the creek. They were talking like the two old friends they were, and smiling—probably over some long forgotten memory.

A vision of Mortimer Greenswaith striding up to them and announcing just exactly who owned the gold flitted through Dannie's head. Undoubtedly one of them would smile like a giddy old fool, and the other scowl with rancor and vengeance. She quickly pushed the image from her mind. Things just couldn't turn out that way. She looked around at the smiling, happy crowd, everyone seeming friendly despite their previous predilections.

Jake and Mr. Greenswaith finally rode up ten minutes later and a quiet hush fell over the crowd. All eyes turned to them in expectation. Dannie hurried toward them as they swung down from their horses, and she was disappointed to discover that they were both wearing expressions that were impossible to read.

Jake gave her a reassuring smile and laid his arm over her shoulders. "Ladies and gentlemen of Shady Gulch. I give you Mr. Mortimer Greenswaith, the official surveyor of Denver and all surrounding towns and counties."

Mr. Greenswaith cleared his throat. He set a pair of pince-nez on the tip of his nose and peered down at the notice in his hands. The babbling of the creek seemed to be the only sound for miles as everyone sat breathless with anticipation.

Mr. Greenswaith looked up, his eyes searching the crowd. "Mr. Sherman Potter?"

The crowd remained silent as Sherman Potter rose to his feet. "Here!"

"And Mr. Dreyfuss Storm?"

Dannie wasn't aware that she was clenching her fingers so tightly that they were turning white until Jake took one of her hands and began to make soothing circles on her palm with his thumb.

Her father rose and shouted. "Here!"

"Good," Mr. Greenswaith mumbled. "I see that all parties are present, so I shall continue." He cleared his throat again and there was a slight surge forward in the crowd as they strained to hear his quiet voice.

"'In the matter of Potter versus Storm with respect to the mineral of gold found in the vicinity or whereabouts of Spangle Creek, located in the city of Shady Gulch, in the county of Denver, I hereby proclaim that the claim be null and void and be posted as such immediately so as not to—'"

A murmur rose up in the crowd. "Null and void?" people began to whisper.

Mr. Greenswaith cleared his throat loudly, and the murmurs died down. "If you would please refrain from remarking until I have finished, it would be greatly appreciated!" he said in a surprisingly sharp voice. "Now, where the hell was I? Oh, yes, '. . . proclaim that the claim be null and void and be posted as such immediately so as not to cause undue havoc and rioting among the people of this town or any other.'"

He lowered the paper from his face, removed his pince-nez and slipped them in the breast pocket of his jacket. "Any questions?"

The crowd errupted into a barrage of questions and shouts, some demanding to know the meaning of this notice—and the term *null and void*—and others remarking on Mr. Greenswaith himself, including his ability to perform his duty considering how obviously blind and dim-witted he was.

Dannie was now wrenching Jake's hand as if she wanted to strangle the life from it, and he finally had to disengage his fingers for their own safety. "This can't be happening," she whispered. "Just when they'd all finally calmed down." She cast a disparaging look at Jake. "It's starting all over again!"

He squeezed her shoulders and pulled her close. "Everything's going to be all right, Daniella," he whispered in her ear. "I promise."

Jake gave a loud ear-piercing whistle and the crowd fell into an angry silence. "If you want your questions answered, you're going to have to ask them one at a time. Let's start with Mr. Potter. Do you have any questions?"

"You bet your great-aunt Sarah I've got some questions! What the hell did all that mean?"

"On which point were you unclear, sir?" Mr. Greenswaith asked with amazing calm considering the entire town wanted him lynched.

"Let's start with the gold claim being null and void!"

"I lack sufficient evidence to mark this as a mining site."

"Sufficient evidence!" Dreyfuss Storm shouted. "There's a nugget of solid gold sitting in the bank vault as we speak!"

The crowd broke into mutters of agreement.

"I have seen the nugget of which you speak, sir. It is that which I am basing my final judgment on."

"Your final judgment," Sherman Potter said with a snort. "Are you trying to tell us that a hunk of gold like that won't have sisters and brothers—and maybe even a mama and a papa—lying in the bottom of that creek!"

Mr. Greenswaith's heavy gray brows rose a fraction. "A nugget of gold that size should very well lead to others of its kind, however—"

"However there ain't no however!" Dreyfuss Storm bellowed. "What the hell's goin' on here, Kiley? Give me back my nugget!"

Dannie straightened as her father pointed his finger at Jake. All eyes turned to the two of them, and she slipped her arm protectively around Jake's waist.

"You want the rock?" he said. "You can have it. I don't have any use for it."

"I'm afraid no one will have much of a use for it, Mr. Storm. Mr. Potter. The nugget is nothing but pyrite."

The hush that now fell over the crowd mirrored Dannie's own astonishment. She pulled back from Jake to better see his face. "Is that true? Is it nothing but fool's gold?"

Jake kept his eyes on the crowd when he answered. "That's right. It's not gold. You've been fighting over nothing but a chunk of worthless pyrite."

Looks were exchanged and heads were shaken. Dannie was aware of a deep sense of shame threading its way through the crowd. And then somebody started to chuckle. "Well, I'll be!" somebody else shouted, and, little by little, the entire town erupted into laughter.

Dannie blinked, not sure if she could believe what she was witnessing. The laughter grew and grew until people were falling over each other on the way to their wagons. She glanced warily to where her father was standing with Sherman Potter. They looked as stunned as she felt. Then her father shrugged, slapped Mr. Potter on the back, and they shook hands amiably.

The crowd soon began to disperse. Jake shook Mortimer Greenswaith's hand and sent the surveyor on his way, and the Potters and the Storms, newly reunited in spirit and in marriage, wandered toward town to drink to what they called their "monumental stupidity."

After the last wagon had left, Dannie stood alone with Jake on the bank of Spangle Creek, shaking her head. She kicked a pinecone into the deep water, and then looked up into his gleaming eyes.

"See," he said, flashing her a smile. "I told you everything would be all right."

She crossed her arms and tilted her head at him. "What just happened here?"

He shrugged and looked away. "I'd say all your problems were solved."

"Well, then I suppose I should say thank you."

He glanced sideways at her. "For what?"

She looked down at her feet and moved closer to him. "For charging into my life and making everything so perfect." She brought his hand to her mouth and grazed his knuckles with her lips, watching as the familiar fire of passion leaped into his eyes. "You keep doing all these nice favors for me, Marshal, and I'm going to start thinking that you actually like me."

He laughed and drew her closer. "Now, why did I think you might be upset with me over the news?"

"Because you haven't gotten used to just how much I love you."

He growled low in his throat and pulled her close. "Kiss me, woman. Before I die from need in your arms."

She pressed two of her fingers to his mouth. "Can I assume that you and your deputy won't be leaving anytime soon?"

He smiled. "Not likely."

"Good." She wrapped her arms around him. "This town can use a jail-happy marshal."

"Not to mention the fact that the Merriweathers won't have a date for Founder's Day if Bean left."

"He's taking both of them?"

Jake shrugged. "Bean figures, he's got two arms, so why not?"

Dannie leaned toward him and nibbled on his lips. Life was definitely taking a wide turn toward wonderful. "And what about the nugget? Shall we bury it, or use it as a doorstop?"

He kissed her deeply and then whispered, "How 'bout if we keep it?"

"Keep it? For what?"

"For our children."

"For our—" She ducked her head to hide her pleasure and fiddled with the top button on his shirt. "But which child do we give it to? the firstborn? the second? the third, the fourth?"

He laughed and pulled her into a tight embrace. "What's say we let them fight over it when the time comes? Why break with tradition?"

She giggled, and he suddenly swept her up in his arms.

"And now," he said, "I believe there's still a little matter of that bucketful of water you placed over my door."

Dannie's eyes widened. She looked down at the creek below her and then back into his intent gaze. "You wouldn't."

He grinned.

And then a shriek of female laughter echoed against the walls of the gulch as Jake hefted Daniella through the air and tossed her into Spangle Creek.

Suzanne Elizabeth returns to time travel . . .

Watch for **Destined to Love**

Coming soon from HarperMonogram

COMING NEXT MONTH

CHEYENNE AMBER by Catherine Anderson

From the bestselling author of the Comanche Trilogy and *Coming Up Roses* comes a dramatic western set in the Colorado Territory. Under normal circumstances, Laura Cheney would never have fallen in love with a rough-edged tracker. But when her infant son was kidnapped by Comancheros, she had no choice but to hire Deke Sheridan. *"Cheyenne Amber* is vivid, unforgettable, and thoroughly marvelous."—Elizabeth Lowell

MOMENTS by Georgia Bockoven

A heartwarming new novel from the author of *A Marriage of Convenience* and *The Way It Should Have Been.* Elizabeth and Amado Montoyas' happy marriage is short-lived when he inexplicably begins to pull away from her. Hurt and bewildered, she turns to Michael Logan, a man Amado thinks of as a son. Now Elizabeth is torn between two men she loves—and hiding a secret that could destroy her world forever.

TRAITOROUS HEARTS by Susan Kay Law

As the American Revolution erupted around them, Elizabeth "Bennie" Jones, the patriotic daughter of a colonial tavern owner, and Jon Leighton, a British soldier, fell desperately in love, in spite of their differences. But when Jon began to question the loyalties of her family, Bennie was torn between duty and family, honor and passion..

THE VOW by Mary Spencer

A medieval love story of a damsel in distress and her questionable knight in shining armor. Beautiful Lady Margot le Brun, the daughter of a well-landed lord, had loved Sir Eric Stavelot, a famed knight of the realm, ever since she was a child and was determined to marry him. But Eric would have none of her, fearing that secrets regarding his birth would ultimately destroy them.

MANTRAP by Louise Titchener

When Sally Dunphy's ex-boyfriend kills himself, she is convinced that there was foul play involved. She teams up with a gorgeous police detective, Duke Spikowski, and discovers suspicious goings-on surprisingly close to home. An exciting, new romantic suspense from the bestselling author of *Homebody.*

GHOSTLY ENCHANTMENT by Angie Ray

With a touch of magic, a dash of humor, and a lot of romance, an enchanting ghost story about a proper miss, her nerdy fiancé, and a debonair ghost. When Margaret Westbourne met Phillip Eglinton, she never realized a man could be so exciting, so dashing, and so . . . dead. For the first time, Margaret began to question whether she should listen to her heart and look for love instead of marrying dull, insect-loving Bernard.

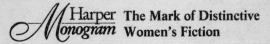 **Harper Monogram** The Mark of Distinctive Women's Fiction